Scorpions Hunt By Night

Second Edition

Book One of The Four Part Series

Soulless

Summer Seline Coyle

SCORPIONS HUNT BY NIGHT
Copyright © 2017 by Summer Coyle

Typing, Formatting, Technical Support: Lyla Coyle

This novel is dedicated to my beautiful daughter Lyla, who is a joy and an inspiration to me.

SCORPIONS HUNT BY NIGHT
SECOND EDITION

BOOK ONE OF THE FOUR PART SERIES SOULLESS

TABLE OF CONTENTS

The year is 1976, and the Sexual Revolution is in full swing. Sensitive teen Dorothy is coming of age amidst the turbulence of a soulless town. SCORPIONS HUNT BY NIGHT is the first book in the four book series SOULLESS. It chronicles the journeys of four complex women whose lives intersect. An elusive newcomer's perilous liaison with a member of the town's elite sets the wheels in motion for lives to spin out of control in this multigenerational tale of love, loss, betrayal, redemption, and hope.

SEXUAL THEMES, VIOLENCE, STRONG LANGUAGE.

Prologue

Clay flower pots, overflowing with scarlet geraniums, lined the wide ledge of the side porch, which was painted custard yellow. A hanging planter beside the kitchen door was bursting into splendor with miniature gramophones: demure white trumpets of morning glories. A marmalade cat slept on a frayed, muddy green woven mat under the kitchen window.

On the sidewalk, a tall woman in an immaculate powder blue suit stood in the scorching afternoon sun, eyes transfixed on the brown Victorian house facing an elm-lined residential street of stately homes.

With tentative steps, she ascended the wooden steps to the square front porch. A hanging planter on the right side of the heavy wooden door was an explosion of fuchsia. To the left was an aging wicker chair spray-painted brown. Green and cream striped awnings, like the half-shut eyelids of screen sirens, hung over the front windows facing the park, where children played a boisterous game of baseball.

Her hand came up in mid-air, however, did not make contact with the doorbell. Through the square pane of glass in the door, she detected a shadow drawing nearer. She instinctively recoiled when the door opened and a red-haired, freckled woman in a seafoam green sundress stood before her, a faint glimmer of recognition flitting across her round face.

"Hello, love. How can I help you?"

"My grandmother used to live in this house." she spoke very quickly, as though afraid of not getting the words out fast enough.

"You have her eyes." the woman smiled broadly, "And her height."

"You knew her?" her enormous dark eyes grew even wider.

"I certainly did. Why, you were just an itty-bitty thing when I saw you last."

After a moment of hesitation, the younger woman's face broke into an enormous smile of recognition.

"Peggy! You're Peggy McGuire!"

"Last time I checked. Good to see you again, love!" she opened her arms to enclose her.

"I'm so glad I found you."

"There's a fresh pot of tea brewing in the kitchen. Let's get caught up, if you have the time."

"All the time in the world, Peggy...I'm sorry I didn't keep in touch..."

"Don't worry about that, dear." she stood aside and held the door open.

The younger woman stood in the vestibule, her eyes taking in every detail with tenderness: the gleaming dark wood of the wainscoting, the warm honey oak of the floors, leaf green walls, geometric print scatter rug in the russets, golds, and olives so popular three decades earlier.

"I'm afraid there have been quite a few changes made to the house since your grandmother lived here."

"It doesn't matter. I just needed to feel her energy." she smiled whimsically, "There's still a part of her here." she turned to face the other woman, looking her directly in the eye, "Did you know her well?"

"Not as well as I would have liked...you were so little when you lost her."

"I've been trying to piece together her life. There are still so many blanks."

"Has your mother provided you with most of the information, dear?"

"My mom passed away when I was fifteen."

"I'm so sorry." Peggy placed a hand over her elbow.

"Soon after Mom died, I was packed up and sent off to a boarding school in Connecticut by her adoptive parents." she paused, "I use that word for lack of a better one."

"I'm aware of the circumstances."

"They tried to have my name legally changed to one of their own choosing: Matilda. My nickname is Tilly, so they thought it would be a clever exchange. Dad put his foot down and objected. Legally they had no leg to stand on."

"I think I understand. There was so much bad blood between them and your grandmother. They were a toxic couple."

"She passed away three years ago, and he is remarried. He cut off all contact with me and Dad when he married Monique."

"That's just as well. You're liberated now. You were given a beautiful name, dear. Your mother wanted you to carry on your grandmother's legacy."

"I've had a chance to get to know some of her relatives and find out from them what Grandma was like as a little girl and a teenager. She was pretty terrific. Spunky and funny. Fiercely loyal, generous to a fault."

"Do you remember her at all? I know you were very young, but sometimes, certain images remain with us."

"I remember how much love she had to give, and how happy she made me...she had a big heart."

"That, she did."

"Today would have been her ninety-fifth birthday." she smiled wistfully, "All my life, people have been evasive about her life. I get the feeling there are some dark secrets."

"No dark secrets. She was just human. Maybe more human than most people dare to be. Most people can't deal with that much honesty."

"Was she really a very controversial figure?"

"Honey, your grandmother turned this sleepy hollow on its heels." Peggy laughed softly, "She caused quite a sensation."

"She was so beautiful."

8

"Tilly, dear, she was the most beautiful woman I've ever laid eyes on."

"She must have had many admirers."

"Beautiful women attract a type of energy that can be devastating. Not only was she breath-taking, she was feisty and free-spirited. This brought her into constant conflict with people. Even after her death, people wouldn't leave the poor soul alone."

"I wish I could've had her longer, had a chance to really know her." Tilly twirled the long, thin strap of her pearlized cream colored pocketbook between the well-manicured thumb and forefinger of her left hand, lowering her moist eyes to the rug, "I would've liked to learn what life was like back in those days, to walk in her shoes, experience what she experienced, to feel closer to her."

"I would be glad to fill in the blanks for you, love. Your grandmother was a great lady. Why don't we adjourn to the kitchen for some tea and fresh blueberry muffins?"

"Thank you." Tilly followed her into the sun-drenched kitchen. "This place is so lovely. You've done some very nice renovations. It's not quite the way I remember it."

"Looks smaller, doesn't it?" Peggy winked at her as she placed a basket filled with muffins on the table. "Have a seat. How do you take your tea?"

"Just black, please." she took the sturdy captain's chair beside the window, and peered out at the small patch of green. A meticulously trimmed primrose bush separated the garden from the neighbor's, its pink blossoms dancing like wild gypsy girls.

Peggy returned to the table with two steaming handcrafted mugs of tea with a lighthouse design against a bright blue sea.

"Things were quite different back then." Peggy encircled her mug with both hands, "People were more rigid, more punitive, more sanctimonious. This town had not grown into the modern, multi-cultural city it is now. It was a small town filled with small minds. Your grandmother found it stifling and judgmental. But she stayed, initially for her kids and later for love. She never seemed to find

9

peace. And she only truly found love at the very end of her life. She was like an exotic gazelle. The poor woman lived under a magnifying glass, under constant scrutiny."

"Was life really dreadful back in the seventies?"

"It wasn't all bad, love. Nice folks were genuinely good, solid, salt of the earth types. But the world was changing at such a frantic pace, and everyone was confused. In some ways, people were more innocent, yet, in other ways, more decadent, and far more hypocritical...Seeing you here after all these years brought back so many memories...I can almost see them now, hear their laughter; I almost expect them to come through the door at any moment...it was a decade of alarming changes, and we were all casualties."

"My mom said she always felt safe in this house, sheltered from the turbulence of the seventies."

"I'm so sorry about your loss, dear. It's not difficult to see what a terrific mom she was: I need only to see how well you've turned out. Your grandmother would be so proud of the exquisite young woman you've grown into."

"Thank you."

"Her story is so intertwined with the stories of the others, it would be impossible to tell you about her without telling you about the others."

"I would like to know about all of them."

"Everyone's gone...I'm the only one left...I'll take you back to the April of 1976, to the day all of our lives were changed forever."

Chapter 1/ City Of Willows

The aging silver bus devoured the torn, abused pavement under its belly with renewed gusto upon leaving Kingswood, a gritty military town built on a scenic riverbank, its rare linden and mulberry trees largely ignored by its inhabitants. The brunette in the second row smiled in recognition of its name. Several years back, an elusive co-worker named Renata with an endearing overbite and earnest brown eyes had told her of another lifetime spent there as a high school teacher and wife of an attorney. Escaping the stifling milieu of sameness, and the endless peccadilloes of her husband, Renata had somehow ended up at McGill University as a medical student, and briefly tended bar at the club until another marriage had elevated her social status and dissolved her association with herself. Kingswood, Renata had told her, through the blue haze of cigarette smoke from the patrons, was the most red-necked, vulgar town on earth. Its residents were oblivious to the natural beauty that surrounded them, and the spiritual beauty shining through the weary eyes of strangers. Women locked away the stench of infidelity in ivory inlaid boxes; men bronzed their fists; adolescents procreated with the ardour of rodents. Alcohol flowed freely, to disinfect gashing wounds. In this picturesque military town; the higher ranks sharpened their linguistic spears for war on the less fortunate; the lower ranks adopted arson as a pastime. Friendships of convenience flourished, nurtured by common contempt for misfits. Souls became dispossessed in this merciless maze of brick bungalows and row houses. Renata had escaped with her sanity, and little else. Years after her departure from the club, she had run across her at a shop. She was still smarting from the awkward denial of recognition in Renata's eyes. Another flicker of friendship fallen by the wayside.

Like all the others. Friendship: an empty, bitter word. As oblivious to inner beauty as the soulless military town they had just left behind.

On this final stretch, the bus sounded more benign. The passengers behind her were growing restless, diving into their carry-on bags, chattering, moving about in their seats. Then, it became discernable slightly ahead of them: the green sign that bore hope. "The City Of Beavertown – Population 23,000." It could hardly be called a city, however, a provincial capital would have that designation, regardless of size, she thought. Renata had spoken briefly of Beavertown, as well, on less disparaging terms. She had described it as dull, claustrophobic, and uppity. The depiction had held little interest for her at the time. Not in her wildest dreams could she have predicted she would one day find herself on an SMT bus, all of her meagre earthly possessions squashed into her tan overnight bag, her destination Beavertown.

Past an industrial park and rows of non-descript bungalows, the road curved by an aging, weather-beaten motel and a turquoise bridge, to a gracious thoroughfare with a park of weeping willows extending its entire length on one side by the riverbank. Sumptuous Victorian mansions lined the opposite side of the road like wedding cakes on display, all of them sugar white, lace-trimmed, and curved. Soon, the road became one with the main artery of this town forgotten by time. Gingerbread cherry-brick storefronts replaced the cake display. The park ended and restarted past grey stone edifices, no doubt under a new identity, and eventually relinquished the riverfront to other gingerbread stores. The bus turned left at a shabby corner of tired tenements and came to a grinding halt.

She could learn to be happy here. Even if her quest proved to be futile. The slow pace of a small town could be a salve after the razor cuts of Montreal. No matter what the outcome. A clean start was what she needed. Her utmost concern was avoiding homelessness at all costs.

The weary passengers disembarked: fringed underfed university students returning from study week to write exams, elderly tourists in Kelly green and crisp white polyester travel separates, lethargic men in mismatched cast-offs with alcohol-soaked breath, prematurely aged women in stained halter tops with the aroma of tomato soup, stale cigarettes, and grease emanating from them. As she often did, at such moments of stark reality, she asked herself why she had been spared the same fate.

The terminal was musty and grey. She bought a newspaper from the machine and tucked it into the exterior pocket of her bag. In the grimy glass of the teal painted door, her own reflection caught her eye. The lack of sleep from her travels clearly showed on her face. During the train ride from Montreal to John's Bay, she had remained awake, her hypervigilance exacerbated by her lone status. Now, she longed for a clean safe room to call her own, a bed to lay down her head.

She approached the thin, middle-aged woman behind the counter.

"Excuse me. Would you happen to have a street map of the city?"

"Take this one." she passed her a folded, wrinkled map across the grimy brown counter.

"How much do I owe you?"

"Promotional maps are free." she smiled, "This was the last one left."

"Thank you."

"First time here, honey?"

"Yes."

"Visiting?"

"Something like that."

"Hope you like it."

She stepped out to the sundrenched sidewalk and glanced at the cover of the map with the black and white photo of a stately cathedral and the writing: "Beavertown Tourist Map/ Carte

Touristique...The City of Willows/ La Ville Aux Saules... New Brunswick/ Nouveau Brunswick Canada." As she unfolded it horizontally, the inner page greeted her with: "Provincial Capital, Beavertown/ Capitale Provinciale: Welcome to Beavertown, The Cultural Centre of New Brunswick. The City of Willows offers a pleasant, relaxing atmosphere, an unhurried pace, and friendly people." French translation followed. Black and white photos of historic buildings were splashed across the two pages. On the opposite side of the map, photographs of parks, beaches, and one of a tender fawn nuzzling a child captured her interest far more. She opened up the map to the grid work of streets and was amazed by the meticulous way the streets were arranged, as close to a real grid work as would be possible. At the top of the page, she read: "Note: This map does not show all of the city streets, nor the entire forty-one square mile city area."

Pinpointing her location on King Street, she charted a mental path to her approximate destination: the three block shopping district on Queen Street. The list of lodgings on the map were out of her reach, even "The General's Inn" three blocks from the bus terminal would be a last resort. Affordably priced downtown hotels were more frequently than not, flophouses for derelicts desperate enough to cause harm, not to mention a popular spot for prostitutes who were not above committing theft.

She needed to find an affordable lunch counter first. The modern white stucco shopping complex next door would most likely have overpriced, over-decorated eateries with meagre portions of tasteless food. She folded the map with painstaking precision and slipped it into a narrower outer pocket of the bag. Surveying her immediate surroundings, she sighed. Most of the buildings on King Street were bleak wooden structures housing a variety of Mom and Pop operations, from shoe repair to locksmith to used goods. The aged forest green and baked bean brown paint of the decaying wood filled her with inexplicable dread. Maple and elm trees grew strategically to soften the blight. Even in the bright sun, the tears of the decaying structures were evident. She followed King Street to the inner section of Regent Street and walked one block to Queen Street, passing by "The General's Inn" on her way, a gritty red brick tenement with dormer windows on the top floor and a shabby front lobby visible through the front window. It was sandwiched between a drycleaner on one side, and a post-war era bar and grill on the other.

The architecture of Queen Street was an eclectic mix of aging brick buildings housing high-end specialty shops, sturdy blond brick and sandstone mid-century structures housing the post office, the customs building, the home of the professional theater troupe, as well as crumbling World War I era tenements. Hand painted signs were used on almost every shop in an attempt to authenticate the Victorian flavor of Beavertown. "Johnson's Footwear", "Belding's Fine China and Gifts", "Millicent's Dress Shop For Ladies", "Foster's Men's Wear", "Violet's Millinery", "Duplissea's Finest Wools", "McCoy's Imported Tea and Coffee"...She came upon the lone restaurant, an Asian place bearing perhaps the only neon sign, emblazoned with the name, "Mimosa Gardens". Beneath it, was written: "Licensed Restaurant – Finest in Chinese, Polynesian, and Canadian Cuisine". The lush bottle-green interior and tropical plants visible through the window caught her eye and she paused. The faint strains of Vic Damone singing "The More I See You" could be heard as the door was opened and a woman with two small children in tow came out, providing a glimpse of the claret plush seats, mint green tablecloths and bud vases of pink carnations. Well-coiffed, middle-aged women with linen shift dresses, and little girls with beaded ponytail holders the color of strawberry jam appeared to be enjoying elaborate cherry-topped sundaes in parfait glasses. She could hear her stomach rumbling. Sighing inwardly, she trudged along. Turning her gaze to the park across the street, she admired the enormous fountain with fat concrete beavers around it, shaded by weeping willows. Freshly painted park benches in sun-drenched blue sparkled. She had heard about the early and hot Beavertown summers. She did not anticipate difficulty in adjusting to them. Beyond the trees, near the military museum mentioned on the map, were monuments, John F. Kennedy's being the only discernable one form this distance.

She crossed Carleton Street. Proceeding along the next block on Queen Street, she peeked in shop windows like a curious child, gazing in longing at diaphanous dresses in ice cream pastels in the window of "Jenny's Fashions". She smiled when she came upon "Ivy's Sweet Earth", a flower child haven filled with wicker furniture, local crafts, chunky wood jewellery, handmade soaps, and woven cotton mats in plums and fuchsias. Then, she came upon it: sandwiched between "Turnbull's Jewellery Store", and an insurance broker, it displayed an unassuming sign in gold block letters above the door: GOLDSTEIN'S MUSIC SHOP. In the window was a display of band instruments against red velvet. The wheelchair ramp at the entrance caught her eye. With trepidation, she pulled the door open. On her left, was a bin of records reduced for clearance. On the back wall was a poster of a blond young man with wounded eyes, bearing a striking resemblance to Robert Redford. She was not close enough to read the print, and was about to remedy the situation when a nasal female voice inquired sharply:

"Yes, may I help you?"

She was a wiry woman with cat glasses and an oversized grey bun on her head.

"Yes...I ...I was looking for Mr. Goldstein, please..."

"If you're looking for a job, there are no openings. You can leave an application with me, but I can't say if or when there'll be anything available."

"No – it's not that...It's...personal..."

"You leave your name and number with me, and I'll pass it along to them."

"I...I think I'll come back later."

"Don't waste your time, dearie." she said sternly, "Mr. Goldstein doesn't spend much time in here. He's in and out. You'll never catch him."

"Are... are you...Mrs. Goldstein?"

The woman shot up a glance of contempt. Then she retorted:

"I don't think so. Now are you going to leave your name and number?"

"No thank you." she backed away unsteadily, sighing in relief at her last response.

"Suit yourself." the woman said icily, "I was only trying to help."

In her haste to escape, she realized once outside, that she had not learned the identity of the man with the wounded eyes. She crossed the intersection of York Street, and continued in her search of a greasy spoon or an affordable lunch counter. Coming upon "Flowers by Lyla", she paused to inhale the scent of the pink and white hyacinths in the outdoor display.

"Nice day." a statuesque young woman with an Irish porcelain complexion greeted her as she came outside to add more flowers to her colorful display.

"Your flowers are lovely." she inhaled deeply.

"Thank you."

She walked by "Parker's Department Store", "Moe's Meat Market", and "Perry's Family Shop". Then, past the bank was the Five and Ten, housed in a shabby turn-of-the-century building with a sooty brick façade. She pulled the door open and stepped into the dingy interior. The floor was soft wood with wide planks. On her right was a large clearance table filled with cheap gadgetry and figurines of children often displayed on window sills. On her left were the flamingo pink wooden doors of the three dressing rooms. In the middle were rows upon rows of colorful baubles, beaded handbags, and discount cosmetics, a sight all too familiar. She smiled fondly. Like an old faithful dog, the Five and Tens of the world could always be relied upon for comfort and reassurance. She glanced around for signs of a lunch counter however, was unable to detect anything resembling one, and the only discernable scent was that of glass cleaner, not food.

A wholesome-looking young woman sporting horn-rimmed glasses and a tortoise-shell hairband to tame her thick black locks, noticed her hesitation, and promptly approached her.

"May I help you?"

"Do you have a lunch counter?"

"I'm sorry, we don't." she smiled in understanding, "But Zeeman's Department Store does. It's two doors down, the new building after the bank."

"Thank You."

She returned to the street and followed the clerk's directions. The imposing new structure with the majestic green marble exterior appeared fresh and clean. Stark white terrazzo floors greeted her. The lights were bright, the ceilings high, and music was piped in. Minnie Riperton's girlish voice singing "Loving You" was muffled by the shoppers' drone. Toward the back of the store was a sign with a spatula and an arrow signifying the location of "The Spatula Restaurant". She strolled past the cosmetics on her way. A higher end line was sold here. Plexiglas Lazy Susan displays of Revlon's "Extra Extra Crystalline" summer pastels for nails were sumptuously rich, frothy shades of dusty rose, silvery lavender, baby pink, buttercream, and cocoa. The aroma of fried grease directed her to her destination: a white Formica counter with orange and chrome stools. At two forty-five, there were few customers. She selected a stool away from the others, and removed her newspaper and her pen from the outer pocket of her bag. Placing her bag securely under her feet, she spread out the newspaper on the counter and located the Classified Ads. Where to start? Employment or Rooms For Rent? Three seats away, a fiftyish blonde with heavy eye makeup, wearing a mint green polyester pantsuit, was diligently filling an aluminum ashtray with scarlet-trimmed cigarette butts. A plump young waitress with smooth full cheeks in a salmon uniform filled her scarlet-trimmed white porcelain cup with fresh coffee.

"Hey, Thelma, how's the shoulder?" the blonde took a puff of her current cigarette.

"Still sore."

"You'd better see a doctor about that."

"Can't get the time off. It'll go away on its own eventually." she returned the coffee carafe to the coffee maker and called out, "Be with you in a jiffy, Ma'am."

The rents for the rooms and small apartments were steeper than she had anticipated for a town this size.

"What can I get you, Ma'am?" the young waitress was in front of her with her notepad.

"A BLT, and some of that coffee the lady's having." she smiled.

"Comin' right up."

She wondered if Thelma had chosen the peach-colored frames for her eyeglasses to match her uniform, or to emphasize her lovely peaches and cream complexion.

"Thelma's coffee's the best." the blonde turned in her direction, "Good'n strong."

"Strong is precisely what I need."

"Whatcha lookin' for in that paper, honey?" she gestured toward the newspaper.

"You name it, I'm looking for it."

"Sounds like the story of my life." the woman burst into a deep, earthy laughter.

Thelma returned with a full white cup and placed it beside her newspaper.

"You're not from around here are you, honey?" the blonde seemed to have regained her composure.

"No."

"I could tell. You've got that big city look. Got a job lined up?"

"I'm looking. I can't believe how much they want for rent. How does anyone find reasonable accommodations?"

"Hon, in a university town, they charge anything they want, and get away with it. Highway robbery, I tell you. You wouldn't believe the dumps they're renting to students. Don't waste your time with them rooms in the Classifieds, honey. Your best bet is word of mouth. Check out Daisy Parker's place on Needham Street. She's a sweetheart. It's the green house next to the brick apartment building between Regent and Carleton Streets. Tell her Shirl sent you."

"Thank you. I appreciate that." she reached for a napkin to write on and scribbled down the information.

"What's your name, honey?"

"Valentina." she pronounced it as they had in Montreal.

"Ah! Sounds so French! So romantic!" Shirl sighed, "I'm just plain old Shirley McCumber. I knew you weren't from around here. You don't even have a French accent. I couldn't tell you were French, but I should have known."

"Half French. That's probably why." she smiled uncomfortably.

A portly man with a blue baseball cap sauntered in and straddled the stool on the other side of Shirley.

"Hi, Mac. How's it goin'?" Shirley turned to him.

"Hi, Shirl. Can't complain."

"Your usual, Mac?" Thelma carried an empty cup and a coffee carafe to him.

"Yep."

"Did Mavis get her bulbs in?" Shirley lit up a new cigarette and took a long drag.

"Yep. Twenty-four blue iris, and twelve glads in that funny color. Spic and span, they call it."

"Should be coming up in July or August."

"Awful lot of work. I had to lug all that peat moss in the wheel barrow, with my sore back, too."

"It'll be worth it."

"It better be. Had to take my Atasol this mornin' or I never would've made it into town."

"I'll get you stronger coffee for your refill." said Thelma, "There's a pot there with only a cup left in it, and, boy, it sure is strong when it sets there like that."

"There's caffeine in them pills, so the doc says. I ain't never noticed it." Mac shifted on his stool.

"It don't matter." laughed Shirley, "Thelma's coffee can give you enough rocket fuel to launch one of them space shuttles."

"You're bad." Thelma shook her head, "Mac, after I get this lady's order served, I'll take care of your soup."

"No hurry." he slurped his coffee loudly, "So, what's new with you, Shirl? Gord still on Compensation?"

"He's gettin' better. I been thinkin' 'bout takin' a job, you know, to tide us over 'till he gets back on his feet. Maybe sellin' clothes."

"They're lookin' for people over at the mall."

"Got no transportation. It's gotta be somethin' around here. This lady here's lookin' for work, too. Meet Valentina...Valentina...?" she searched her face for the surname to fill in the blank.

"Bertrand." she offered reluctantly.

"Ain't that a glorious name? So French! This here is Mac Cousins."

"Nice to meet you." she smiled conventionally.

"Likewise." Mac nodded, "Why don't you try them government offices over at the Centennial Building? They're always hirin' French ladies for secretaries."

"I'm afraid I have no secretarial training."

"Neither do they!" Shirley burst into another bout of laughter.

"Shirl, you're bad today." Thelma returned with the BLT on a white platter with a generous serving of home fries and coleslaw on the side.

"I'm always bad." Shirley winked at her.

"Hey, Shirl, why don't you apply for the singer's job over at Chandler's?" Thelma said, "There's an ad in the paper."

"Wouldn't that be a hoot?" Shirley roared with laughter. "Me in a low-cut number in red satin, beltin' out "Moon River"!"

Valentina discreetly scanned the employment section of the Classifieds and found the block ad:

WANTED – Singers: One male, one female. Must be familiar with the standards. Auditions: April 15, Thursday, 2 – 6 PM. Apply in person at Chandler's Lounge, Willow Place. No telephone calls.

Folding up her newspaper, she wolfed down her meal in silence.

"Who are they replacin'?" asked Shirley.

"Stephen, the queer fellow." Mac spoke stoically between slurps of soup.

"He was too big city." Thelma said, "I don't think he gelled with the audience."

"Chandler's goin' on tour in Europe for a year. He's lookin' to hire a temporary fellow to work his sets, but he wants a lady to replace the queer."

"Not much of a change. Stephen was a lady, too!" Mac laughed.

Valentina sighed inwardly. What was she getting herself into? Small towns were undeniably intolerant and judgmental. Pierre would not have fared well in this climate. Even with all of its rough edges, the big city suited him best. She wondered how they were reacting to her disappearance. It was not difficult to visualize Sven and his cohorts cursing loud enough to be heard by the entire staff. Pierre would not betray her confidence. Her trail had already grown cold. Now, it was time to retire Valentina. Middle names were not customarily afforded the privilege enjoyed by Valentina. She blinked away tears at the awareness that she would never see Pierre again. Once the opportunity presented itself, he too, planned to make a run for it. Wherever he ended up, she hoped he would be happy.

"Them artsy-fartsy types, they're all queer." Mac wiped soup from his chin, "Not too discriminatin' either. Drop their drawers for anyone."

"They're different." Thelma said, "That's for sure."

"They use drugs, too. I sure don't want any of them freaks in my neighborhood." Mac frowned.

"Theresa told me Arnie and Flo's girl's one of them lesbians." Shirley whispered deliciously, "She's moved in with some artist over in Vancouver."

"Arnie and Flo, they're such nice folks, too. They must be heartbroken." Thelma said.

"Youngsters today." Mac grunted, "All goin' to hell on roller-skates."

"Gotta run." Shirley gathered up her pack of smokes and her orange disposable lighter, "Gordie's stories are over around now. I play gin rummy with him every day at four. Beat 'im good every time, too."

"He must be a glutton for punishment." Mac said.

"He married her, didn't he?" Thelma's eyes twinkled in mischief.

"One o' these days, missy..." Shirley shook a nicotine-stained index finger at her.

"See youse later" Mac said.

"Say hi to Mavis for me."

"Will do."

"Be good." Thelma said.

"See you, honey." Shirley adjusted the fraying strap of her dirty white shoulder bag, "Good luck, Valentina."

"Thank you. And thanks for the information."

"You're welcome. You'll love Daisy."

"I'm sure I will."

"Good luck with the job huntin'."

"Thank you. It was nice to meet you."

"See you 'round, honey."

Before she rose from her seat, Valentina reached in her bag to pay for her lunch, and left a tip for Thelma. She located the ladies' room before leaving Zeeman's. The broken yellow tiles, and the abundance of toilet paper on the floor instead of the roll in the malodorous space had no impact on her. She had seen much worse. As she was preparing to return to the main lobby, on an impulse, she took a detour to the jewellery counter. On her left was a clearance bin with trinkets: clunky, gaudy, over-sized necklaces, thick cuffed bracelets, and two-inch initial brooches in a vintage script with a wavy flourish. It appeared that mostly "O's", "I's", "U's", "Z's", and "Y's" were left, however, upon a concentrated excavation, she discovered an "S", and promptly took it to the bespectacled clerk, who rang in the 75 cent purchase.

"Can you tell me where I can find Willow Place?" she inquired as the clerk handed back the quarter change to her dollar bill.

"Sure. It's the white stucco building right across the street from 'The Center for Performing Arts'. You can't miss it."

"Thank you. Could I wear it?" she intercepted her as she was about to place it in a bag.

"Of course." she scraped off the sticky orange price tag and handed it to her.

Meticulously, she fastened it to the lapel of her navy blue blazer.

"It looks lovely on you." the clerk smiled, "Have a nice day."

"Thank you. You, too."

Outside, she inhaled deeply, and murmured inwardly:

"Good-bye, Valentina."

Remembering she had not checked herself in the mirror, she cast a glance at her reflection in the plate glass window. Her chin-length Flapper bob appeared to be in place. It was, without a doubt, the most carefree hairstyle on earth, even without the customary heavy bangs. It fell into place with minimal fuss. Her Visa Polyester classic suit had retained its shape through her travels, and her wedge pumps were exceptionally soft and comfortable, despite their low cost. Her square-necked white and navy nautical blouse was cool and breathable. She was presentable enough, she reminded herself, and began her walk in rewind mode past the buildings she had observed on her way. Despite her quicker steps, she made it a point to peek into the music shop, only to find the same sour woman behind the counter.

The uncluttered contemporary lines of Willow Place were unmistakable. How could she have missed it before? Through the heavy wooden door, she entered the majestic marble foyer, where a sign was posted in a prominent spot by the entrance to "Chandler's Lounge" on her right: "Auditions" was hand-printed on poster board in block letters with an arrow pointing toward the back of the building. On her left was a restaurant with rich Bordeaux décor and impeccably attired waiters moving with utmost efficiency. Billie Holiday singing "God Bless The Child" was being piped in from an old scratchy recording. Past the restaurant, and past the potted tropical trees, she spotted another sign with an arrow pointing straight ahead in the direction of the beige carpeted stairs to the basement. As she tiptoed down, a youthful female voice struggling with "I've Got You Under My Skin" became audible. She followed the singing to her left, to a room lined with metal office chairs. There was a closed door to her right where the auditions were held. Three young men and four women turned expressionless faces toward her. She took a chair as far away from the others as possible, and kept her head down.

The door opened and a short, stocky man came out to the waiting area, followed by a thin young woman in a see-through blouse with brassy, stiff hair, who scampered up the stairs.

"Next!" the man called out, glancing at his clipboard, "Mark Spinney".

A short young man with blond curls rose hesitantly. The man motioned him into the room, and approached herself.

"Write your name here." he handed her the clipboard and a pen, "Your real name, not your stage name. Write your phone number beside it."

He snatched it back without noticing the absence of a phone number, and without giving her the opportunity to explain. He disappeared into the room again, closing the door behind him.

Mark was singing "Luck Be A Lady". She listened to the next young man belting out "My Way", a thirtyish woman in expensive attire and excessive makeup purring "Diamonds Are A Girl's Best Friend", a flaxen-haired teenaged girl reciting an anemic rendition of "It Had To Be You", an East Indian woman overdramatizing Carly Simon's contemporary hit "You're So Vain". She sighed. A dark-haired young man's rich rendition of "My Funny Valentine" was a welcome relief. The final applicant before her was a fidgety, bird-like woman in her forties, who sang "Witchcraft". Then, as the woman ascended the stairs following her audition, she rose from her chair, expecting the surly man to summon her. However, she found herself face-to-face with the strangely familiar green eyes she had seen earlier.

"Miss Bertrand?" he stood before her, "I'm Jack Chandler." he extended his hand and shook hers firmly, "Please come in."

Once in the room, he offered her a softer chair and a glass of water.

"I'm afraid we didn't get your phone number." he lowered his eyes apologetically.

"I don't have one yet. I've just arrived in town today, and don't have a place to live yet."

"I'm sorry about that. Please meet Richard, my manager." he motioned to the gruff man she had met earlier, who nodded, "And this is Chuck, our accompanist."

A balding man with thick glasses wearing a captain's uniform saluted her. His captain's hat was on top of the piano.

"Where did you work before?" Richard wanted to know.

"Various clubs in Montreal." her heart skipped a beat. What if he pressed the issue further?

"What would you like to sing, Miss Bertrand?" Jack Chandler intervened.

""But Not For Me". "

"It's refreshing to have someone sing a Gershwin song for a change." he smiled.

"You haven't heard me yet. I hope I can do justice to his music."

"You'll do just fine."

Her trembling legs threatened to give way, however, did not betray her. She sang only Gershwin songs for auditions. Only he had the power to lift her out of dismal reality and enable her to transcend.

"You've got the job." Jack said immediately upon her completion, "You are by far the best singer we've heard today."

"I do? I am?" she beamed, "Thank you!"

"Before you leave, I would like to ask you to please accept this advance on your salary. It should cover the cost of a room at "The Queen's Hotel" for a week." he wrote out a cheque swiftly.

"Mr. Chandler, I can't."

"It's Jack. And I insist. I wouldn't feel right letting you go out there without a proper roof over your head."

She was speechless. He placed the cheque in her hand.

"I'm afraid I'll be leaving first thing in the morning, so I won't be here when you come in tomorrow. I want to say "Break a leg" now." he laughed softly, "We open at seven and close at two AM. If you come in at six or six-fifteen, Richard can orient you to the new place. You will be one of the two full-time principal singers. Brett Morrow, our other full-time singer is an old veteran at this, and can provide you with the answers to any questions or concerns you might have. You both work seventeen hours per week for five nights. That gives you three hours on three nights, and four hours on two nights, with the extra hours frequently being on Fridays and Saturdays. That is when we have the most business, and people come from out of town, so we try to feature our main attractions. You and Brett have one day off each. We have also hired a new part-time singer: Danny Minucci, the chap who sang "My Funny Valentine." He has eight hours per week, three in the two nights you and Brett don't work and one hour each on two other nights. Some details are negotiable, as long as all parties agree. I hope you'll enjoy working at Chandler's."

"I'm sure I will, Mr. Ch..."

"Jack."

"Jack. Thank you."

"I hope to see you again when I return from my tour."

"I hope your tour will be wonderful."

"I appreciate that. In the meantime, you'll be in good hands."

Stepping back into the sunshine, she felt happy, happier than she had been in a very long time.

Chapter 2/ Lush Life

Audrey pulled back the heavy drapes and sighed deeply. Her Ted would have known what to do now. He had always been skillful at handling these delicate matters. How she wished he were with her now. Outside, the wind was blowing the warm April rain against the windows. The slender silver maple was reaching skyward, its bare branches a haphazard road map. She hoped May would bring timid buds of tender green to hold the promise of rejuvenation. Her eyes wandered to the photograph of her grandparents over the mantle, peering out from their antique frame, stiffly posing against an artificial pastoral backdrop in their Sunday best. Robert Horncastle's stern countenance and Henrietta Horncastle's strong chin were a daily reminder of her breeding and good fortune. Her indulgences in self-pity rarely exceeded these fleeting moments.

In the opposite corner of the room adjacent to the dining room, above the antique rosewood piano was the photograph of her achingly handsome son. Mildred lifted solicitous eyes from her intricate crochet work to smile knowingly at her. Audrey released the burgundy brocade curtains and resumed her seat beside her on the cream and burgundy striped Queen Anne sofa.

"You're doing just fine, dear." Mildred patted her on the knee maternally.

"Divorce number five... and it appears he's swiftly headed for number six."

"Don't put your cart before your horse, dear."

"I detect a definite pattern, Millie. Although I must admit I am pleased to see the last of Tracy, this Linda worries me. She appeared too soon after his breakup with Tracy. He barely had time to process the ending of his marriage before he became seriously involved with Linda. As soon as one relationship sours, he rushes headlong into a new one. He was dating Tracy two weeks after Kate walked out on him."

"That Kate was a piece of work, as young people would say."

"Don't even get me started on her, Mildred, dear." Audrey rolled her eyes.

"There's certainly no shortage of attractive women around him. I dare say, he's a frightfully handsome young man. It's inevitable, what with women being so brazen these days... It's that Women's Lib stuff, you know."

"Gold-diggers, all of them. They reel him in every time. I wish he could meet a woman with no hidden agenda. But nice women do not go chasing after men, so he ends up with whoever seeks him out. He's too shy to take the initiative. And, I reckon, respectable women would be intimidated by his good looks and fame, not to mention his groupies."

"He's suffered so many losses in his young life, Audrey, dear."

"When I first met him, just six months after Sylvia had passed away, he was a scrawny little lad of twelve, with the most soulful eyes, and unruly blond hair. Even at that tender age, he possessed an air of other-worldliness. He was always so courteous, and generous to me, though I was taking his mother's place. He accepted me unconditionally and allowed me to dote on him. Then, sixteen years later, he lost his dad too."

"He's very fortunate to have you, Audrey. You've provided him with a stable, nurturing environment. He knows this is a safe haven. He can always come home when things don't work out in the outside world."

"It's the times we're living in, Millie. There's no right or wrong anymore. Those hippies eroded the fabric of our society. Look at the way Garrett's turned out! It just breaks my heart. You and I are blessed. I wouldn't want to be in poor Annette's shoes for anything in the world."

"I agree, dear. Our boys have their troubles, but they're good boys."

"You must be very proud of Anthony, you and Willy."

"We are. I only wish he wouldn't work so hard, have a little fun once in a while."

"I would have thought he'd had sufficient time to get over that woman by now, but he appears to be stuck. He's a slow healer. Takes things hard. Always wearing his heart on his sleeve. He was the same way after Adele. In death, Adele loomed larger than life. No one measured up to her memory."

"That gave him an excuse for not picking up the pieces and moving on. Only, this time it's worse. She's not dead." Mildred's lips were taut.

"When he falls, he falls hard."

"What are you two prophets of doom and gloom up to now?" a somewhat younger, plump woman with teased blonde hair and heavy makeup stood in the doorway.

"Hello, Annette, dear." Mildred smiled, "Just commiserating."

"You sourpusses!" she flung her alligator pocketbook on the ottoman and headed for the bar in the opposite corner of the room, "Let's have some brandy!" she poured herself a drink, "After that perfectly dreadful parent-teacher meeting, I need a stiff drink!"

"Is the bar open for business?" a dimpled man with a thick dark mane leaned against the wall beside the piano, "Two hours of sheer torture, listening to parents lamenting over their Johnny or Susie's history marks...what an unfair teacher I was, how misunderstood their fair-haired brats were...I need a drink."

"How is Dottie making out, Annette?" Audrey asked.

"Not too well. She's still daydreaming in class, and not passing in any homework. She's not getting a passing grade in Math or Biology. She's barely passing History. She's scraping by in English and French. Her elective is Art, the easiest course on earth. And, she's getting below average in that."

"She has only another year left." Mildred said, "Then, she'll be off to university."

"For Pete's Sake, Millie, she's failing high school! How can she get into university?"

"She may just surprise you." the dimpled man, who had been listening silently, leaned back in his leather chair relishing the fine flavor of his quality scotch.

"Warren, Dottie doesn't have an academic mind. It's not realistic to expect too much from her." Annette poured herself another brandy.

"She may actually find university stimulating enough to be worth applying herself."

"Let's face it, Warren: Dottie has no potential, no ambition, no motivation."

"Actually, doing poorly in our school system is more an indication of giftedness than slowness."

"He's saying that because he was such a bad student himself at that age." Audrey said.

"No wonder. I had you for a sister, didn't I? I was traumatized." he winked at her, "Where's the Boy Wonder? Isn't he back from the club yet?"

His smile met Audrey's icy glare. A youthful female voice was heard from the hallway.

"It should be according to ability to pay...all services...The poorest should get everything free. The middle class should pay a certain percentage according to income level, and people like us should pay the full amount. That way, we won't be a drain on the system and take away from those who need it more. Those who can pay have an obligation to contribute, to make it better for those who can't. It's only fair." the voice found its home in a diminutive figure.

"In some parts of the world, you would be imprisoned for voicing such convictions." Warren said.

"I think the world needs more idealists like you to make it a less ugly place." the man with closely-cropped black curls beside her placed a fraternal arm around her.

"Where have you two been all this time?" Annette demanded.

"Making all the snooty girls from school green with envy, because I have such a handsome cousin."

"Speaking of school, Dottie, your performance is a disgrace." Annette refilled her brandy.

"Cut her some slack, Annette. She's trying to save the world." Warren said, "Are Don and Willy still playing chess in the library?"

"I think so. I saw Shawn carrying a tray in the direction of the library when I came in." Annette returned to her seat by the window.

"They enjoy it immensely." Audrey remarked, "I remember Ted and Father spending evenings in the library, playing chess."

Dottie, who had been curled up with her feet tucked under her, on the buttery leather loveseat, bolted at the sound of the front door being shut against resistance from the wind.

"Let me take these for you, Sir. Dreadful night, isn't it, Sir?"

"Thank you, Shawn. Pretty nasty out there, yes, and doesn't show any signs of easing up."

Both Dottie and Audrey ran to greet him the moment he appeared, his gentle smile illuminating the room.

"Hello, darling." Audrey kissed his cheek.

He kissed her back and placed an arm around her shoulder. Dottie snuggled into his free armpit, and he squeezed her to himself.

"You look all tuckered out, dear." Audrey stroked his cheek, "Get things all wrapped up at the club?"

"Anthony, dear, please get him a drink." Mildred glanced up from her crocheting.

Audrey led him to the sofa and instructed him to sit between herself and Mildred. Dottie took a seat on the ottoman in front of Warren's chair, where she was facing the trio.

"We hired two youngsters to fill the positions." he took the drink Anthony offered him, "Thanks."

"Were there many who auditioned, dear?"

"About twenty-five or so. Most were in high school musicals years ago and were under the impression that they had talent. We were getting pretty discouraged. We had filled the part-time position, but no one suitable had come through the doors for the full-time one. Chuck was threatening to walk out, when in walks this young lady, the final applicant, with luggage in tow, fresh off an SMT. She sang Gershwin, and warmed all of our hearts."

"She came to seek her fortune in Beavertown, the Hollywood of Eastern Canada." Warren stretched out his legs with one foot on either side of Dottie on the ottoman.

"Where is she from, dear?" Audrey asked.

"Montreal. She's been singing in various clubs. I could be jumping the gun here, but she might have some connection to the missing woman...perhaps the next generation."

"What makes you think so?" Annette piped up.

"Same name. It's not exactly common."

"Most likely a coincidence." she frowned, "That detective combed through Montreal thoroughly. He found absolutely no trails leading to her."

"She loves Gershwin."

"This reeks of an imposter." Warren remarked.

"What's the last name?" Annette wanted to know.

"Bertrand."

"Doesn't mean anything. There can't be a connection."

"Could be a husband's surname."

"Women don't take their husbands' surnames in Quebec." Warren said.

"Unless they want to. Maybe she wanted to. It's the perfect cover for someone who doesn't want to be found." Annette mused.

"Why wouldn't she want to be found?" Dottie asked.

"There could be other people looking for her, too...like Roy and What's-Her-Name..." Annette bit her lower lip, "She might be afraid they could find her daughter and do the same to her."

"If this is her daughter. And it is a very big if." Warren said, "She might have heard about the investigation and snooped around for information, so she could impersonate a member of her family."

"She really seems like a very nice young woman."

"Jack, dear, you're so trusting." Mildred said.

"I'm sure she has no connection to this, and it's all one big coincidence."

"I'll keep my eyes and ears open." Tony said, "If she is an imposter, she's bound to contact the family sooner or later."

"It's wise to keep this among ourselves until we know more." Warren scratched his head, "No need to get their hopes up or cause turmoil for those two. They've been through enough. We need hard cold facts. It may be time to get Sherman on the job again."

"Brett might be able to do some spy work. After all, they are going to be working together." Dottie suggested.

"Let's leave Brett out of it." Mildred said coldly.

Warren met her gaze and winked at her. Mildred shot back an icy glare.

"I'll get you another drink, dear." Audrey broke the uncomfortable silence.

"No, thanks, Mom. I must go up and finish packing. My plane leaves early in the morning." he rose to his feet.

"How many cities are in the European leg of the tour, dear?"

"Twenty-four."

"Oh – please send me postcards from Moscow and Istanbul!" pleaded Dottie.

"For you, my favorite cousin, I'll send one from every city!"

"I love you, Jack!" she sprang to her feet and kissed his cheek.

"I love you, too, Dots." he kissed both her cheeks. "I'm afraid I really do have to go upstairs and finish packing."

"See you in the morning, dear." Audrey embraced him, "Good night."

"Good night, Mom." he kissed her, "Good night, everyone."

"Tony and I are coming up to help you pack." Warren volunteered, "Want to come along, Polka Dot?"

"Sure I do!"

Once they were out of earshot, Warren snickered.

"Gotta watch out for those scheming La Rocque dames – no offence, Polka Dot. I wonder just how and when Edna's old sucker of a husband caught on to her deception and plotted a whopper of his own. Now, there's a con artist on the loose, lurking around, trying to cash in on the entire fiasco. I can blow her right out of the water and send her packing back to Montreal."

"What if she really is the next generation?" Dottie reminded him exuberantly, "Wouldn't it be wonderful to have her here?"

"If she is the daughter, I suppose it's better for her to turn up than our missing person." Tony mused, "Can you imagine how damaged she must be by now, if she's even alive? It's for the best that she's never been found. Sometimes we need to leave well enough alone."

"I'm sorry I ever mentioned it." Jack loosened his tie and opened his door.

"No, it's a good thing you did." Tony said, "In case there is a scam, we can be on our guard."

Jack hung up his blazer on a hanger and placed it on the clothes rack by the door connecting the sitting area to his sleeping quarters. His suite was in the turret, above the grand ballroom. It was decorated in Jack's understated signature style in shades of blue and straw yellow. The sitting area contained sparse contemporary style furnishings from the 1950's. A gold circular ottoman in tufted velvet, reminiscent of those found in hotel lobbies was the center piece of the space. The sectional sofa was upholstered in a heavy nubby royal blue fabric and decorated with gold velvet tasselled toss cushions. A wing chair with blue and cream stripes was placed by the window. The drapes were a royal blue check in a loose-weave fabric. The walls were flaxen grass cloth. The carpet was a lush royal blue. An oak console stereo and a matching record storage cabinet were opposite the wing chair. Abstract art in vivid colors and black and white autographed photographs of celebrities lined the walls: Tony Bennett, Ella Fitzgerald, Frank Sinatra, Pearl Bailey, Mel Torme, Peggy Lee, and Rosemary Clooney.

"You have my itinerary, don't you, Tony?" Jack said, "I have an attached sheet with all the phone numbers of the hotels."

"Don't worry. I'll find you if I need you."

"I'm cutting it shorter than planned. After Europe and Asia, I'm in South America, not Australia. Then, by Mid-October, I'll be in L.A., producing the new album, doing promotional tours in the U.S. for another six months. It feels strange not having Stephen there ever again."

"You know he did the best thing he possibly could, by leaving." Tony said, "It was an altruistic, noble act. He didn't want your reputation tarnished. Let's finish getting you packed, shall we?"

There was a myriad of questions Dottie was longing to ask Jack, but she knew better. Being with the three of them, surrounded by their love, she was acutely aware of how happy she felt at that moment, and wondered if she would ever experience this sense of security and well-being again. She wondered what she needed to do in order to keep life precisely as it was at this very moment, with those she loved most: The sensitive, nurturing Jack, the gentle, dependable Tony, the outrageous, dashing Warren, though she was aware that others' perceptions of her cousins and uncle might vary considerably. For this moment, all was as it should be.

Chapter 3/ But Not For Me

Daisy Parker's house was on a short, narrow one-way street spanning two city blocks. Only pedestrians could enter it from Regent Street, the corner with the majestic red and white gingerbread mansion housing a law office on the ground floor. She was across the street in front of the white mini supermarket with apartments above it. The houses on both sides of Needham Street were built close to the road and tightly knit together. Most appeared to be of Victorian vintage, though plainer and smaller than her mental image of houses of the era, albeit well-maintained on a limited budget. They were almost identical, with peaked roofs, clapboard siding, and symmetrical windows. A white two-storey on the opposite side of the street appeared out of place with its fresh, clean, mid-century architectural style, respectable sized lot, and abundant shrubbery. It even had an attached single car garage with an ornately fenced deck on its roof accessible only through a second storey bedroom. What could have been on this lot for half a century before someone had painstakingly built this lavish home?

Continuing her stroll, she admired the tiny patches of flower beds under oblong front windows. A block up the street, another refreshing example of mid-century architecture peered out at her from between two imposing structures set claustrophobically close on each side. The pristine red brick bungalow with sparkling white trim was set back from the street, and situated directly across from the red brick apartment building Shirl had mentioned. The post-war monstrosity had the battle-worn appearance of a building once respectable and well-maintained, however, one which bore the scars of the passing years, the neglect of new ownership, and the decline of the quality of its tenants. Then, past its driveway was Daisy Parker's house, just as Shirl had told her. It was painted a faded mint green, another classic example of the predominant architectural style on the street, with an extension built on the back. She gingerly rang the doorbell. Following what felt like an eternity, the black heavy door opened and a diminutive woman with a white chignon and blue eyes peeked out.

"Mrs. Parker? I'm Sydney Bertrand, the one who called you last night about renting a room."

"Oh, yes. Shirley's friend. Well, come on in, dear." she stood aside to allow her entry into the dingy slate foyer, which was separated from the interior of the house by yet another heavy door.

"I work evenings. I hope that is not a problem."

"Not at all. What is it you said you did, dear?"

"I'm a singer."

"Sounds lovely." she led her through the second door into the enormous dining room with rich mahogany antiques. On the left was a curving staircase, and on the right, two doors led off the room. Visible through the first open door was a generously-sized living room filled with dark antique furniture. The second door was closed.

"You must be an industrious girl to find work as soon as you arrived in town."

"No. Just very lucky."

"Now, don't worry about the hours, dear. I've had university students who kept late hours, factory workers who worked shifts. At the moment, I have no other boarders, so you have your choice of three rooms upstairs. I sleep down here." she pointed to the closed door, "Why don't we go up and see the rooms? You might decide you don't like any of them."

"I'm sure that won't be the case. I'm grateful to have found a safe, homey place to live."

"Looks like you and I are going to get along just fine, my dear. I was looking for only one female boarder who doesn't smoke – a clean-living, dependable girl."

"I don't have a life outside of work, so you don't have to worry about men coming around."

"Oh, I'm sure things will all change, once you've been here for a while. A lovely girl like you...why, in no time at all, young men will be lining up outside."

"You're very kind. I don't smoke, and I wouldn't dream of having a hot plate in my room. I'm familiar with the basic safety rules. And, I don't use a blow-dryer or a curling iron. I know they can be fire hazards."

"You're certainly very knowledgeable. I don't plug in too many things. Just my stove and fridge, my toaster, iron, spin-washer, lamps, my radio, and my phonograph."

"I've always lived in buildings with knob and tube wiring, so I've learned to be very cautious, even with upgraded wiring."

"I don't have any upgrading here, dear. I'm glad you're cautious."

"Mrs. Parker, I'm grateful that you're open-minded about my line of work. You don't have preconceived notions about singers."

"Singing is a God-given talent. You have to use what God gave you. Why would anyone hold that against you? They must be jealous. I don't care how you earn a living; it's how you live your life I'm concerned with. We were going to see the bedrooms. They're not fancy, but they're clean."

She followed Daisy up the curved staircase to the claustrophobic upper floor with the low ceilings and gables. The wide metal column of the antiquated heating system in the hallway lent the space an industrial air. The rooms were of a respectable size, one being only slightly larger than the other two. Sparsely furnished, each had a narrow twin bed with an unadorned metal headboard painted aquamarine. The bedspreads were chenille, each in the predominant color of the respective room. A Shaker style chair and a small vanity table in well-worn wood, as well as a sizable chest of drawers were diligently placed in each room. The floors were old maple, with oval scatter rugs placed strategically to conceal flaws.

The pinch-pleated drapes were lined cotton print. The largest room, "the green room" had mint green walls, a mint green bedspread, and striped drapes in varying shades of green with a rug in the same hues. The window faced northwest. The blue and the pink rooms were across the hall, smaller but brighter, and almost identical in size. "The blue room" had white leno curtains with delicate blue flowers, and the "the pink room" had pink daisy print curtains. The washed-out pastel walls made each room feel cold. She leaned down to open her travel bag, and produced a crumpled bundle of bills, which she placed in Daisy's palm.

"One month's room and board. I'll take the pink room."

"It's my favorite, too. Why don't you leave your things here, and come down for some tea?"

"Thank you. I'd love to."

"Yes, you and I are going to get along famously, dear. I've had some trouble in the past. I was thinking about giving up taking in boarders."

"I'm so glad you didn't. Where would I be now if you had?."

They descended the stairs cautiously.

"The world isn't what it used to be. I had girls doing drugs up there. I could smell it. I called up to Danielle, asked her what the smell was. She said she was ironing her blouse and scorched it. I wasn't born yesterday. I knew she was up to no good. Gave her her notice right then and there. Betty and John next door in the peach house used to take in boarders. They had trouble, too. I asked Betty what that smell was, and she said it was marijuana. It smelled like burning rope. She told me she and John weren't having any more girls boarding with them. Those girls were sneaking men into their rooms."

"Don't worry, Mrs. Parker, those will be the least of your worries. I absolutely abhor drugs, and when it comes to men, I'm invisible."

41

"What type of music do you sing, dear? Is it that new yippie music? Do you sing those songs like "Feeling Gravy" and "Yummy in My Tummy"?"

"Oh no. I sing the old standards. Gershwin, Rodgers and Hart, Jerome Kern, Billy Strayhorn."

"Do you sing Cole Porter? I just adore Cole Porter."

"Yes I do."

"How lovely. Where is it that you sing, dear?"

"Chandler's Lounge."

"I'm afraid I don't get out much. Where is it? What is it like?"

"It's in Willow Place. I haven't actually seen the lounge yet. I start tonight."

"Isn't Willow Place owned by the Horncastles?"

"I don't know very much about it yet. The owner's name is Jack Chandler."

"Ah, yes. He is Audrey Horncastle's stepson. She was married to an American widower, Edward Chandler. The Horncastles had that place built a few years back. The other Horncastle boy, Willy's son, owns the restaurant part. The Horncastles are the founders of this town. Robert Horncastle was the Lieutenant Governor back in the 1930's. Their name is synonymous with Beavertown."

"I hope you can come to the lounge with me sometime."

"I would love it, dear. Come." she took her hand and led her to a small room to the left of the dining room, "I want to show you something."

It was a tiny space tucked away behind the staircase. Had Daisy not shown it to her, Sydney might have missed it. Three of the walls were lined from floor to ceiling with robin blue shelves filled with records. Under the window was the stereo console and a divan with plum silk cushions.

"This is magnificent!" Sydney's face lit up.

"I listen to music in here most afternoons. In the summer, I open this window, put a record on, and sit outside the kitchen door. People from the apartment building sometimes stop by and chat.

Why don't we go into the kitchen and have our tea, dear?" Daisy led her to the back of the house to an enormous country kitchen, the entire floor space of the extension built onto the back of the house. Sydney wondered where the original kitchen might have been.

The inexpensive plywood cupboards, which had been de rigeur until the present decade, and were often painted a glossy alkyd white, were painted mint green. The thin white arborite sheets glued over the black gummy counters were secured with chrome edging. The oversized white porcelain sink had a faded green geometric print skirt under it. Home-grown plants in aged earthenware pots lined the window sills. The clutter of rusting muffin tins, frying pans, and stock pots lined the yellowing counters. In the far left corner was the door leading to the narrow strip of lawn facing the apartment building. On the back wall, standing alone was the double sized Moffatt range with six burners and two ovens, and the rounded corners from the post war era. The walls were painted the color of baby chicks. The ruffled curtains on the window above the sink were yellow gingham. Through the window, she could see the peach Cape Cod with the exterior stairs leading to the second floor.

"Your name is far from ordinary, isn't it?" Daisy was filling an aluminum tea kettle with water, "when you told me over the telephone your name was Sydney, I got to thinking: You don't hear it much anymore. There were some lasses named Sydney when I was a wee one back in the old country. My aunt had a servant girl, a pretty little slip of a thing. The lads sure came around an awful lot. Then, she got in a family way and married this scraggly chimney sweep. He went off to fight in World War I and was killed in action. I don't know what happened to Sydney after that...Such a beauty she was...Back then, only ladies spelled it with a "Y", and men with an "I". Later, it fell out of use with ladies altogether. I thought it such as shame. I've always liked that name for a girl. You are the first Sydney I've met since then. How did you come by it, dear? Is it popular in Quebec?"

43

"I might have been named after my father. I've never met my parents."

"I'm so sorry. Did they die?"

"I...don't think so."

"Did they put you up for adoption?"

"Not exactly."

"I'm sorry, dear. I didn't mean to pry."

"Mrs. Parker, when I am able to talk, you'll definitely be the first one I'll be talking to about it. But not yet. I'm sorry."

"No, I'm sorry."

"It's perfectly all right."

"I had no right to press you."

"No problem. By the way, I've never met another female with my name, either."

"That makes you one of a kind." Daisy opened a tin of Dutch shortbread cookies, "You can move in any time you wish, dear. You can use two rooms, if you like."

"I can move in right now. The bag I left upstairs contains all of my worldly possessions."

Daisy glanced up in astonishment.

"I'm like a turtle." Sydney said, "I don't accumulate things, and what I have, I carry on my back. The only valuables I have are my record albums."

Daisy placed two jadeite mugs, the type sold in every five and ten, on the white ice crackle Formica table.

"Do you take milk and sugar, dear?"

"No, thank you." she enclosed the mug in her hands and savored the warmth spreading through her.

"You are welcome to use my phonograph anytime, dear."

"You are very kind." she bit her lower lip, overwhelmed by this kindness.

"We sensitive souls need music for nourishment."

"It can sustain you through the darkest times."

44

"It sustained me through two world wars. How's your tea, dear?"

"It's wonderful."

"I only buy Darjeeling. It was my Oscar's favorite." her eyes were moistened, "I married him after World War I, and came with him to this new and strange land. We had a farm in Ontario for many years. Times were hard, but we somehow managed to raise our daughters and put them through university. One is a lawyer in Toronto, and so is her husband. The younger one is a nurse in Alberta. We moved here once my Oscar got too weak with rheumatism, and we had to sell the farm. His sister was living near here, so we came out and bought this house eighteen years ago. My Oscar left us soon after that. He only got to enjoy his retirement for two years."

"I'm sorry."

"We had a good life together. We were happy. I have wonderful memories of him."

Tears welling in her eyes, Sydney savored the soothing aroma of the tea, feeling her pores tingling with the steam. This was now her new home. She could learn to be happy here. Happier than she had ever been.

...Overheard snippets of a conversation from the table behind her at the patisserie might not have been a solid foundation for embarking on this journey, yet the time had been right to leave grimy old Montreal behind. She had been there too long. Not that it had been without its perks. She smiled in nostalgia, revisiting her afternoons at the patisserie, and her warm conversations with the elderly Portuguese couple who had bought it two years earlier. Even in her dismal apartments, she had found the joy of solitude revitalizing. Music and literature had never betrayed her. And neither had Pierre. Her few outings to the park and inexpensive eateries had been with him. She smiled, remembering the way people had mistaken them for a couple, and how embarrassed she had been for him, but he had never allowed her to feel his own discomfort. Secure in his own skin as a gay man, he was not hesitant about being seen with a woman and possibly discouraging potential lovers. He had treated her with the utmost respect and brotherly solicitude, protected her from lecherous men. Her eyes stung.

Long ago, she had arrived in Montreal in the same fashion she had arrived here. On a fruitless mission with even fewer leads, she had ended up staying, a part of her hoping against hope that the answers she sought would miraculously materialize there, her mother's birthplace.

Daisy had been talking all this while, enlightening her about the layout of Beavertown, and the best pedestrian routes.

"I've been there so long, I watched different families come and go. Especially the apartment building. No one stays long. But I remember a little girl who sat by a long narrow second-storey window day and night, slumped over a desk for three years. Oh, this must have been thirteen or fourteen years ago or more. I still remember her as if it were yesterday. She must have been ten or eleven when I first spotted her. She had two long golden braids down to her waist, and thick glasses. She occasionally came outside and talked to me about how much she enjoyed my music. I don't remember her ever talking about her family. Her clothing was shabby and outdated. Her eyes were sunken with dark circles under them. It seemed she always had a cast or a sling or a bandage. She said she was clumsy, but I think she kept a lot of secrets. She didn't seem to have anyone who cared about her. She had a most unusual name, too. I wish I could remember it. The name of a tree...Magnolia? No. Wisteria? No. It'll come to me, one of these days. Then, one day, she just disappeared. I've been saying a prayer for her every night since then. I'm afraid she might be dead."

"It's a haunting image...A child in pain...I hope she was able to get out of her circumstances and build a life for herself."

"I hope so, dear." she took the mugs to the sink, "I'll give you a chance to unpack and get settled in, dear. I'll start supper."

"Let me help."

"Not today. You'll have plenty of opportunities to help later."

"Thank you."

Her modest wardrobe did not take up much space in the generously sized closet. Once she removed her two polyester-knit dresses, robin blue and peach, yesterday's nautical set, her long white cardigan, light blue jeans, burgundy oriental peasant skirt, and her ecru Turkish cotton peasant tops from her bag and hung them up on the wire hangers provided, the bulge on the bag was deflated. She removed her tan wedge sandals and white gum rubber boots and placed them on the closet floor. From the opposite side of the bag, she removed the manila envelope of vital documents and slid it in the top drawer of the chest of drawers. Two cosmetic bags containing costume jewellery, lipstick, eyeliner, comb, razors, toothpaste, toothbrush, and deodorant, she placed in the two vanity drawers. Her bag of undergarments and the bundle of T-shirts and tops, she slid into two other chest drawers. Her records found a home in the bottom drawer. She slung her small pocketbook over her shoulder and placed the now empty travel bag on the closet floor. She did not own an item of clothing suitable for her new job. She had left Montreal with only the bare essentials and given away the work dresses which held only painful memories. There was enough time to shop for a dress and return home in time for supper and a shower.

"Mrs. Parker," she called out from the bottom of the stairs, "I'm going out to buy myself a decent work outfit. I'll be back for supper."

"You go right ahead, dear. You want to leave a good impression on your first day." Daisy emerged from the kitchen, wearing a green apron with enormous flowers.

"Is it all right if I look in your telephone book?"

"Help yourself. It's right there on the credenza, beside the telephone." she returned to her cooking.

Sydney turned the pages with trembling fingers. The only listing for Goldstein was the music shop. No home number.

"Sydney, dear, I forgot to give you your house key!" Daisy opened one of the credenza drawers and produced a Yale key on a plastic chicken keychain.

"Thank you." Sydney tucked it into her pocketbook and made a mental note to buy a replacement keychain for the duration of time she was going to be living there.

She decided to walk to the other end of Needham Street and journey downtown via York Street. Past Betty's charming Cape Cod, the street became bleak. Dilapidated shacks with verdigris asbestos shingles leaned wearily toward one another. The two houses at the end of Needham Street were of the nondescript shabby variety with multiple extensions built haphazardly onto one another until collision with the neighboring house in either direction prevented further sprawl.

She turned the corner to York Street, which, like Regent Street was one of three main arteries running the full length of town from Queen Street to Prospect Street on the hilltop. Prospect Street housed the only high school, completed four years earlier. It was an unwieldy building resembling a prison, she thought, from the newspaper clipping she had seen tucked into the telephone book, dated March 1972. Why had Daisy saved an article about the newly-built high school?

On Queen Street, she found her way back to the same location and peered in the window. She recognized the surly woman with her back turned, speaking with a grey-haired, bespectacled man in a wheelchair. The door had been propped open to allow fresh air into the tiny store. Her heart was pounding a jungle drum beat, as she strained her ears for fragments of their conversation, to no avail. The woman turned around to retrieve a book from behind the counter, and caught a glimpse of her. An expression of indignation swept over her face.

"It's that pesky girl again! What is she doing back here?"

"What is it, Agnes?" the man wheeled himself around to get a better view of the street, and look directly at her. She stepped back instinctively.

"It's that crazy girl. I told her to scram when she came around yesterday."

"What was she looking for?"

Pressed against the wall, out of their field of vision, she listened.

"Who knows? Who cares? She wouldn't tell me. I told her to leave me her name and number, but she insisted she had to see you in person."

"Did she indicate what it might be about?"

"No. I saw her lurking outside this morning, shortly after I opened up. She didn't come in, but if she hadn't moved along when she did, I would have called the police. She's some kind of a lunatic. I think she's still out there. I'm going to call the police right now and get this sorted, once and for all."

"No, Agnes. I'll speak to her. I'm the one she asked for."

"No, sir. I don't think that's a good idea. She's a nutcase."

"She looks harmless to me." he wheeled himself to the threshold, "Hello?" he peeked his head out.

She was trembling, unable to steady herself.

"Is there anything I can do for you, Miss?" he smiled benevolently, "I'm afraid I'm at a disadvantage. You know my name, but I don't know yours."

She wept silent tears, taking in every detail of his features – his long nose, elongated ears, soft brown eyes, tired, sloping shoulders.

"Miss, it's obvious that you are in distress. Please let me help. What can I do?"

"It's not important. I'm sorry I disturbed you."

"You did not disturb me in the least."

"I'm sorry. I have to go." she turned to run, however, tripped on the uneven sidewalk.

He reached out his arms to catch her, and she instinctively gripped his hands to steady herself.

"Why don't you come in and have a glass of water?"

"No thank you. I've been too much trouble. Thank you for your kindness. I appreciate it. Good-bye."

His eyes followed her with a pained expression until her pastel print dress dissolved into the crowd like a watercolor in the rain.

Chapter 4/ The Siren

From the tablecloths and the curtains, to the wallpaper, everything was in soft shades of blue. Even the flowers on the tables placed in curved glass vases were freshly-cut blue hyacinths. Waiters in formal attire were serving drinks efficiently. He waited until the two couples ahead of him were seated, and the maître D' caught sight of him.

"Mr. Horncastle, what can I do for you, sir?"

"Is Brett around, Johnny?"

"Yes sir. Please have a seat. I'll send Andy over to take your order."

"Thanks, Johnny."

"I'll get Brett for you, sir." he led him to the best table in the house, by a large window overlooking the window, and with the best view of the stage.

A fresh-faced young man was belting out "Volare" to the adoring female audience members in his ill-fitting baby blue suit.

"May I take your order, Mr. Horncastle?" a young waiter was promptly by his table.

"A dry martini, please, Andy."

"Coming right up, sir."

He leaned back in his chair and observed in amusement as the youthful singer curtsied at the end of the number, and broke into song once more with another Dean Martin standard, "Amore".

A tall, striking brunette with dramatically arched eyebrows and eyes like a gazelle's emerged from the discrete path leading from the basement to the main seating area. In her deep rose silk gown, she dazzled like a 1930's Hollywood siren.

"Hello, darling. To what do I owe this honor?" she kissed his cheek, leaving a red imprint.

"Hello, Brett. You look lovely as ever." he gazed longingly at her as she took the chair he held out for her and seductively tossed back her luxuriant shoulder-length hair.

"You've been avoiding me, darling. You show up here at odd hours during the day and always leave before the lounge opens. You only come here to do paperwork, and conveniently vanish before the show starts. Jack left you in charge during his absence. That doesn't mean just the paperwork. How are you going to know we're not all singing off-key and getting booed by the audience? We could start losing all our customers to "The Beaver Room" next door. You'll have to get the whip out and keep us on our toes."

"Judging by the audience's reaction to Danny, I don't think I have too much to worry about."

"The kids' good, isn't he? Big hit with the ladies. Another Dino in the making."

"Buy you a drink?"

"It's a start. You're learning." she winked.

"Your drink, sir." Andy had returned with his martini.

"One for the lady, Andy."

"Make mine extra dry, Andy, baby doll." she batted her eyelashes at the young waiter.

"Most of my evenings are tied up at the restaurant. I rely on Richard to let me know if something's amiss. I'm only next door."

"Just funning you, hon." she winked, "You could drop in to visit me at home, you know, darling. I'm home Sundays."

"So are Keir, Toby, your lodger, and the lady next door."

"You could make those reservations at Silverwood, sweetheart." she tapped the side of her nose playfully.

"Brett...Brett..." he held her exquisite face in his hands tenderly, "You know why."

"Why do you have to spoil it, Tony? Why can't we just..."

He placed a finger on her lips.

Andy returned with her drink. She took a swig of her martini and proceeded to twirl the swizzle stick between her fingers, her eyes on the slayed olive at the end of it.

"Brett, you know you can put an end to all this by saying one simple word."

"Tony, you know why. Can't we just go back to the way it was before? It was just swell. Why do we have to spoil it?"

"You're running like a frightened fawn."

"I'm on in a little while and I need to be composed."

"You'll be fine. You're a pro."

"That's me, Brett, the old pro. Everything slides off my back...considering what type of woman I am."

"Brett, it's not easy for me, either."

"What was so important that you broke your vow to avoid me to come to the club, then?"

"Brett..."

"I know you're after information, and you want my help." she savored her olive, careful to avoid his gaze.

"I'm doing a background check on Sydney Bertrand."

"If you hadn't been so busy avoiding me, you could've met her yourself a long time ago. Why the curiosity? What has she done?"

"Nothing that I'm aware of."

"You're a big boy now, Tony. You can arrange your own social calendar. You don't need Aunty Brett to find dates for you."

"Did she tell you why she left Montreal for an obscure little town? Did she mention any family or friends she has here?"

"Why all this interest? Is she a fugitive from the law?"

"No."

"Then, leave her alone. She's a nice girl."

"We're trying to determine whether she's out to fleece Edna and Sid by impersonating their granddaughter."

"Granddaughter! Those aren't that ancient! Daughter, maybe."

"Jack said she was barely out of her teens."

"Leave it to Jack!" she threw her head back in laughter, "How old does he think I am?"

"You know you're ageless, Brett."

"That's what you say to all the girls."

"You know I only have eyes for you."

"Sure, hon. How many of those martinis have you had?"

"What is her real age?"

"She says she's thirty-seven. And that's all you're getting out of me."

"This is serious. She could be a con artist. That puts her at the right age to be their daughter."

"Whatever gave you such a lame-brain idea?"

"Her name is Sydney."

"Good one. Anyone with that name is a con artist."

"She's also from Montreal."

"Heaven forbid!"

"You know Edna's from Montreal. People who knew her might have been talking about her frantic search for her daughter. Sydney might have overheard something and decided to capitalize on it."

"A modern day Anastasia." she shook her head incredulously, "Wouldn't she have contacted them by now, if they are, indeed, the reason she came here?"

"She might not have been able to track them down. She might not have enough information to act upon yet. It can't be a coincidence that she would turn up for an audition here."

"How could she possibly have known Jack was connected to them? That's not something she could have overheard in Montreal."

"This can't all be a coincidence."

"It could. Did Jack believe all this nonsense, too?"

"He assumed she was the real deal."

"Did it ever occur to you he might be right? You highbrows live in constant paranoia. You think everyone's an extortionist. You think there's a criminal lurking around each corner. Who came up with this cockeyed theory, anyway?"

"Warren."

"A ha! There. That says it all."

"Do you think you could put your feelings about my family aside for once and look at this objectively? Edna and Sid are not Horncastles. Don't you want to protect them from opportunists who want to cash in on their misfortunes?"

"Of course."

"Do you think you could get her to open up to you more?"

"I am not going to be your spy, Tony. It's unethical. If she is their daughter, there might be a reason why she hasn't come forward all this time. She might not be ready yet."

"Brett, Edna and Sid have been going through hell for years. Your protectiveness is noble, but it is not fair to them."

"It's not fair to Sydney to be poked and prodded by your family. I don't want to see that poor little flower set up for a heartbreak. Your family'll pick her bones dry. If it turns out that she's not "their" Sydney", and it's all a coincidence, you'll toss her away like yesterday's news. And if she is "their" Sydney, you mucky mucks will set up unrealistic expectations she can never meet. You'll try to make her over, scrutinize her every move, and imprison her in your enchanted kingdom. And, should she ever step out of line and have lapses of humanity, you'll persecute her and banish her from the kingdom."

"If it turns out that she's their Sydney, then both families would welcome her with open arms."

"Knowing that bunch, I wouldn't hold my breath."

"You don't even know my entire family."

"I know enough. I've met your parents, your Uncle Donald and his addle-brained social-climbing wife Annette, not to mention their psychopathic son with the peculiar name...I've met your loutish Casanova of an uncle, dear old Warren. Need I say more?"

"We're not all bad. There's Jack."

"He's not a true Horncastle. I don't know how little Dottie ever grew out of that tribe. She's such a doll. She must take after Edna."

"How do I fit into the picture?"

She shot up a wounded glance at him.

"Brett, when are we going to stop playing this charade?"

"Tony, this is not the time or the place."

"It never is, is it?"

"I have to go on in a few minutes. Danny looks exhausted. He's enrolled in intersession courses. When he gets home, he has to read four chapters and write an essay. Then he has to be in class at 8 A.M. No break for the poor devil. I wouldn't want to be young again for anything in the world."

"We've already paid our dues."

"If you won't turn into a pumpkin, you can stay until closing and meet Sydney for yourself. She's doing the final set. But I want you to go easy on her."

"Don't worry. I trust your judgment. If you think she's honest, I'll assume she is."

"You're learning. Why don't you buy Shayleigh a drink? I see her coming in now." she rose from her chair and waved wildly to attract the attention of a young woman with light auburn hair.

Noticing her, Shayleigh smiled and waved back.

"Keep that lecherous Umberto, the Spanish prof at that table away from Shayleigh. Pretend you're her date." Brett whispered to Tony, "He starts drooling the moment he sees her, and puts the moves on her shamelessly."

"That old geezer?" Tony appeared perplexed.

"He's married with a daughter older than Shayleigh. Just act like you're her date."

"Wouldn't that make you jealous?"

"You wish." she laughed, "Make those reservations at Silverwood, sweetheart!" she turned to embrace Shayleigh, who, by this time, was at their table. "Hello, sweetheart. I'm glad you got here okay. Tony's going to be your date for the evening."

"He is, is he?" she glanced over at him, "What does he have to say about it?"

"It will be my pleasure." he courteously pulled her chair out for her.

"We're all going to stay till closing time and have a few drinks with Sydney." Brett told her.

"That sounds good."

"Tony'll love having three gorgeous women by his side." Brett slithered away, blowing kisses in the direction of the table.

Following the drumroll, Richard appeared on the stage vacated by Danny, and announced with a scowl:

"Ladies and gentlemen, Chandler's Lounge is proud to present the captivating Ms. Brett Morrow."

Amidst the applause, she appeared, blowing kisses at the audience. In her smoky voice, she broke into strains of "We'll Be Together Again".

"What are you having, Shayleigh?" Tony motioned to Andy.

"A Manhattan, please."

"Are you sure you're legal? Wouldn't you rather have a soft drink?"

She burst into laughter.

"I'm sorry but you look the same age as my little cousin, Dottie."

"How old is she? Twelve?"

"A Manhattan, and another martini, please, Andy." he turned to the conscientious waiter, "I'm sorry." he said, once Andy had left. "Dottie's sixteen. And very innocent. I'd like to keep her that way for as long as possible."

"That might be difficult in the seventies."

"I'm aware of that."

He was struck aware of how little he knew about this young woman. She had always been just Shayleigh, Brett's lodger, who, at times, was the one to open the door for him on his visits to Brett. Her age, occupation, and personal life remained unknown, insignificant and irrelevant within the framework of his relationship with Brett. If it could still be called that now.

"It's been a while since you've come around. The boys have been asking where you are." she said.

"Say hi to them for me, will you? Tell them I'll take them to see the next action flick."

Shayleigh treaded cautiously around the issue of their relationship. Brett and Tony's was certainly an unusual one at that. But, then, Brett and Tony were unusual people. The fluidity of their boundaries intrigued her, and confused her. Possessive and exclusive by nature, she questioned the merits of such elasticity, and wondered how she herself would cope in a union that dictated it. Whether the ground rules had been set by either Brett or Tony, or mutually agreed upon, she had difficulty fathoming the relaxed way the two of them had of relating to one another. Perhaps she herself lacked the self-assurance and life experience to be contented with such a non-traditional arrangement.

Andy served their drinks. Mild mannered and soft featured, he appeared barely legal.

"How's Jack doing on his tour?" she asked conversationally.

"They love him in Europe."

"I imagine. He's underappreciated in these parts. People around here either want to go to smoky pubs and listen to country music, or consider themselves highbrow and only attend symphony concerts. No one has class – just affectation."

"You sound like Brett." he said, gazing longingly at the doe-eyed siren on the stage, lost in the haunting melody of "Lush Life".

"You and Jack are single-handedly responsible for bringing sophistication to this backward little place."

"That's precisely what Brett says."

"I still wouldn't want to live in a big city again – unless it's New York. Places like Toronto and Vancouver are too stilted, plastic, too self-conscious, too caught up in their own sense of self-importance. New York just is."

Sipping her drink, she wondered how it must feel for Tony to see other men lusting after Brett and flaunting it before his eyes.

"How is the new girl making out?"

"Sydney? She's fitting in well."

"What's your impression of her?"

"She's nice. A bit guarded. But pleasant. I like her."

"Is she good-looking?"

"She has a cute girl-next-door look. You'll meet her soon."

Brett, who was between songs, was speaking to the audience.

"I would like to dedicate this next song to my very dear friend and fellow former New Yorker: Shayleigh Wallace." she broke into strains of "Autumn In New York".

"You must get homesick for the hustle and bustle of New York." Tony said.

"A part of me will always be back there. Brett really understands that feeling."

"We all miss our roots. Jack enjoys his time in L.A. even more so, because that's where his roots are." he took the last sip of his drink, "I'm fortunate. I'm a local boy through and through."

"Is Jack's divorce final?"

"At last. What a mess."

"Was this his fourth or fifth? I lost track."

"I know how it looks, but Jack only has the opportunity to meet a certain type of woman, due to the circles he travels in."

"In the plastic, superficial world of celebrities and groupies, there's no substance or depth. I think Jack needs that. He's not like the other people in those circles."

"Very astute." he remarked in admiration.

Brett was singing "More Than You Know". Her enormous coal-black eyes were transfixed on Tony. Flawless beauty such as hers was more of a curse than a blessing, Shayleigh mused. Brett possessed the power to captivate completely. She studied Tony's finely chiseled features. Beavertown's single women dreamed of marrying the town's dark-haired prince and living in his family's mansion. Brett possessed his heart, yet appeared reluctant to commit herself emotionally. Shayleigh resented her own youth and lack of experience for making it so awkward to navigate her way in the world.

Brett was now crooning "East Of The Sun". Other men had been calling for her at the house of late, and Shayleigh wondered how Brett could stomach any of them. She was secretly delighted by Sydney's arrival on the scene, as she seemed to be a kindred spirit in these matters. If anything, she appeared oblivious to all men.

Brett had begun "How Deep Is The Ocean", yet Tony's attention appeared to have been diverted elsewhere, to something by the entrance to the lounge.

"I don't believe it!" he said.

Following the direction of his eyes, she spotted a dimpled man with a thick, dark mane, and a flashy brunette on his arm.

"He swore he'd never set foot in this place." Tony murmured incredulously.

"Are you referring to the Winston Rekert lookalike at the door with the big slut?"

"You cut right through the chase. No pussy-footing around." he smiled, "Yes. That's my dear Uncle Warren."

"Uncle? He looks too young."

"He's the youngest sibling. My father, Dottie's father, Jack's stepmother, and their other sister, who, we all pretend doesn't exist, are all considerably older than Warren."

"You certainly have a fascinating family."

"Much to my chagrin."

"Brett never mentioned this Warren."

"They don't get along. I thought everyone knew about him."

"Not me. I'm out of the loop. I rely solely on Brett to keep me up to date."

"This is one nugget Brett must have deemed unsuitable for your ears."

"Why? What has he done? Now you've piqued my interest."

"How long do you have?"

Brett was singing "Love For Sale". Warren, who, by now, had spotted Tony, waved. Turning to his companion, he whispered in her ear. She reluctantly slinked toward the bar, the skimpy scarlet fabric of her dress hugging her posterior in an unbecoming fashion. Warren's eyes followed the woman's buttocks as he made his way to Tony and Shayleigh's table.

"How old is he?" Shayleigh whispered to Tony.

"Fifty-two."

"He's handsome, I admit. He's attracted a lot of attention from the women in here."

"He's well aware of the effect he has on women and he knows how to exploit it."

Warren, who, by now, was at their table, flashed a very white, even set of teeth at them.

"Hey, Tone – how are things? What are the old fogies up to, tonight?"

"What are you doing here, Warren? I thought you were too hip for this place. Why aren't you at "The Metro", doing the hustle with your lovely date?"

"I wanted to see how my favorite nephew was doing. Aren't you going to introduce me to your beautiful date, old boy?"

"Shayleigh, this is the infamous Warren Horncastle. Warren, meet Shayleigh Wallace."

"Enchanted." Warren kissed her hand and gazed intensely into her eyes.

"Why don't you ask your date to join us?" Tony said.

"Samia seems to be doing all right for herself." he glanced back at the bar, where the olive-skinned beauty was laughing and nuzzling with a moderately handsome man.

"Don't you want to rescue her from that interloper?" Tony suggested.

"I don't think she needs rescuing. He's welcome to her." Warren smiled, settling back in his chair, "I thought I'd check out the new dish. Some of the fellows at work said she was quite a looker. I had to see for myself. Has she been on yet?"

"She's next." Shayleigh said.

Her set complete, Brett was blowing kisses at her audience amidst hearty applause and shouts of "We love you, Brett!", particularly from the younger men. She slid behind the curtain. "Gene And The Matchmakers", the club's band, struck up with a soft rendition of "Corcovado".

Samia was slinking toward their table with an exaggerated swivel of her hips.

"Warren, darling..." she purred, expertly manoeuvering her scarlet talons through his abundant mane, "Why didn't you come back? I ordered you a drink and put it on your tab, but you never came back to drink it. So, I drank it. I was getting lonely, but a very nice gentleman kept me company. Aren't you going to introduce me to your friends?"

"Samia, this is my nephew Tony. And, this is Shelley Wallace."

"Shayleigh" Tony corrected him.

"My apologies. This is Samia El Khazin."

"Charmed, I'm sure." Samia simpered, "Warren, honey, come on, let's split this joint. It's like the Lawrence Welk show. All the beautiful people are at "The Metro". I don't want to listen to old people's music. I want to disco, do the hustle, and boogie."

"All in due time, baby. Sit back and relax. You can have another Singapore Sling on Tony. For your information, I don't have a tab here."

"I want to go to "The Metro"." she pouted.

"I'll call you a cab." he rose reluctantly.

"Wuzzy-Bear, you're no fun." she whined, "You'd better make it up to me tomorrow night."

"I'll call you." he led her back to the entrance, "Johnny, call the lady a cab, will you?"

"Yes sir."

"Warren." she clutched his sleeve.

He was gone. Tony and Shayleigh glanced knowingly at each other. Warren returned to the table.

"Where did you ever pick up Scarlett O'Hara, Wuzzy-Bear?" Tony laughed.

"At "The Metro"."

"What escort service does she work for?"

"She's a hairstylist at "Fashion Cuts". She's a complete moron."

"I almost feel sorry for her." Tony shook his head.

Upon hearing the drumroll, Warren averted his eyes to the stage. The bags under Richard's eyes were even more pronounced than usual. His lacklustre voice announced:

"Ladies and gentlemen, Chandler's Lounge presents Ms. Sydney Bertrand."

Almost gliding onto the stage, a remote half-smile on her full lips, Sydney broke into song with "Someone To Watch Over Me" in a voice more girlish and ethereal than her predecessor's.

"Wow..." Warren murmured, transfixed, "She's a knockout."

"Warren, if you don't slow down, someday your fast and loose ways with women are going to catch up with you."

"I'm much too slick for that, dear nephew."

Brett, who, by now, had changed into her street clothes, appeared, her curls pulled away from her face with a black velvet hairband exposing her broad forehead. She was dressed in a black and gold geometric print button-down blouse and black palazzo pants. At the sight of Warren, she stopped dead in her tracks.

"Be still, my heart."

"Nice to see you, too, Brett." Warren winked at her.

"Is the wolf on the prowl again, in search of defenseless lambs?" she remarked with disdain, seating herself between Shayleigh and Tony.

"You're jealous, Brett, because you're over the hill, and wolves don't pay attention to you anymore." Warren winked at her, "I have a great title for a movie: "An Aging Trollop In Beavertown"."

"That's enough, Warren." Tony intercepted, "Why don't you return to "The Metro" and see if you can pick up another hairdresser?...Get you a drink, sweetheart?" he turned to Brett with tenderness.

"Hit a nerve, didn't I?" Warren smirked.

"One of these days, Warren..." Brett narrowed her eyes at him.

"Admit it, Brett. We all know you're lusting after me."

"In your dreams."

"Stop playing hard to get. Everyone knows how easy your virtue is."

"Do you want to be carried out on a stretcher?" Tony leapt to his feet.

"She's got you twisted around her little finger, Tony. I hope you come to your senses before she destroys you completely. Don't worry: I'm leaving. I'd rather listen to the songbird from the bar." he blew a kiss at Brett.

"Let's not allow that vermin to ruin our evening." Brett leaned back, "Let's have a round of drinks...Andy, sweetheart! Over here, hon! Three martinis, please – all extra dry."

"Warren has designs on Sydney." Shayleigh informed her.

"That slime ball! He's the last thing she needs. If he touches a hair on her head, he's going to answer to me!"

"Don't get too worked up over him. He's not worth it. You were wonderful." Tony's hand closed on hers.

"Thank you, sweetness." she kissed his cheek, "What do you think of Sydney? No one can belt out a Gershwin tune better than she can."

"She's a top-notch entertainer."

"That Warren's quite a character." Shayleigh remarked as Andy brought their drinks, "Don't worry, Brett. I've been duly warned by Tony to stay clear of him."

"He showed up with a woman of questionable origins that he had picked up at "The Metro"." Tony shook his head, "Then, he tried to unload her on some unsuspecting patron. But she proved to be a bigger handful than he had predicted."

"He wanted to check out Sydney." Shayleigh joined in, "But his hooker was so clingy. She had a sleazy name, too: Samia Ala Kazzeena or something. He ended up putting her in a cab and sending her on her way...You should have seen the dress on her...and her makeup."

"I'm heartbroken I missed it." she rolled her eyes, "With Warren, the wonders never cease."

"What does he do for a living?"

"He teaches high school history."

"I never would have pegged him as a school teacher. He's too flamboyant...too much of a playboy."

"Warren's a mass of contradictions." Tony said.

"He must sleep with all his female students." Shayleigh laughed.

"He's very particular about age." Tony said, "It may be his only redeeming quality, but when it comes to the age of his conquests, he has his scruples."

"Warren and scruples cannot be mentioned in the same sentence." Brett said.

"He's intriguing." Shayleigh mused.

"Bite your tongue!" Brett admonished her, "Don't even joke about that!"

"He is nothing but trouble." Tony explained paternally.

"Someday, Warren's going to die the loneliest old man." Brett sighed, "I probably ought to pity him, but I have far too much contempt for him."

"I must admit Sydney sings those slow numbers with so much emotion." Tony attempted to change the subject.

"Do you take back all your allegations now that you've seen her?"

"I take it all back." he gazed at her tenderly, "For you, anything."

Shayleigh's eyes searched the bar area for a glimpse of Warren. Her view was obstructed by the two rotund men on the first two barstools. She was twenty-six years old, and had never experienced love. Or anything remotely resembling it. She had never been on a date with a real man. Slimy reptiles from her university days did not count. Even a handshake with one of them had been nauseating. She wished she could be more like Brett.

Amid the applause, bowing shyly at her audience, Sydney scurried off the stage and down the corridor to the stairs leading to the basement dressing rooms, when a seductive baritone beckoned her.

"You were terrific."

She turned around sheepishly to Warren's intense dark eyes.

"I'm Warren Horncastle." he took her hand and kissed it, "Jack obviously knew what he was doing when he hired you."

She was speechless.

"That color is very becoming to you." he eyed her appreciatively, his gaze lingering on her curves under the sumptuous chocolate velvet gown. It was one Brett had persuaded her to buy on a day she had gone shopping with her to assist her in expanding her work wardrobe. She had felt uncomfortable spending more money on one dress than she had ever spent on an entire year's wardrobe in the past. Had Brett not been with her, she would have placed it back on the rack.

"What do you say you and I slip out the back door after you get into something more comfortable, and get a bite to eat?" he winked.

"I promised to have drinks with Brett and her friends."

"So? You're a free agent. She doesn't own you. I would really like to become better acquainted with you. I find you absolutely captivating."

"There are no restaurants open at this hour."

"Haven't you ever heard of "The Admiral" on Woodstock Road? If you're really adventurous, "Al's Truck Stop" on the Trans Canada is always open. They've got the best home fries."

"I'm sure they do. Thank you, but I really can't."

"How about tomorrow then?"

"I'm really not sure, Mr. Horncastle."

"Warren, please."

"Warren."

"May I call you Sydney? It's a delightful name. Will you grace me with the pleasure of your company by having dinner with me tomorrow night?"

"I..."

"Don't you trust me? Do you want references?"

She smiled weakly.

"I must be doing something right. I thought I saw a smile. You should smile more often." his index finger traced the outline of her mouth, "You are too lovely to hide behind a solemn expression."

She peered up at his handsome face, feeling herself being flung from a roller coaster.

"We can meet here, if you like, and eat at "The Castle". How does that sound?"

She smiled feebly.

"Is that a yes? A maybe perhaps? Yes?"

"Yes."

"Seven o'clock by the front entrance sound all right?"

"Yes."

"Until then." he kissed her hand and held it in both of his, "Bon nuit Mademoiselle."

She watched him disappear up the stairs with quick, purposeful steps.

Recorded instrumental music was playing in the lounge when she ran breathlessly up the stairs in her street clothes and rushed to the table, appearing flustered.

"I'm so sorry it took me so long, Brett." she apologized profusely, her cheeks noticeably flushed.

"It's okay sweetheart." Brett embraced her, "You look so pretty in that pink dress. Just like a flower. Come, sit down." she helped her to the seat vacated earlier by Warren, "Sweetheart, I would like you to meet Tony Horncastle, Jack's cousin and business partner."

"It's nice to meet you, Mr. Horncastle." she extended her hand.

"Tony, please." he shook it firmly, "I enjoyed your singing immensely. Gershwin himself would have been touched by your sensitive rendition of his music."

"Thank you. You're very kind."

"Hi, Sydney." Shayleigh waved with a flutter of her fingers.

"Hi, Shayleigh." she smiled congenially.

"What'll you have, sweetness?" Brett flagged down Andy, who was bussing tables.

"A pink lady, please."

"How apropos. You've got it. Andy, cutie, could you please get us a pink lady and three more martinis? You're a doll."

"Stormy" was being played over the P.A. system. Sydney's eyes wandered to the bar where Warren was standing, watching her intently. As their eyes met, he winked. She looked away, trembling. Aware of this exchange, Brett turned to her.

"Watch out for that one, hon. Wouldn't trust him as far as I can throw him."

"Warren? He doesn't seem so bad."

"When did you meet him?"

"He came downstairs after the show. He was very nice."

"He's a wolf in sheep's clothing. Stay away from him. If he tries to chat you up again, run as far as you can."

"They've given me plenty of warning about him, too." Shayleigh remarked, "He came in here with the biggest slut, then went through a big song and dance to ditch her. He told me and Tony he was here just to check you out. He's a sex fiend, a heartless Casanova, according to both Brett and Tony. I know he's easy on the eyes, but he spells danger."

"I don't want to see you hurt, sweetheart." Brett reached across the table to touch her hand.

"I'm afraid it might already be too late. I have a date with him tomorrow night."

"He certainly moves fast." Tony shook his head.

"Oh, honey, that frightens me." Brett squeezed her hand.

Andy returned with their drinks. The few remaining patrons were dissipating as the staff attempted to tidy up before closing. Sydney glanced sideways at Warren again. His eyes were still on her. His crooked smile, his deep dimples were all she could see. One dinner with Warren was not dangerous. It would never lead to a liaison. Just one evening at a restaurant. What was the harm in that? It was not as though he would call her for a second date or attempt to sleep with her. He would move on to his next, worldlier conquest. Brett had no reason to worry. It was just dinner. Nothing more.

Chapter 5/ Stormy

He was seated on a bench under a weeping willow outside the entrance to Willow Place. One leg uncomfortably placed over the other, he was leaning back with an air of detached self-satisfaction. Across the street, at the first sight of him, her heart missed a beat. She slid behind an elderly woman at the crosswalk to escape his eye, however, he was far too quick for her, and leapt to his feet to meet her at the curb.

"You actually showed up." he flashed his dimples as he took her arm.

Would it not be the other way around, Sydney thought: His dates would be the ones to wonder whether or not he would keep his commitment. Why would a man like Warren ever fear being stood up? She had been the one with her heart racing in trepidation, so certain he would not be there. Experience had taught her men could not be relied upon to honor their commitments, even the smallest ones. She hoped the veins in her arm under his hand did not betray the pounding of her heart.

"Can you imagine what kind of an idiot I would have looked like, sitting here waiting, all dressed up and no date?" he said.

She knew that feeling well.

"I can't imagine you ever looking like an idiot." she lifted liquid eyes to his face.

In his beige summer suit, he appeared tanned, trim, and even more handsome than she remembered from the night before.

"You look lovely." he said, his gaze lingering on her ample bosom, "Even lovelier in the sun. A lot of women who pass for beautiful under dim lights barely look passable in the bright sun, with every flaw magnified tenfold. But, you...You are breath-taking."

"Thank you."

"That, and short hair. Long hair can conceal many flaws. But a woman who bares her face and still looks beautiful is the genuine article. With your flawless features, you must never hide this face behind hair."

"Thank you." she repeated sheepishly, at a loss for anything else to say.

"Shall we go in?" he led her up the front steps.

In the lobby, heads were turning in their direction.

"People are staring." she whispered, "Is something wrong with the way I'm dressed? Is it inappropriate for this place?"

"Around here, it's a down-home tradition to look unfamiliar people up and down and try to make them feel as uncomfortable as possible. Don't worry. You'll get used to it. By the way, you look scrumptious. They're all jealous." he observed the fluid lines of her bias-cut champagne dress.

They were greeted by the Maître D', and led to a table in a secluded corner with a view of the weeping willows along the river. She felt his dark eyes burning through her as she attempted to busy herself admiring the view.

"A bottle of your best champagne, Alfred." Warren said.

"Yes sir. Mathew will be here shortly to take your order, sir." the middle-aged man in formal attire placed menus before them.

"Do you see anything you like?" he asked her, observing her fascination with the menu.

"What do you recommend?"

She did not want to reveal the fact that she had never been in a posh restaurant before, or heard of most of the items listed on the menu. She did not know salmon could be prepared in such a variety of ways, with such unlikely and exotic ingredients, or that there could be so many different types of steak and seafood.

"What I'm having: Steak Tartare."

That, she knew about.

"Isn't that raw meat?" she lifted enormous eyes to his face.

"You bet. Nothing like it. Increases the stamina." he winked.

71

"Raw meat?" she made a face.

"This is the only place in town you can get it. They prepare it exactly the way I like it."

"I think I'll pass."

"In that case, I would recommend the Filet Mignon."

She liked the name, and agreed to try it. She secretly hoped it was something that had been cooked.

The Maître D' returned with the champagne and two traditional wide, shallow champagne glasses. Warren reached across the table to clasp her hand as Alfred opened their champagne and poured it.

"To us." Warren lifted his glass when Alfred was gone, "Welcome to Beavertown, Sydney Bertrand."

"Thank you."

"Are you ready to order, sir?" a solemn young man appeared at their table, pad and pencil in hand.

"The lady will have the Filet Mignon and parsley potatoes, with a Mediterranean salad and house vinaigrette dressing...I'll have the Steak Tartare and oysters on the half shell."

"Yes, sir."

"Too bad they can't get "Leche di Burro"." he smiled when the waiter was gone.

"Lechy...what?"

"Leche di Burro. Donkey's milk. Gives a man super powers with the ladies. It's a delicacy in Chile."

She was not sure whether he was putting her on. She smiled uncomfortably.

"What do you think of Tony's business venture?" he asked her.

"It's very elegant." she admired the crystal chandeliers and heavy velvet drapes in her favorite color: burgundy.

"He caters to a far more sophisticated, cosmopolitan bunch than his competitors. He juggles his law practice and this business quite skillfully, not to mention, he's also Jack's business partner at Chandler's. Don't get on his bad side. He has the authority to hire and fire people in Jack's absence. And he's definitely much more on the ball than Jack."

"They're both very nice," she said diplomatically, "and very smart."

The recorded music was unexpectedly changed from instrumental to Tony Bennett singing "They Can't Take That Away From Me".

"Would you like to dance?"

No one had asked her to dance before. She had studied some basic steps by analyzing diagrams of feet, however, had not been given the opportunity to put her knowledge into practice. Until tonight, she had not even dated a man who could pass for respectable. In the black holes she had inhabited, men cursed, pinched, groped; and those were the tamer ones. No one had taken her out for a meal, complemented her on her appearance, or any other aspect of her being. She had been forced to fight off their advances. Their touch had repulsed her. She shut her eyes in pain as Warren helped her up and with an arm gently around her shoulder, led her to the dance floor.

"You don't have to look so sad. I promise I don't bite."

She avoided his gaze by burying her face in his shoulder. Unlike the men in Montreal, he smelled of fresh botanicals, crisp, laundered fabric and moist, warm, earthy skin. His left hand slid down to her hip and subtly caressed her. Her heart was threatening to burst out of her chest.

"You're trembling." he murmured, "Are you all right?"

She was speechless.

"Sydney...you smell divine."

As his lips touched her neck, a lightning bolt shot through her. She wished at that moment she could be transformed into someone else – anyone other than herself.

"I think our appetizers have arrived. We can return to the dance floor later."

Reluctantly, she pulled away from the warmth of his scent. He led her back to the table by the hand. She eyed his oysters with scepticism, much to his amusement. He lifted one deftly and placed it her mouth. It was tasteless. She revealed no expression.

"You know what they say about oysters." he winked.

She smiled and pierced a tomato wedge with her fork.

"So, how did a creature like you ever end up in Beavertown?"

"I was tired of life in the big city."

"Why Beavertown? How did you even find out about it? No one outside of the Maritimes knows it exists."

"It is the capital of New Brunswick."

"The rest of Canada doesn't even recognize New Brunswick. This is the "have-not "province. They think we're all half-wits living in log cabins."

"I met people who lived around here. A lady who used to teach school."

"You must've followed a Frenchman here! Why else would you leave everything behind and come to a new place on a whim?"

"Nothing like that."

"A broken heart? Did you leave Montreal because of a man who left you high and dry?"

"No. I was simply fed up. My life was going nowhere. I wanted a drastic change, live in a small town for once. And, from what that lady said, this sounded like a nice place to live."

"Did you grow up in Montreal? Do you still have family there?"

"No. I don't have family anywhere. When I was growing up, the family I was with moved around a lot."

"An army brat, eh?"

"No. The man worked at temporary jobs. We went where the work was – usually industrial cities throughout North America. We didn't stay in one place too long."

"Must've been very difficult. I find this intriguing. It's not often that fascinating women like you turn up in this neck of the woods." he leaned back in his seat, "No wonder Jack hired you on the spot.

Until I met you in person last night, I was expecting another lush like Brett."

"Brett's not a lush!" she flung her fork indignantly.

"You're fiercely loyal to your friends. I like that. Perhaps you will have occasion to defend me some time. I want you in my corner."

"I don't take anyone for granted." she looked him in the eye.

"Very admirable."

"Thank you."

The waiter served their meals. Warren observed her daintily cutting her meat into small portions.

"Have some?" he offered her a morsel of his delicacy on his fork.

"No, thank you." she shook her head emphatically.

"You don't fool me for an instant, Miss Goody-Two-Shoes." he mused inwardly, "You're lying through your teeth. You came to Beavertown for a specific reason, and I intend to find out exactly what it is before anyone else does."

Reaching for her water glass, she caught his gaze. He winked. She smiled and returned to her meal.

"All of this could belong to Brett's unruly brats someday. They'll probably turn it into a punk rock drug haven." he cast a forlorn glance at the river.

"You really don't like Brett, do you?"

"She knows she's got Tony exactly where she wants him."

"Brett's not like that. I'm sure she cares just as deeply about Tony."

"It's hard to believe all that time in Montreal hasn't hardened you. Brett's very smooth and charming on the surface, but when you dig deeper, what you find is quite different."

"I always dig deeper. I ignore what's on the surface and look into the soul."

"You're frightening me. Does that mean you can read my thoughts? Can you tell what I'm thinking about doing later in the evening?"

She blushed and picked at her remaining vegetables.

"I think those carrots are dead by now. You don't need to stab them anymore."

"Why don't you and Brett get along?" she looked up at him unexpectedly.

"She's a woman with a past. My nephew's no match for her. He wears his heart on his sleeve."

"Brett would never hurt him."

"I have my reasons for being concerned about Tony."

"Brett's a beautiful person. He couldn't possibly find anyone better."

"It's complicated. Maybe someday, I'll tell you. You're a woman of many mysteries and surprises. Someone I definitely want to know better."

"I'd like to know you better, too." she murmured shyly.

"What would you like to know? Ask away." he leaned back.

"What do you do for a living? Are you a lawyer?"

"I broke the family tradition. First Horncastle male not to take the legal path. I teach school. High school history, to be precise."

"All the young girls must be infatuated with you."

"I don't go for young stuff."

"You prefer women of the world."

"I don't go for strumpets, either."

"I'm going to quit while I'm ahead."

"Aren't you going to ask me what my type is?"

"Only if you want to tell me."

"You are my type, Sydney."

She froze, her fork still in her hand, raised in mid-air.

"Yes, you. There's much more to you than meets the eye. You have an intensity I have never seen in another woman. I think you've known the gut-wrenching depths of hell, and emerged, through the sheer force of your strong will. There are depths of your soul no one can ever come close to fathoming. There's pain there no one can touch."

This, from a man reputed to be a cad and a narcissist?

"You can tell all of this in the short amount of time we've known each other?"

"I've always known you, Sydney. No one will know you or understand you the way I do." his dark eyes were strangely lambent.

She shut her eyes, but his gaze bore through her. At that moment, she was acutely aware of her long denied need to merge with another, to transcend herself.

They began playing "But Not For Me". Matthew brought the check.

"Who is that singing?" she asked.

"You don't know who that is?"

"No. Should I?"

"Think about it."

"It's not...is it Jack Chandler?"

"The one and only."

"He sings like an angel."

"That's my nephew, the angel. Unlike Yours Truly, the devil." he observed her trembling, "You're nervous. That's sexual tension. I have a remedy for that."

She lowered her eyes. He produced a small package from his inner breast pocket, a white paper bag with "Chester's Drugs" in red lettering. He slid it under the table and placed it on her lap. His hand found her thigh and lingered there.

"Use this in the ladies' room while I settle accounts."

Jack's song had ended. She rose unsteadily. As she walked past his chair, his hand brushed against her rump. In the privacy of the cubicle, she clumsily inserted the applicator of gooey mess into the designated cavity. She expected to awaken any moment from this dizzying, desperate journey. Warren had known hundreds – perhaps thousands of women – the most desirable, worldly women. What was he doing with her? Was this all a joke for him? Perhaps a bet? Was he making fun of her? Would he laugh about her with his friends afterwards? He was smooth as silk. Brett had warned her. Men like Warren left a string of broken hearts across the globe. She was trapped, powerless, at his mercy tonight. All she could do now was prepare herself for the worst possible outcome.

She returned to the table. They began playing "Stormy".

"Why don't you sit down and listen to the song before we leave?"

She agreed gratefully. She wanted to postpone the inevitable as long as possible.

"Do you like it?" he wanted to know.

"Very much."

"It's your song."

"My song?"

"You're Stormy. Beneath your shy, reserved exterior is a raging storm. You're a Scorpio, aren't you?"

"How did you know?"

"I'm a Scorpio, too."

She was silent.

"Well, my little songbird," he rose and helped her out of her chair as the song changed to "Traces Of Love", another Classics IV hit, "Shall we proceed to phase two of our evening?"

The scent of his cologne was frighteningly intoxicating. He led her outside by the hand, to the warm and still evening air. Under a willow, he pulled her to himself kissed her savagely. She moaned in longing. His hand slid under her dress and tugged urgently at her panties. He led her through the lobby of "The Queen's Hotel", into the empty elevator, where he kissed her until her legs could no longer hold her up. He unlocked the door to the room awaiting them. Vases of calla lilies were placed on the dresser, the desk, and the night tables. He pressed the play button of the tape recorder on the desk, and smooth instrumental jazz filled the room. The street light shone through the slats of the venetian blinds. On the seventh floor, they were above all human activity on Queen Street. Neither made an attempt to close the blinds. His suit coat was tossed nonchalantly on the mahogany chair, and his red silk tie loosened. She placed her evening bag on the dresser and removed her shoes. He pulled her closer for another kiss as he untied the sash of her wrap dress. It landed at her feet. His shirt was urgently pulled off and flung across the room. He unhooked and removed her satin bra and bit her breasts playfully as it fluttered like a butterfly before landing. In one smooth movement, his trousers and shorts fell to his feet. He ripped at her satin panties and tossed them in the air. She longed to be overtaken, devoured. They fell feverishly on the bed. His chest hair was smooth and downy. She opened herself up to him like trusting, tender orchid petals reaching out to the sun. When he entered her, a torrent of tears overcame her. With every thrust, her heart threatened to burst out of her ribcage, and her urgent screams overpowered the music. He finally collapsed on her chest, his pounding heart beating in unison with her own. She twirled a perspiration-soaked lock of his hair between her fingers.

"I'm not through with you, yet, Princess." he said, "There are more delights to come. The night is still young."

"It must be the Steak Tartare."

"You're absolutely delightful." he turned his face to her, his curly eyelashes silhouetted against the window.

She did not want their evening to end. She wanted to dissolve through his pores and become a permanent extension of him, take up residence in his interior regions.

"Sydney, get on top of me." he murmured.

It was not a position she preferred. Yet, with Warren, it felt natural and safe. When he exploded inside of her, she fell into his arms.

"I have a special treat for you." he coaxed her onto her back and buried his head in the moist darkness between her legs, his tongue flickering, sending her into spasms and screeches of ecstasy.

"I'll be back." he whispered seductively and slinked away.

When he returned from the bathroom, he removed the now silent cassette from the player, and inserted another one. He lay on his back and turned to her with a gleam in his eye.

"Come here, Stormy. Get on top of me again." he masterfully guided her back on top of himself and silenced her with a kiss. His tongue tasted salty, like the ocean. Like her salty center, where his fingers were now navigating purposefully.

"Move down." he murmured, "Lower...lower...that's it...now, take it in your mouth."

She complied. It tasted salty, too. She wanted to give him pleasure, to show him her gratitude. She wanted to take her time with him, just as he had, with her. She did not move her head until he was satisfied.

"Do you know how amazing you are?" he beckoned her to his side, "Not too many women can keep up with my voracious appetite."

They lay in silence until the end of the cassette.

"You may need to top it up." he said, gesturing toward her handbag.

She complied. He rose slowly and deliberately to tend to the music. When she re-emerged, from the bathroom, Warren was sprawled out on the bed, a complacent lion after the kill.

"Come here, my lovely." he opened his arms to enclose her, "I know what you want."

He guided her into the protective cocoon of the missionary position. When he pierced her again, she wound her legs around his neck.

"You're driving me totally wild!" he bit her breasts hard before releasing himself.

When he rolled over, he propped himself up on one elbow.

"Have you had enough, or are you up for more?" he smirked.

"I'm up for more."

"You're a handful. I'll bet not too many lovers can keep up with you."

She kissed his smooth cheek.

"Have you ever been married?" he asked her.

"Once. A long time ago."

"What was he? A foreign diplomat?"

"Hardly."

"A woman of many secrets. How long were you married?"

"Not long."

"You must've worn him out."

"Were you ever married?"

He shook his head emphatically.

"Engaged?"

"Commitment, fidelity...Not my scene."

"Any children?"

"God forbid!" he roared.

"I'm sorry." she pulled away.

"No, I'm sorry." he smiled, "I didn't realize how sensitive you are...come back..." he patted the spot on his chest now vacated by her head.

She complied cautiously.

"Get on your stomach." he ordered her, "Time for a massage." he reached into the top drawer of the nightstand and produced a jar of cream.

She shut her eyes and let Andre Gagnon's instrumentals soothe her as Warren's skillful fingers wove their magic.

"Let me massage you, too." she said, fumbling with the jar of cream.

"Hmm..." he stretched out on his stomach and shut his eyes, a contented smile across his face.

She focused all her attention on his back, trying to emulate all of his moves. At intervals, she kissed his musky skin.

"Hmm..." he stirred, "Why don't you get your stuff topped up and come back again?"

The music had stopped. The clock on the nightstand was flashing a red 12:11.

"Get back in the same position." he told her when she returned.

"On my stomach?"

"Yes."

She obeyed hesitantly. He mounted her forcefully.

"Don't be afraid." he said, piercing her with such brutality that she was certain her insides were ruptured.

"Ahh..." he sank into her, "Am I hurting you?"

"No." she lied, biting her lower lip.

"This is new to you, isn't it? Don't worry, you'll get used to it. You'll learn to love it."

In silence, she waited for it to be over. When he gathered her in his arms, and stroked her hair, she buried her face in his chest.

"Tonight's just an appetizer. I have so many other delights in store for you...You haven't seen "nothing" yet. Come on. Look at me."

When she turned wide, child-like eyes to his face, he had to look away. He guided her on to her back and kissed her feverishly. His tongue found her salty center once again and he remained there until her screams were loud enough to disturb other guests at the hotel, though he had booked an entire wing to prevent them from being heard.

"You're insatiable." he sat up, wiping contraceptive foam from his mouth with his hand, "A woman after my own heart. You give in to unbridled passion and pull out all the stops! You're a fiery temptress, but soft and vulnerable, too. You could well be dangerous."

"I'm not dangerous, I assure you."

"Don't underestimate yourself." he rose, "Do you want to clean up in there first?"

She complied. When she returned, he had packed up the tapes, the player, and the cream in a cobalt blue flight bag. As he accosted her on his way to the bathroom, he caressed her hip. She dressed efficiently, and gathered his clothing from the pile on the floor, placing each item on the bed neatly. When he returned, she cast an appreciative glance at him.

"We've been here for four hours. Your landlady must have a search party out for you." he zipped his fly and reached for his shirt,

"What would she ever think if she knew what you've been up to, you naughty, naughty girl?"

She handed him his tie and stroked his dimpled cheek.

"Does Daisy always wait up for you?"

"No, but, I have a feeling she's waiting up tonight."

"Is she familiar with my reputation as an ogre?" he knotted his tie with a flourish.

"You're not an ogre."

"No one in Beavertown would agree with you." he put on his blazer and his shoes.

"Their opinion doesn't matter."

Slinging the flight bag over one shoulder, he turned the doorknob, "My car's in the hotel parking lot."

On the way back, both spoke little. He glanced sideways at her complacently at red lights and stop signs.

"Where's the house, again? Saunders?"

"Needham. Five fifty-four."

"That's a one-way, isn't it?"

"Yes."

They were silent the rest of the way. When they arrived in front of Daisy's house, she saw that all the lights on the main floor were lit.

"Good night, Stormy." he reached across the bench seat to kiss her lightly.

"Good night, Warren."

"I'll call you. Dream about me." he winked and drove away swiftly.

As she was fumbling in her handbag for her house keys, the door opened and Daisy stood before her, smiling broadly.

"Mrs. Parker...Hello..." she blushed.

"I hope you had a nice evening, dear."

"I'm sorry I kept you up."

"It's all right. Your friend's been keeping me company. We've been having a lovely chat."

"My friend?"

"Yes. The tall, pretty one with the noble cheekbones."

"Brett's here?"

Brett emerged from the music room in a long orange print jersey dress with bell sleeves.

"Hi, sweetheart. I hope you're not upset with me."

"Why would I be upset?"

"For meddling."

"I'm lucky that you care enough to meddle." she embraced her, tears filling her eyes.

"Are you all right, sweetheart?" Brett stroked her hair, "Did he behave?"

"He was impeccable. I'm sorry I worried you both."

"We had plenty of reason for being worried. I'm glad you're all right." Brett said.

"We've been having a grand time, listening to Cole Porter." Daisy said, "Brett called around ten looking for you, to see if you were back. I told her you were still at your soiree with Warren Horncastle. She sounded concerned, so I invited her over to have tea and biscuits with me while we waited. How was your evening, dear?"

"Oh, it was lovely."

"Where did he take you?" Daisy inquired innocently.

"To "The Castle". It's a very elegant restaurant."

"All this time? Don't they close at eleven?"

"They...let us stay longer...Warren's nephew is the owner, so Warren has a key, and he agreed to lock up...We played music and danced...we talked so much, we lost track of time..." she despised herself for lying, but the truth was much too shameful.

"Was he a perfect gentleman, dear?"

"Absolutely."

"How romantic!" Daisy beamed, "I've seen his picture in the newspaper's society pages, attending charity balls and such. He's a very handsome lad. Didn't I tell you your luck would change in Beavertown, dear, and you'd meet all sorts of fellows?"

"Yes you did." Sydney embraced her tenderly.

"Maybe he'll propose marriage." Daisy said dreamily, "I told Brett there was no need to worry. He's well brought up. He'd never take advantage of you. Now that you're home safe and sound, I shall retire to my room and give the two of you time alone."

"You don't have to leave."

"You don't need an old lady like me around when you youngsters want to have girl talk. Brett's staying overnight with you, dear. It'll be good for you to have a heart to heart. I'll say goodnight now. You girls have a lovely time."

"Good night. Thank you." Sydney kissed her cheek.

"Thank you." Brett hugged her.

"Let's go up to your room." Brett led her to the hallway and unhooked her handbag from the bannister.

"Are your kids okay with you staying away overnight?"

"No problem. Shayleigh and Maggie from next door are babysitting the monsters. When the boys go to bed, they're going to watch Garbo in "Grand Hotel" on "The Late Late Show". I bought three flavors of ice cream for Maggie. They're having their own party."

"I'm grateful you're here, Brett." she embraced her, "Thank you for thinking of me."

"I thought you'd be angry with me and tell me to mind my own business."

"I would never do that, Brett." she opened the door to her room, "Did you bring an overnight bag?"

"No, sweetheart. I don't need one. I travel very light." she glanced around the room, "This is a lovely place, Sydney. It's cozy and inviting."

"It's a lot better than all the places I've lived in before."

She had never been close enough to another woman before to share confidences. She had wondered what it would be like to feel secure in the knowledge that one was assured of unconditional friendship. Brett had a way of melting away her insecurities and fears.

"This is like a slumber party." she said, "Maybe we should do each other's hair and nails."

"We can do anything you want, hon." Brett sat on the edge of the bed and kicked off her metallic sandals.

"I've never been to a slumber party before."

"You and I can have loads of them. Honey, I grew up on a big old farm. Our place was always filled with visiting relatives and other people's kids. You look heavenly, sweetheart. Come on, give me the real dirt on Warren." She leaned back on her elbows.

"Brett, I'm so confused." she sat beside her.

"I'm not buying that "perfect gentleman" stuff for an instant, sweetheart. It's written all over you."

"You can see right through me."

"You slept with him, didn't you? I sensed it the moment you walked in. I smelled it when I hugged you."

Sydney squirmed like a schoolgirl caught passing notes in class.

"I knew it." Brett shook her head, "I knew he'd get you into bed."

"There must be more to him than just a heartless womanizer."

"Sweetheart, if you ever find out what that is, please let me know. I hope you used protection."

"He's the one who thought of it. He bought it before our date. I wasn't prepared. I didn't think I was going to sleep with him."

"If you date Warren, you always have to be prepared. Did he use condoms?"

"No. He bought spermicidal foam for me."

"I should have known. Honey, that stuff's not effective unless you have a diaphragm or he uses condoms in conjunction."

Sydney's face grew pale.

"I don't want to worry you, but you may want to get a diaphragm if you're going to be seeing him regularly."

"He may not be interested in seeing me again."

"You never know. I'll take you to my doctor. Unfortunately, they don't put women over thirty-five on the pill. Nothing else is as safe. I just don't want you to have any surprises. The last thing you need is a Warren Junior."

"Brett...do you think I had enough protection?...We... did it multiple times."

"I should have known!" Brett threw her hands up in the air, "That pervert! Don't worry, hon, I'll take you to the hospital for a morning-after pill."

"Everyone there is going to find out I had sex."

"Wait a minute. You may not have to go through that. I just remembered: I filled a prescription for it last year when a partner's condom broke, but I never used it. I started my period the same day. I kept it for future use. It doesn't lose its effectiveness for a couple of years. I'll give it to you in the morning. We'll go to my house first thing. But, be prepared: you may be vomiting like mad. It's not really one pill, but several birth control pills. You take frequent, massive doses in a short period of time."

"There's always a price to pay."

"Oh, poor flower." she embraced her.

"I haven't been with anyone in fifteen years."

"You sure made up for it tonight. I don't want to alarm you, hon, but if you're with Warren, you need to get yourself checked for Venereal Disease. I don't know how to put this delicately, but he travels extensively throughout Europe and Asia, and has escapades with prostitutes. You're playing Russian Roulette. I'll make sure my doctor takes good care of you, sweetheart."

"Why would man like Warren need prostitutes? He can have any woman he wants."

"He's insatiable. It's an addiction – a disease. He's not relationship material. Don't get too emotionally involved. I don't want to see you hurt."

"I'm not going to fall in love with him. He's out of my league. But he was incredible tonight. I had never imagined it could be like that. My ex-husband was the only other man I had ever slept with, and I had never enjoyed it with him."

"No one enjoys it with her ex-husband."

Sydney laughed softly.

"I think he deeply loathes women. That's why he takes delight in debasing them." Brett said, "You deserve so much better than that cad."

"Brett, you have no idea how much this talk means to me. I never had one with anyone else before. I feel blessed to have a friend like you."

"God love you." she stroked her cheek, "Don't let Warren mess up your life."

"I won't. I know there can never be anything deeper, and I don't feel comfortable being in a relationship based on nothing but lust. It's not easy for me to give myself. This was the first time. But I have no illusions."

"I heard somewhere that having a lover who is not your friend is worse than having an enemy."

"Wise words to live by. I need to be friends with someone first."

"Warren's not anybody's friend."

"I realize that."

"Being physically intimate with someone without an emotional connection is the loneliest feeling in the world." Brett shuddered, and crossed her arms across her chest.

"And, yet, it's our loneliness that drives us to do these self-destructive things. Even when we know the loneliness can only get worse in the long run, it seems alleviated in the short run."

"Loneliness is our worst enemy. Sometimes, we do what it takes to survive, even if it's harmful to our well-being."

"Men think we're created purely for their pleasure. Sometimes I think they're not worth all the trouble they cause. I don't know which is more painful: being all alone, or at the mercy of someone who doesn't care about our well-being." Sydney dried her tears with the knuckles of her thumbs.

"You can date him to alleviate that gut-wrenching loneliness, as long as you keep your perspective. As long as you keep your emotions in check. If you're not vulnerable to him, he can't do as much damage. We need to take charge and use men for our pleasure and nothing more. We need to turn the tables. When they realize they can't destroy us, they'll move on."

"Thank you for this talk, Brett."

"You're welcome, hon. I'm always here for you no matter when or where. I'm always available if you need me. I'll drop everything. You come first. Remember that."

"Brett." she threw her arms around her.

"It's going to be all right, hon." she stroked her back, "You must be exhausted. Let's get some sleep. We'll have many future sleepovers like this. You use the bathroom first."

"You're the guest. You should."

"Okay, hon."

"Would you like to wear one of my nighties?"

"No, thank you, hon. I sleep in the buff."

"Brett pulled off her dress over her head and placed it on the chair. She was not wearing a bra or a slip underneath, only blue panties, the color of the morning glories in the fabric of her dress. She produced a toothbrush from her handbag. Tall and slender, Brett's figure was shapely and in perfect proportion. Her breasts were small, firm, and separate with tiny pink nipples.

"The bathroom's right across the hall." Sydney said.

"I won't be long, hon."

While Brett was out of the room, Sydney was debating whether or not to do the same. Her nightgowns were tattered and faded. It would be more embarrassing to be seen in one of them than to be seen au naturel. She undressed, and placed everything in a pile on the closet floor, to be hand washed later. Brett returned without her makeup and every bit as beautiful. She slid under the white coverlet.

"Bathroom's all yours, sweetheart."

When Sydney returned and slid in beside Brett in the narrow bed, she was struck aware of the warmth and reassurance of having someone beside her.

"Make sure you tell me about the X-rated dreams you're going to have about Warren." Brett said, guiding her into a spooning position and placing a reassuring arm across Sydney's abdomen.

Feeling Brett's warm breath on her neck and back, Sydney smiled inwardly, filled with peace and calm. Warren was already a distant memory.

"Good night, Brett."

"Sleep tight, sweetheart."

As long as Brett was in her life, nothing and no one could harm her. Sleep came upon her without struggle. She had no dreams that night.

Chapter 6/ The Gift Of Music

She was awakened by the singing of birds outside the window. The sun was streaming into the room. She stretched her arms luxuriously, with feline movements and yawned.

Sydney, who had been by the window, turned around to greet her.

"Good morning, Brett."

"Good morning, sweetheart. How long have you been up?"

"Not long. Did you sleep all right?"

"Like a log. How about you? I hope I didn't disturb you by snoring or moving around."

"Not at all." she turned away from the window and picked up the tray on the vanity, "I hope you like cheese omelettes and lukewarm coffee." she awkwardly placed the tray on the bed beside Brett, and propped up the pillows under Brett's head.

"Sweetheart, you didn't have to do all this for me." she sat up, making no attempt to cover her exposed breasts.

"I wanted to." she sat at the foot of the bed, making a deliberate attempt not to look at her breasts.

"I come here to interfere in your life, and you bring me breakfast in bed." she poured milk into her coffee and stirred it, "I feel guilty."

"You can interfere any time you like. You're very nice about it."

"God love you." she gazed at her with tenderness.

"If it tastes awful, you don't have to eat it."

"It's delicious, hon." she placed the fork in her mouth, "I intend to eat every last morsel. But you shouldn't wait on me like this, sweetheart."

"You are the perfect person to wait on."

"Sweetheart," she reached for her hand, "I think you and I were always meant to be friends."

"I think so, too."

"Fate brought you here, so you and I could meet."

Brett placed her empty tray beside her and slid off the bed covers.

"Would you like to bathe first, hon?"

"No, you're the guest. You must go first."

"If you're sure, hon." Brett slid out of bed.

"I'll take this stuff downstairs." Sydney picked up the tray and looked away.

Like the sun, extreme beauty could be blinding.

"Help yourself to the towels and everything else in the linen closet, Brett. I'll wait till I hear the water stop before I soak the dishes.

"Ok, sweetheart."

Downstairs, Daisy was listening to Mozart and reading Jane Austen in the music room.

"Good morning, Mrs. Parker." she peeked her head in the door.

"Good morning, Sydney, dear! How did you girls sleep? Is there anything I can get for you?"

"Everything's fine, thank you. We've both eaten, and Brett's drawing her bath now. Once she's in the tub, I'll soak these dishes. Then, I'll get my bath, and clean up down here in the kitchen. I hope we didn't keep you awake with our talking."

"No, dear. I slept like a baby. You girls have a nice day together. Brett's a very fine person."

"Yes she is."

She could hear that the water was no longer running.

"I guess I'd better tend to the dishes."

The steam from the sink rose to her face. The mixing bowl, whisk, frying pan, spatula, and her own breakfast dishes had been soaking all this time. She scrubbed them with the limp yellow dish rag. Overhead, Brett was singing "It Never Entered My Mind". She smiled.

What was she doing, trying to convince herself she belonged with glamorous people like Brett and Warren? Who was she fooling? Brett felt sorry for her; she would soon tire of her and return to her own circle of friends. As for Warren, there had never been any question about the fleeting, elusive quality of their union. It was only a matter of time before all of them would begin excluding her, making excuses to avoid her. She stacked the dishes on the mustard-colored plastic dish rack...Dating a Horncastle...The thought was preposterous. Other women would give anything to be in her predicament now: For having Brett as a friend, the friend all women dreamed of, and only a select few rarely found, for working as a jazz singer, for dating Warren, and hobnobbing with the elite of Beavertown society. It had not been her desire to move in such circles; in fact, she would have preferred to avoid the privileged altogether, however, the work environment provided by the elite was a safer, cleaner, more congenial one than the dives of Montreal, and, for that, she was grateful. She knew only too well, all good fortune was short-lived, and happiness came with a high price tag. Permanence was an illusion. Letting go had become second nature to her: Friends, jobs, social engagements, men. This, too, could vanish in the blink of an eye. She could let it all go – except Brett. Her, she would miss deeply, more deeply than any of the friends she had lost in the past. Brett was the anchor, the beacon all woman needed in their lives to survive the injustices life presented around every corner. Without a Brett in their lives, women disintegrated, or worse still, survived, only to morph into beings they no longer recognized.

Would she drive Brett away, too, just like all her former friends? She had never been accepted into the fold, considered an equal. An oddity and an outcast, she had never belonged. Ostracized and patronized for being shy, considered unintelligent and defective for her lack of pretense and her childlike vulnerability, she had not been deemed worthy of friendship by other women. Only gay men seemed to appreciate her unaffected, brutally honest approach. Was she only postponing the inevitable by allowing herself to grow close to Brett, knowing only too well it was a matter of time before she lost her, too? Only, this time, the pain would be greater than she could bear.

She washed Brett's breakfast dishes and placed them on the rack with the others. For now, it appeared she had it all. But for how long? How long would she be permitted to keep it? When would her world crash around her? She dried the dishes with a green checkered tea towel and placed them in the cupboard overhead. People were careless with other people's hearts. They treated them like toys, tossed them around, and smashed them to pieces. Once broken, they were of no use, and thus, were discarded in the trash bin.

Thinking Brett would likely be dressed by now, and wondering about her whereabouts, she returned upstairs.

"Daydreaming about Warren, sweetheart?" Brett accosted her at the top of the stairs, "You were gone so long, you must have had some real censored fantasies."

"No, no, nothing like that..." she blushed.

"No reason to be embarrassed. Go ahead. Splurge. Pay no mind to me. As long as you protect your heart and your body from him, allow yourself to have some fun."

"It...wasn't exactly fun...More scary and confusing."

"Of course it is. I'll draw your bath. A nice soak'll clear your mind." Brett returned to the bathroom.

"I'm not deserving of all this good fortune." Sydney undressed slowly, facing away from the vanity mirror in the room.

"Don't you ever say that, hon!" Brett called out from across the hall, "He's not deserving of you!"

"I didn't mean him specifically...I meant...all of this...everything...the job, the room, the kindness, your friendship...especially your friendship."

"Sydney, honey, don't ever say such things!" Brett ran across the hall to gather her up in her arms, "Don't you ever say you're not good enough! It's the rest of us who are not good enough for you! Come on. Your bath's ready." she led her to the discolored claw foot tub and sat on the toilet seat, pulling up her dress to her knees to keep it off the floor.

Sydney immersed herself in the warm water.

"Why don't we spend the whole day together?"

"Brett, you don't have to do that. You have to work tonight."

"I have the last set. That gives us plenty of time. Once we get you the dreaded morning after pills from my house, we can pack a picnic lunch and take it to Wilmot Park. It's a lovely spot. You'll love it. Why don't we have another sleepover at my house?" She picked at a hangnail on her thumb, "The boys are going to spend the night at their dad's tonight. He has all the cable channels. Shayleigh's staying with her friend Mindy. The house should be all ours."

Sydney smiled.

"And if Loverboy phones here when you're out, it'll keep him on his toes." she winked.

"I don't think he'll be phoning here any time soon."

"I have a feeling he will." she held a towel for her as she stepped out of the tub, "Let's find you something to wear. One of those new sundresses, maybe."

She chose a cherry print cotton sundress and a white cardigan for the anticipated evening chill. She wore it with its sleeves wound around her neck until then.

"All you need to bring is a toothbrush, sweetheart. I'll have whatever you need back at the house, anyway. If those pills make you sick, I have some Pepto. I want to get that stuff into you fast before Warren's seed does some real damage."

"Maybe I should bring a change of clothes for the club. Even if I'm just in the audience, I need to adhere to the dress code."

"You could wear something of mine."

"I could never get into your clothes, Brett!"

"I don't have a glorious bosom like yours, but my jersey dresses would look gorgeous on you. Full circle skirts, elastic waistbands, spaghetti straps...You'd look delish in the fuchsia one. You could wear it with my ivory sandals and matching handbag, my pearls and my shawl. Tony'll be there to keep you company and protect you."

At the foot of the stairs, Sydney called out:

"Mrs. Parker, Brett and I are leaving now. I'll be spending the night at her place. I've left the phone number in the credenza drawer. Do you need anything before I go?"

"I'm fine, dear. You girls go on and have a nice time."

On Regent Street, passing motorists slowed down to admire Brett's striking beauty.

"Everyone's admiring you." Sydney remarked.

"How do you know I'm the one they're admiring? Have you seen yourself in the mirror lately?"

"Brett, the only time men notice me is when I step on their feet."

"They do notice you, sweetheart. I see the way they look at you at the club."

"They never approach me. They never have."

"Sweetheart, I grew up in the US of A where there are plenty of red-blooded men. You grew up in Canada, where most men are zombies."

The shops on Queen Street were opening their sleepy eyes. Employees in perky polo shirts the colors of a summer landscape, vacuumed carpets and dusted countertops.

"I need to pick up something at "Goldstein's"." Brett remarked casually, taking Sydney's quivering hand in her own and leading her.

A stunning fortyish blonde with sparkling green eyes emerged from behind the counter and smiled.

"Hi, Brett."

"Hi, Greeney. How are you, sweetheart?"

"Just fine. How are you? How are the boys?"

"Can't complain."

"Your sheet music came in. I'll get it for you." she produced a flat brown paper bag from under the counter with Brett's name written on it.

"Greeney, this is Sydney Bertrand. We work together at the club. This is Grace Greene, but everyone calls her Greeney. Anything that is difficult to find, she'll move mountains to order for you."

"I've caught your act. You're terrific. Very nice to meet you." Greeney smiled and shook her hand.

"Nice to meet you, too."

"I hope you like Beavertown."

"It's lovely."

"Thanks, sweetheart." Brett paid for her purchase, "Say hi to Leonard."

"I will. Say hi to the boys."

"Take care, Greeney."

"You, too, Brett. Nice to meet you, Sydney."

"Nice to meet you, too." Sydney mouthed sheepishly.

Once out of Greeney's earshot, Brett turned to her:

"Your secret's safe with me."

"How did you know?"

"Tony. The Horncastles have been snooping around since the day Jack hired you."

"The Horncastles? What do they have to do with it?"

"You don't know, do you, hon?"

"Know what?"

"Sweetheart, you and I need to do some serious talking." she placed a protective arm around her, "It is true, then, isn't it?"

Sydney nodded.

"You haven't come forward in all this time."

"It's not that I haven't tried. A nasty old woman named Agnes kept kicking me out."

"That old battle-axe!"

"Brett, how do the Horncastles tie into it? Do they own Goldstein's, too?"

"No, hon. The Goldsteins do. But Mrs. Goldstein's sister is married to one of Warren's brothers, who also happens to be Mr. Goldstein's childhood friend."

Sydney was speechless.

"Honey, they've been searching for you relentlessly since the day you disappeared. They hired all sorts of detectives, but they couldn't get any leads."

"We moved around a lot."

"They never gave up on you, in spite of what everyone said. They never stopped believing you were alive. How did you find out who you were?"

"Once I turned eighteen, Donna gave me all my authentic papers and kicked me out. Then, the two of them disappeared again. I went to Montreal, believing my mother to be there, but couldn't get any information."

"What led you here, sweetheart?"

"I overheard a conversation between two women who had known my mother's entire family. One of them said she had heard my mother had married the father of her child and had been living here...and that all sorts of detectives had been around the neighborhood at that time asking questions, trying to track down Roy and Donna, but no one seemed to know anything. They were reminiscing about their schooldays, and that's how my mother's name came up and all of this was discussed. They said she had lied to Roy and told him she was pregnant with his child, and he had married her. Then, when he realized he had been deceived, he divorced her, abducted me, and hit the road. I don't understand why my parents didn't get married when she first realized she was pregnant. Obviously, they loved each other."

"Things were different in those days, hon."

"Once I heard all of that, I packed up and came here. What tipped them off about me?"

"Your first name. There are no other women named Sydney. And, the fact that you were from Montreal. Your last name threw them off at first. They thought you were the next generation."

"I took my ex-husband's last name, because in my legal papers, I still had Roy's last name, since he was married to my mother when I was born. I wanted nothing of his."

"Makes sense."

"Do they know?"

"No. The Horncastles have been tight-lipped. They wanted to be certain of who you were before getting your parents' hopes up. It's been very painful for them."

"I saw him once, Brett...He came to talk to me, but I froze. He was very gracious. I wanted so desperately to tell him, but I couldn't..."

"That's understandable, hon."

"If the Horncastles suspected I was me, why didn't they just ask me?"

"With the Horncastles, nothing is that straight forward."

"Do I...look anything like my mother?"

"You have her coloring, and her delicate little nose. But Edna's a tiny, petite lady. You get your height from the Goldsteins. From what I hear, all the women in your father's family were tall and curvaceous like you."

"I've missed a lifetime. I'll seem like a stranger to them."

"No, hon. They've held you in their hearts all these years. You'll take to each other naturally. There's nothing like the bond between parents and children."

"Do you think they'll like me?"

"They'll love you! Both of them are very fine people. Nothing like the Horncastles. Would you like me to be with you when you meet them?"

"I would appreciate that. Brett, I'm terrified."

"That's natural. I could invite them to my house, so you can meet them privately, away from prying Horncastle eyes. Honey, this reunion is long overdue."

"Thank you, Brett."

"Do you want me to call them this afternoon and arrange for a meeting tomorrow or the next day?"

"That would be very nice."

"I have just one more stop to make before we go to my house." Brett said, "Why don't we make some chicken salad sandwiches for our picnic? I have a quarter watermelon we can take with us. And some Perrier. Does that sound okay to you?"

"Sounds perfect."

At the intersection of Queen and Westmorland Streets, Brett led her diagonally to the opposite side of Queen Street to a curved Art Deco building. The sign above the door read: NBLCC. A thirtyish man behind the counter greeted Brett with alarming familiarity:

"How's it going, Brett?"

"Hi, Ron."

Brett went directly to the back of the store and returned with three bottles of Prince Igor Vodka. Ron smirked knowingly as he rang in her purchase. Sydney cringed at this claustrophobic exchange.

They crossed Queen Street once again, following it past a medical office building, a locksmith, a supermarket, a car dealer, and a junk shop. Then, at the intersection of Smythe Street, Queen Street came to an abrupt end. King and Brunswick Streets, the next two streets parallel to it, converged here to become one, and Brunswick Street was victorious in passing down its name to their offspring.

"Are you sure you're okay about working my sets next week, hon?" Brett said, "I feel very guilty about you and Danny having to work longer hours, but I promise I'll make it up to you."

"I appreciate the extra pay for extra hours. Don't worry about anything. Just enjoy your daughter's graduation."

"I haven't seen Laurie for a long time. She never wanted to come up here for a visit, and managed to be away with friends any time I visited. I've just been biting my tongue. When she chose to attend the boarding school in Connecticut, my ex-husband Josh and I gave our full support. It was close to my sister Vera. She spent all her holidays with her. Now she's graduating, and wants to take a year off to travel in Europe. She doesn't know what she wants to do with her life yet. She says she needs time to find herself. Her generation's obsessed with that. My generation didn't have that luxury. We were living through the war."

Brunswick Street ended where it met Odell Avenue, an unexpectedly lush oasis encompassing three blocks of gingerbread houses and majestic trees along one side and a park on the other. Past the tired brick building of obscure identity, Brunswick Street resumed its journey under the new identity of Woodstock Road, extending toward a sparkling modern subdivision past the park. Brett stood in front of the first house on Odell Avenue, an imposing chocolate brown two-storey. She led her up the steps to the square-shaped front porch, and produced an enormous skeleton key from her handbag.

"The landlord's sending the painters over in two weeks." she gestured toward the peeling paint, "I have to nag him about everything. He'd let the place go to seed and burn it down for insurance. I don't think it's bringing in much of a profit for him. The place is falling apart. Something breaks down every week. When a house is this old, it becomes a money pit. You either sink a huge chunk of cash to bring it up to snuff, or you sell it to someone who can afford to do it. He just lets it coast along. The plumbing's outdated, the wiring dangerous, the furnace ancient. But I love it."

"It's gorgeous." Sydney stood in the foyer, surrounded by rich hues of dark wood: the worn maple floors, the wood plant stands housing Boston ferns under the square window, the antique hall rack, and the mahogany hall table with the mirror. Brown was the predominant color, from the burnished brass ceiling light to the dark-stained wood trim. Brett hung her handbag on one of the knobs of the ornate Victorian hall rack. Straw hats with pastel ribbons adorned the higher knobs.

The living room was modestly furnished in subdued colors. Two of the walls were lined with bookcases bulging with antique volumes. A piano separated the space from the adjoining dining room. Brett arranged her bottles of Prince Igor Vodka in the liquor cabinet at the far end of the dining room beside an antique mahogany desk. An antique cherry China cabinet, a matching credenza and table and chairs faced the living room. In the secluded corner of the dining room were a daybed and a television set on a metal stand.

"Make yourself at home, sweetheart." Brett removed her sheet music from the bag and placed it on the piano, "Do you know "Greenfields"?"

"Of course. It's one of the most beautiful songs I've heard."

"I didn't think anyone knew it, except me. It's very obscure. I've been obsessed with it for fifteen years. I had never been able to get sheet music for it until now. I used to have an LP album of it, The Vogues version, back in New York, but a burglar stole it, along with all of my other favorites. Nothing worse than a burglar with good taste in music. I tried to find a replacement for seven years. Even in New York, it was impossible. Then, we moved here. I checked in some of the well-known, popular record shops, but all they sold was country music. The clerks gave me some pretty strange looks. Then, I discovered "Goldstein's". Now, there's a class act, I said. Sure enough, Greeney pulled out all these catalogues, found it, and ordered it. The only available version was the "Brothers Four" version, a bit folksier, in a forty-five with "The Green Leaves Of Summer" on the other side. I was so elated, I could've kissed her! The sheet music proved to be trickier to find, but Greeney never gave up. She always kept it in mind, and when she came across it, she phoned me up to see if I still wanted it. I told her: "Do I still want it? Honey, I'd die for it!" So, she ordered it for me. Smart as a whip, that girl is."

"That's a fascinating story."

"Now that I have the sheet music, I can get a copy made at the drug store for Chuck, so I can sing it at the club. It's not a standard, I know, but it's so pretty, I don't think anyone would mind. Do you want to go through it once before we make the sandwiches? But, first, I'm getting you the dreaded pills. Wait here, hon."

When she returned with a glass of water and a handful of miniature pink dots, Sydney washed them down obediently. Brett handed her a flat bubble-gum pink tablet resembling a dress button.

"This is for your stomach, so you can keep them down. We'll keep the next dose here." she placed the discretely small purple cardboard box in a desk drawer.

"Now, we can enjoy Greenfields." Sydney sat on the far left side of the piano bench.

"I'll probably mess it up." Brett sat beside her, "I'm no virtuoso. Here goes nothing."

Self-consciously aware of Brett's warm hips pressing against her own, Sydney was filled with a strange yearning. Brett reached for her reading glasses on top of the piano, beside the vase of lilacs. Her skillful fingers caressed the keys with expert dexterity, awakening the entrancing melody of love lost. Their voices filled the fragrant air: Brett's smoky tenor and Sydney's girlish mezzo-soprano in unison. At that moment, a sense of acute familiarity seized the younger woman. Intently focused on her music, Brett possessed an almost ethereal quality. Sydney felt she had been in a room like this before...Sitting with Brett by the piano...This vase of lilacs...This intoxicating, yet frightening sensation...This sense of deja-vu was reassuring, filling her with a sense of being precisely where she was meant to be at this time.

"We can't forget about our picnic lunch." Brett rose and turned on the console stereo on the opposite side of the room, "Have you heard Jack's singing, sweetheart?"

103

"I heard one song at the restaurant."

"I'll play one of his albums for you."

The first song was "I Wish You Love". Sydney shut her eyes and visualized him as he had appeared on the only occasion she had met him. The enigmatic Jack Chandler...She wondered when she would have the chance to know him.

Brett's kitchen was straight out of a 1950s sitcom with ruffled sheer curtains in peach chiffon, inexpensively built plywood cabinetry painted mint green, white Arborite counter tops edged with chrome. The pristine white stove and refrigerator had curved edges. Brett efficiently opened and shut cabinets and drawers and the fridge, pulling out all necessary materials for their preparations. They spread butter on whole wheat bread, piled and smoothed mounds of chicken salad. Each sandwich was then enveloped in wax paper and arranged in the wicker basket on the table. The watermelons slices were placed in a Tupperware container, and added to the basket, along with two bottles of Perrier, the paper plates, plastic cutlery and drinking glasses. Brett closed the basket and shut off the phonograph in the living room. She returned to find Sydney carrying the basket.

"Let me take it, sweetheart."

"Please let me, Brett."

"Okay – but only because you're so adorable." she playfully picked up a straw hat from the hall rack and placed it on Sydney's head; she also picked one for herself on their way out the door.

Jack's voice remained in Sydney's head. Brett smiled knowingly at her.

"Cute, isn't he?"

"I didn't exactly get a very good look at him. It was my first day in town and I was exhausted from my trip."

"I don't believe you for a second."

"Okay – he is very nice-looking."

She longed to ask Brett whether she had been intimate with him, however, was unable to come up with the right words. They decided on a bench under a massive elm tree and placed the basket between them.

"We used to take picnic lunches to Central Park." Brett unpacked dreamily, "The children were very young, then...Those were such wonderful days."

"What made you move here?"

"Josh was offered a teaching position at East Coast University. He had friends here. So, like the fool that I am, I listened to his arguments about the benefits of raising children in a small town."

"What does your ex-husband teach?"

"American Lit."

"Literary types frighten me."

"And so they should. I wish I had possessed the common sense to be frightened before I married him."

"But you have wonderful children as a result of that marriage."

"Children of divorce...Laurie's never come to terms with it."

"She will, in time." Sydney tentatively touched Brett's arm and held her breath. When Brett did not pull away, she inhaled in relief.

"God, this stuffy little town is choking the life out of me!" Brett sighed.

Sydney's hand closed on hers.

"Sanctimonious church ladies telling me in supermarkets that I'm going to hell...Lecherous old men propositioning me...If you're a woman alone, you're fair game...This town is so corrupt, so stagnant."

Sydney reached over the basket to stroke her cheek. Brett placed her own hand over hers and shut her eyes.

"No doubt, Warren's told you I'm an old lush and a trollop, and that you should stay clear of me."

"Who cares what Warren thinks?"

"He's your boyfriend."

"He's not my boyfriend. I don't have any respect for anyone who'd ever say such things about you."

"You're a treasure." she smiled wistfully, "Around you, I feel transported to an Elizabeth Bowen novel, striking up a friendship with the sensitive, fragile heroine whose wings have been clipped. The one I'm thinking of is your namesake from THE HOTEL. That's where I first ran across your name as a woman's name – and I thought, how lovely! It looks so pretty in print with two Ys. You remind me so much of her, too…those big, trusting eyes, porcelain-doll features…a soft, feminine babe in the woods."

"Thank you. I didn't think anyone else read Elizabeth Bowen."

"Are you kidding? Maggie's got her own library. I swear she owns every novel written before 1970. I borrow from her frequently. She recommended THE HOTEL about three years ago. It's one of her personal favorites."

"It's my all-time favorite."

"That's not surprising. She almost seemed to have written it about you – even though you weren't even born yet in 1927. I feel she has a cosmic connection with you. I only hope I can be a better friend to you than that wretched Mrs. What's-her-name was to your namesake."

"Heaps better. You are the perfect friend."

"No, you are, sweetheart. You're one in a million."

"I hope I can be good enough."

"Oh, sweetheart, there's so much pain in those gorgeous eyes of yours." Brett observed, "You must have been so frightened, so lonely all those years on your own in a city like Montreal."

"It was my mother's birthplace, so I thought she'd eventually return there. Some people I tracked down at her old neighborhood told me she hadn't been around since 1955 – a year before I got there. They thought she had spent considerable time in a psychiatric hospital, but they didn't know where. So, I stayed, taking odd jobs washing dishes, cleaning bathrooms."

"You were married for a while."

"Yes. Married at twenty-one, divorced at twenty-two. Jean-Guy delivered supplies to the restaurant where I worked as a cleaner. I thought I had found someone to take care of me. He only married me because I was pregnant. I was doing twice the work, and getting beat up. It was like Roy and Donna all over again. After I had a miscarriage, he left me. The only good thing he ever did. All those years with Roy and Donna, and later with Jean-Guy, music was my only escape. I listened to the radio every chance I had, spent hours in record shops, sang when I was alone."

"How did you get work singing?"

"I was a server at a bar a few years after Jean-Guy left. That's where I met Sven, this middle-aged hippie, a beatnik, as they were called then in the early sixties. He was opening his own club, and wanted me to work for him. Initially, I didn't accept, but the dive I was working in went under, and when he offered me a job again, I accepted. At first, it wasn't bad. The place was actually less seedy than some of the other places. When Sven discovered I could sing, he gave me the job vacated by his singer who quit suddenly. He said he was going to make me a star that he had contacts in the recording industry. I was living in total oblivion. I never doubted him. He was like a father figure – never tried to take advantage of me. I was blind to his faults. So stupid! Didn't even get suspicious. What he did have were ties to organized crime. These two characters became regulars at the club. It turned out, Gus was a drug kingpin, and Marie-France was a madam at a brothel nearby, and Sven's paramour. She wanted to recruit me. Gus convinced Sven to pressure me into taking illegal drugs and dancing nude. When I refused, Sven fired me. I couldn't get work anywhere. Gus controlled all the bars and clubs. Marie-France kept sending goons after me to warn me about what would happen if I blabbed about what I knew."

"Sweetheart..." Brett rubbed her neck, "That's horrendous."

"I finally found work singing in a bar again. Gus moved out to B.C., and Sven's relationships with Marie-France soured. He bought the place I was working in. He kept me on strictly as a singer. I bit my tongue and did my job. The one bright light was Pierre, the accompanist. He's the one who helped me get away. I hope he can get away himself. I still have nightmares about Sven tracking me down here and dragging me back."

"After all you've been through, no wonder, sweetheart. Don't worry, no one can find you here." Brett held her hand, "You are home now. Safe and loved."

"Thank you."

"What amazes me is how you remained so chaste in such an unwholesome environment."

"It's very hard for me to get close to men. I force myself to when I have to. But I'm terrified of most men."

"You weren't afraid of Warren." Brett winked at her.

"There was something different about him."

"You could say that."

"I've been dominating the conversation all this time. How did you choose music as your career? Was it your first choice?"

"I started out as a model. I also struck out on my own at eighteen, and went to the big city, but under totally different circumstances. My family was very supportive. I was seeking my fortune in the Big Apple."

"That must have been so glamorous."

"It's not what it's cracked up to be. I was young and foolish then, just a farm girl from Vermont. The glamor soon wore thin. I desperately needed stability in my life. That's when I married my first husband, Frank, an aspiring actor who mostly waited on tables, like me. A year later, our daughter was born: Martha Evelyn. I called her Marin, just like Marin County, California. She was a delightful child. Each moment with her was a moment of grace. We had her for such a short time."

"Brett, I'm so sorry."

"She was only three when we lost her. That was the beginning of the end for us. Our marriage was not strong enough to survive the death of a child. It crumbled under the weight of our grief. I never saw or heard from Frank again. I don't even know if he's still alive. I'm not angry. He dealt with his pain the only way he could."

"Oh Brett..."

"I put myself through acting school. Then, five years later I met Josh. I was taking an American Lit course from him. He took a shine to me. We were married the following year, and Laurie was born in another year. Soon, the boys followed."

"How old are the boys?"

"Keir's fourteen, Toby twelve."

"It must be nice."

"Some days, I wouldn't say so. But, seriously, they're good kids."

Brett gathered up the trash and deposited it in the bin. Furious hornets circled its rim. Sydney arranged the empty containers back in the wicker basket.

"Let's take a little stroll around the park." Brett took the basket from her and linked her arm through hers.

"Is it all right if I ask how you got the name Brett?"

"Sure, hon. I named myself after Ernest Hemingway's heroine in THE SUN ALSO RISES."

"That's fascinating."

"My real name is Bernadette."

"It's a perfect fit. I love it."

"Thank you. I'm in good company. Another New Yorker has taken the name from the same novel: Actress Brett Somers. Wonderful woman. I'll have to make sure we watch her one of these days on "Match Game", or a late night re-run of "The Odd Couple". I've clipped out magazine photos of her. I'll show you back at the house. She's gorgeous."

Brett's arm was exerting the gentlest pressure on Sydney's elbow. Americans were so fortunate, Sydney mused, to be raised without the hang-ups produced by repressive, obsessively homophobic Canadian culture. She envied the emotionally and physically expressive way women connected and formed warm, genuine friendships. Her experiences as a Canadian had illustrated the shameless rivalry and pettiness of duplicitous female friendship, both in Francophone and Anglophone milieus. Brett embodied all things unfamiliar to her, all things lacking but most needed. She vowed to herself that she would never allow any man to come between her and Brett. Her utmost priority would always be her friendship with her.

* * *

"Would you like me to get started on that lasagna?" she asked Brett, once back in her kitchen.

"Oh, thank you, sweetheart." she removed the box of lasagna noodles from the pantry, "That would be terrific. If you start the noodles, I'll start the meat sauce. All the pots and pans are in the bottom drawer beside the stove."

"Five for supper, right?" she knelt down to inspect the pots and selected one to her liking.

"Yes, five. You'll adore Maggie. She's seventy-nine and sharp as a tack." she was combining her ingredients lovingly in a saucepan, "I hope you don't mind being around so many people."

"Brett, this is your world. I consider myself very fortunate to be included in it."

"Of course you're included in it."

"Your world is beautiful. It's a story book I never want to put down."

"You never have to. It's a much better story book with you in it."

They worked diligently side by side, placing alternating layers of noodles and meat mixture in two rectangular Pyrex lasagna dishes.

"Now, we're ready for company." Brett arranged them in the oven.

They heard a key in the lock, and youthful laughter in the foyer.

"Hi, Brett!" Shayleigh's voice called out.

"Hi, hon." she came out to greet them, "Hi, Mindy."

"Hi, Miss Morrow." a thin girl with amber-tinted glasses stood awkwardly.

"Miss Morrow? After all this time? It's Brett."

"Mindy, meet Sydney." Shayleigh led her to the doorway of the kitchen, where Sydney was standing tentatively, "Sydney, this is Mindy."

Pleasantries exchanged, they resumed preparations.

"I'll set the table." Sydney volunteered, glancing at Brett.

"We'll do it together."

"We're off to get Mags now." Shayleigh and Mindy fluttered by, "See you in a bit."

A meticulously-folded and fragrant linen tablecloth with matching napkins was produced from the credenza. The china Brett removed from the antique cabinet had gilded edges and vibrant pink roses. Brett placed crystal goblets and the centerpiece, an arrangement of dried and silk flowers in pinks and creams from the credenza on the table.

"After supper, when we're alone, I'll call your mother and set up a meeting." Brett said.

"I'm nervous."

"Naturally. That's why, the sooner we do this, the better. They might even have heard about you by now. People could be talking about the new singer at Chandler's being named Sydney, and it could send them into a tailspin."

"No, I don't want them to find out that way. That would be cruel. They need to find out from us. I should have known that with such an unusual name, I would stand out like a sore thumb."

"It's a beautiful name. And very feminine. No man should be allowed to have it. People are so small-minded around here. I think I hear footsteps on the porch."

The door opened and a rotund figure with a pink cherubic face, a white bob with bangs, and thick glasses in cat's eye frames stood, flanked by her two youthful companions. Her crimson shirtwaist dress had a print of tiny white parasols.

"Maggie!" Brett embraced her and kissed her cheek.

"I declare, you look more beautiful every time I see you." Maggie stood back to admire Brett, "You are a vision of grace and utter perfection, my dear. You absolutely take my breath away."

"Thank you, Maggie. This is my friend Sydney."

"So, this is Sydney. I've heard do much about you. My, my, another pretty face. This house is filled with such beauty. What are you doing wasting your time with an old woman like me?"

"You are our guest of honor." Brett led her into the living room with an arm around her and gently lowered her to the sofa, leaned her cane against the armrest, and arranged the cushions around her, "I'm going to check on our meal. You and Sydney can get acquainted while the girls help me out."

Shayleigh and Mindy followed Brett into the kitchen, with Shayleigh carrying the round tin of home-made cookies Maggie had given them.

"Are you a writer, by any chance?" Maggie asked.

"I'm afraid not."

"I'm relieved, for your sake. I should think any other calling should be an improvement over a writer's lot in life."

"I wouldn't know."

"You look like a writer. A sensitive soul. Like our Shayleigh."

"Is Shayleigh a writer?"

"A lovely writer. And, she's had a devil of a time. In this country, established writers have a secret society, and the only newcomers they allow in are those who possess certain questionable traits. If you get on one writer's bad side, he can make your life pretty miserable. If you anger one nasty devil, you'd better watch out! You'll be blacklisted. Little Shayleigh could tell you all about the troubles she's had."

"I'm sorry it's been so horrible for her. I must say, I've never liked established writers. I've found them to be a pompous, narcissistic, morally bankrupt bunch. No wonder decent folks who have talent can't get published."

"It's for jackasses only." Maggie laughed heartily, "I lived in Boston for fifty-five years. It was not like this there."

"What made you move here, Mrs...."

"Maggie. No Mrs., please. Makes me feel old. My mother was a Beavertonian. I lived here until I was fifteen, until my father's work took us to Massachusetts. I stayed there, worked as a nutritionist, got married. After my husband died fourteen years ago, I came back to be with my childhood friends."

"I'm sorry about your husband."

"Such is life, my dear. I'm the only one left now. My entire family, my friends, gone. But life has to go on. I've met Brett and the children. They're my family now."

"They're blessed to have you."

"Look at all these bookcases lined with all the classics. Brett used to teach theater back home, you know. She's knowledgeable in practically every creative discipline. She's quite a lady."

"She certainly is."

"That ex-husband of hers was such a cad. She's better off without him. A while back, it looked as though she might settle down with Tony Horncastle, but as it turned out, it was not meant to be. I thought he would be so good for her, too. Brett's the type of woman who needs someone in her life to give her a sense of continuity and emotional security. She's vulnerable. There are dozens of admirers, but no Mr. Right."

"I hope she finds the right person. No one deserves happiness as much as Brett."

"Dinner's ready, ladies." Mindy was in the doorway.

Sydney helped Maggie to her feet, and took her arm. In the dining room, she helped her to the seat of honor at the head of the oval table.

"It smells frightfully good, dear." Maggie called toward the kitchen.

"Sydney and I made it together." Brett appeared, carrying one of the Pyrex dishes, followed by Shayleigh carrying the other.

Both dishes were placed on cast iron trivets. Mindy brought in the large wooden salad bowl. Sydney retrieved the basket of steaming hot garlic bread from the kitchen. Once Mindy poured the ice-cold water from the pitcher, Brett sat opposite from Maggie. Shayleigh meticulously served them lasagna individually, as the bread and salad were passed around the table.

Following the meal, as the two youngest women cleared the dishes and began washing them, the others adjourned to the living room.

"Lovely meal." Maggie said, "You're absolutely amazing, Brett. You keep a spotless home, raise children by yourself, cook like a chef...I don't know how you do it."

"I get a lot of help from all of you."

The girls returned with coffee and cookies on trays and served the others.

"Shayleigh and I had a marvelous time watching Garbo last night." Maggie smiled, lifting her china cup to her lips.

"I hope we can do that again soon." Shayleigh said, "I enjoyed it immensely."

"I'm a night owl. I'm game for it any time you are."

"What do you girls have planned for tonight?" Brett turned to the younger women.

"They're showing that movie about the two teeny-boppers who play phone games and nearly get killed." Mindy said, "I can't remember the name of it."

"It's something like "I Know Who You Are"?" Shayleigh said, ""I Know What You Did"? I'm not sure."

"It's close enough. We don't have to be in at work until two o'clock tomorrow, so we can stay up to watch it."

"Have fun." Brett laughed, "I hope the boys behaved themselves last night. I know what a handful they can be."

"They were good as gold."

"Are you sure, Maggie?"

"They're growing up, Brett, dear. And becoming fine young men. Their good upbringing shows."

"You're very kind. I couldn't have gotten through these past few years without you and Shayleigh. If the boys are turning out all right, it's thanks to the love and support you two have provided and how you've made them feel secure and wanted."

"It goes both ways."

Sydney observed the look of contentment in Shayleigh's eyes and the level of comfort with which she navigated in her surroundings. It was the product of that elusive state known as a sense of belonging.

"I've had a splendid time, my dear, but now I must go home to my cat." Maggie said, "Thank you for a wonderful evening, my dears."

"We love having you, Maggie." Brett helped her to her feet and handed her dark, aged wood cane to her.

"We'll walk you back." Shayleigh took one arm and Mindy the other.

"Take care, Maggie. I'll see you tomorrow." Brett kissed her cheek.

"We'll be going, too." Mindy said, "Shay's stuff's already in my trunk."

"I'm glad to meet you, Maggie." Sydney touched her shoulder, "I hope to see you again soon."

"You will, God willing."

"Bye, Brett." Shayleigh embraced her, "Bye, Sydney."

"You girls be good. And take care." Brett shook a finger at her.

"Bye." Sydney called out.

"If you don't behave, I'll show you home movies of my brother's wedding." Mindy was saying as the threesome made their way toward Maggie's.

Brett closed the door and turned to Sydney.

"I can phone your parents now, if you like, hon."

"I guess it's best to get it over with."

"I'll try to set it up for tomorrow, then? If not, the next day?"

"Okay. No point in prolonging this anymore."

"That's right." Brett dialed the green wall phone in the kitchen and waited for it to be picked up, "Hello. Edna? This is Brett Morrow. Oh, fine, thanks, and you?...Glad to hear it...Yes, I did. I picked it up this morning. That Greeney's a gem...Edna, the reason I called is I was wondering if you and Sid could come for tea tomorrow afternoon?...Oh, that's terrific. Three o'clock all right?...See you then." she placed the receiver back on the hook, "See how easy that was? You'll see, everything'll be just fine."

In less than twenty-four hours, she would be face to face with her parents. Suddenly feeling dizzy, she sat on the nearest chair.

"Can I get you some water, hon? You look pale." observed Brett.

"I'm all right. It's just so much to take in."

"I imagine it is."

"There's something I need to do." she stood unsteadily, "I'll be right back, Brett."

She went to the living room and searched through her handbag. She returned to the kitchen with an outstretched palm and a pewter Star of David on a leather string.

"I didn't know you had one."

"I've been carrying it around in my purse since I left Montreal, but never had the nerve to actually wear it. I bought it from one of those hippie craftspeople who sell their wares at flea markets and outdoor craft festivals. When I overheard those women at the sweet shop, I went searching for an affordable Star of David. I wanted a symbol of my heritage."

"Your father would be so proud to see you wearing the symbol of his faith. You can start wearing it right now, sweetheart." she fastened the clasp at the nape of Sydney's neck, "There. It's beautiful. Wear it with pride."

"What if Tony asks questions at the club?"

"We'll simply tell him you're Jewish. We'll keep the Horncastles guessing just a little longer. Kind of a final joke. He'll think this is a sign that you're ready to make a move, and get them all worked up. Serves them right for thinking you were an extortionist. From now on, they're all going to treat you like royalty. You are a Goldstein."

"That sounds beautiful. Goldstein. I can't believe it."

"You'd better believe it, hon. Welcome to your life, Sydney Goldstein."

Chapter 7/ Light In French

The drone of teenagers milling about in the orange lobby and slithering through the maze of orange lockers became muted as the familiar strumming of a guitar over the P.A. system alerted them to the end of their lunch break. The crowds dispersed, as if on cue. Sighing in relief, she slammed her locker door shut and bent down to gather the text books on the floor she had removed for the afternoon. Behind her, she heard a cackle of geese, and without turning around, caught a glimpse of long raven hair swinging like a pendulum against a disproportionately large posterior on a thin frame. Clutching her books to her bosom, she started down the corridor toward her first class, however, was unable to get very far when she found herself surrounded by a wall of girls with stringy, unkempt hair.

"Miss Hoity-Doity thinks she's too good for us!" the raven-haired one at the center of the group sneered.

She attempted to squeeze between two of the girls, to no avail.

"What's the matter? Cat got your tongue?" her tormenter continued, "Rich Bitch is too stuck up to talk to us!"

She made another attempt to squeeze through, in vain. She met the raven-haired one's gaze and held icy eye contact without flinching.

"Hilary and I are going to see the new Robert Redford movie on Friday night." her tormenter moved closer, "Hilary's my very best friend in the whole world now. We can go to the movies without a loser like you tagging along. Hilary only hung around with you because she felt sorry for you, but she's washed her hands off you. She doesn't want a fifth wheel, either. Eat your heart out, Dorky. You're not going to see Robert Redford's naked chest."

The other girls appeared comfortable with allowing Raven Hair to have the floor and watching her from the sidelines.

"Ben's telling everyone about you trying to put the moves on him. You'll never get a date with anyone, anywhere, in this lifetime! You're a pathetic weirdo freak loser!"

The sound of another strumming guitar sent a wave of relief through her like a rush of cool air.

"Come on, Darnelle, let's get to class." one of the mousy companions of Raven Hair found her voice, "Mrs. Burtt gets mad if we're late."

In yet another futile attempt to escape, she dropped her Math book on the floor.

"She's not worth talking to, anyway. Dorky's a big, fat loser." Darnelle peered at her from behind octagonal glasses, tossed back her long raven hair, and strutted past her like a peacock, kicking her Math book aside.

She was struck by how much Darnelle's profile resembled that of a witch. She waited for the vultures' footsteps to fade into a diminuendo before picking up her now soiled book. Behind her, she heard visceral laughter. In the corner of her eye, she could make out a group of vaguely familiar boys pointing at her and sharing side-splitting laughter. Her head held high, she briskly walked past the pack of wolves without as much as a furtive glance in their direction. In her high school of three thousand students, she was at the bottom of the pecking order. Girls with obnoxious personalities, worse grades, girls three times her size, girls with unibrows and moustaches, girls with acne all had friends, even boyfriends. All of them considered themselves superior to her and ostracized her. She was still at a loss as to what it was about her that made her a defective specimen. She dressed and appeared quite average. She was spontaneous and unaffected, perhaps too child-like and unsophisticated in the way she interacted with people. She treated everyone equally. What had she done to elicit such contempt?

All of this trouble had started on the day she had asked Ben what she had missed in Math during her absence. Just an innocent casual question by the lockers. His over-inflated ego had kicked into high gear, and, by the end of the day, all of his friends and their girlfriends were laughing in her face. Perhaps a note of insecurity, fear, and desperation had sparked the killer instinct and prompted such visceral an attack. The word around school was that she was "desperate" for a boyfriend, but was too much of a loser to be able to secure one. Yet, the irony of it all had been that, she had only convinced herself to like boys in order to appease the other girls. Her lack of interest in the opposite sex had sparked rumors of possible lesbianism. In order to quash the whispers and stares, she had concocted her fictitious interest in boys in order to be accepted, considered "normal" by the other girls. Her strategy had backfired miserably, and she was at a loss to understand what had gone wrong.

"Where the hell have you been?" someone thumped her on the back, "I waited for you by Madame Vautour's room. You never showed up!" an enormous girl with a menacing scowl and furious eyebrows punched her in the arm.

"Something unexpected came up, Dawn."

"What? Run out of tampons and bled all over your panties?"

"Far worse."

"What? Shit your pants?"

"No. Never mind."

"Come on, Dufus. You're gonna help me with our French assignment before the teacher shows up!" Dawn dug a pudgy index finger with jagged yellow nails into her left nostril and affixed the gelatinous prize on her grease-soaked grey T-shirt.

"I don't know how to do it, either, Dawn."

"I cut my necking time with Brian short because of you, so, you'd better gimme it!" she shoved her through the doorway and all the way to the back of the classroom, "It can't be that hard for you! Your mother's French!"

Dawn snatched her notebook away from her and began copying the contents of the assignment into her own notebook, the smell of bacon grease wafting from its pages. A blonde with corkscrew ringlets stood in the doorway in her cheerleading skirt, kissing a tall, dark-haired boy, a star athlete of some sort. When she unglued her lips from his at last, she acknowledged each one of the girls who had entered earlier, by name. She cast a blank stare at Dawn, and after hesitation, remembered her name. Then, she gave herself a smug look, and spoke.

"Hi, Doris."

Candee was the most popular girl at school: cheerleader, honor student, athlete, social butterfly, beauty queen, slut – all the prerequisites for this dubious honor. As more students began filing in, Dawn flung her notebook back at her. It had absorbed the stale grease oozing out of Dawn's pores. She placed it as far away from herself as possible, on the far right corner of her desk. A group of boys, whose names she did not know, snickered, their eyes turned toward her. She wished the ground would open up and swallow her. Averting her gaze to the parking lot outside the window, she began counting the number of green cars. Had it not been for her English test earlier in the day, she would not have come to prison today. She planned to spend the following day hiding in Peggy's family's living quarters in the basement, watching "Match Game", re-runs of "The Odd Couple", and a few soaps thrown in for good measure. In another year, she would be released on parole, and never set foot in this cesspool again. The year was almost over. For two glorious months, she would no longer need to sneak around to play hooky. A long, hot Beavertown summer with no psycho kids...lazy afternoons in the T.V. room with Marge's famous chocolate chip cookies...evenings spent with Peggy once she returned home from her job as a legal secretary.

"Peggy's only nice to you because her family works for your family." Darnelle had said to her, "Your parents have to pay her to be your friend!"

She had been racking her brains all year to decipher the formula for Darnelle's popularity and inexplicable power over other girls. A degree of superficial charm, turned on and off for the right audience, extreme narcissism, a self-aggrandizing attitude, a sanctimonious streak, a skill in oppressing minorities, particularly the socially inept, uncanny powers of persuasion...One more year...Just one more year and she would be able to make her getaway.

"How would you fill in that blank, Dorothy?" Madame Vautour asked in her mellifluous accent.

Hearing her name jolted her back to reality.

"I'm sorry, Madame?"

"La valise de Philippe est BLANK. How would you fill in that blank?"

Just like "Match Game", she thought. How would Brett Somers fill in that blank? After all, she spent her weekdays filling in blanks on the game show. The suitcase was "left behind at the motel in Encino.". That's what Brett would say. It was an ongoing joke on the show that Brett and the handsome host, Gene Rayburn, allegedly frequented a motel in Encino. It was of course nothing more than a sarcastic dig at the Paparazzi. It would be too difficult to translate that into French. She wished Brett Somers were there to help her come up with an answer. A color, perhaps? The suitcase was a particular color. What would a boy like? A blue suitcase? Why not? Boys liked blue.

"Bleu." she called out with pride, "La valise de Phillippe est bleu!"

Laughter broke out. What had she done wrong?

"Sh-h..." Madame quieted them, "Dorothy, haven't you been following the story? His sister Anne-Marie's suitcase was too heavy. In contrast, Philippe's was..."

"Light!"

"That's right. Now, what is light in French?"

"Lumiere."

More laughter erupted.

"That is one type of light." Madame said, "The type that shines. What is light which means the opposite of heavy?"

It was the same word in both instances in English. Why couldn't it be the same in French? She could remember only one word.

"Um...um...I don't know."

More laughter.

"Quiet, all of you! Let her think."

She shook her head.

"Does anyone know?" Madame addressed the class.

All hands were raised.

"Legere!" Candee called out with complacency, without being called on.

"That is right. Legere. That is all, class. We'll continue this chapter tomorrow."

Everyone filed out laughing boisterously. It seemed, every time she opened her mouth, she ended up making a fool of herself. Why did she ever bother getting out of bed in the mornings? Her next class was Math. She wished she could go home now. Madame's class was so close to the front door, she could slip out and no one would know. But, Mrs. Burger would know. As her home room teacher, she had marked her as present in the morning at roll call, and would expect her to be there now for Math. Ben and Dom would sit behind her, throw spit balls at her and snicker. She would not have a moment's peace. Ben needed to get over himself. It might have been amusing back in October that the most socially inept and most unpopular girl at school had shown an interest in him. Surely, it had to be growing stale by now. Did they not have any other source of entertainment?

Apathetic, slouching figures sauntered in and found their seats through blind instinct. They opened their books with the enthusiasm of garden slugs. She could not remember a time in her life before this year when Hilary had not been her friend. She had always seemed more like a relative. The two of them had a history together, a sense of continuity. As children, they had shared confidences, created outlandish skits and performed them for Hilary's older sister. They had countless sleepovers. She smiled to herself at the recollection of her favorite scenario, inspired by their scavenger hunt in Hilary's attic when they were eleven: her brother's toy gun from his younger days, and her grandmother's crutches from the time she had lived with the family had been priceless treasures. They had taken turns portraying Mrs. Chambers, their demure music teacher, threatening the students with the gun and beating them with the crutches when they misbehaved. Hilary's dolls had been the students.

"Dottie!" Mrs. Burger's voice penetrated her musings, "Can you work with Nancy this period? You got all the questions wrong on your test. Nancy got all of them right. She'll show you how to do them. Move your chair next to her desk. The rest of you, work on the exam review practice problems I've put on the board." She paused, aware of the stirrings from the direction of Ben and his best friend Dom, "Boys, would you like to share with the rest of us whatever is so funny?"

The two fell silent, covering their mouths to conceal stifled laughter.

"I'll have to separate the two of you. Neither one of you can afford to goof off during this class. You both barely passed the test, so you need to pay close attention. Dominic, I want to you to switch seats with Shawn."

The other students snickered as the stylishly disheveled Dom gathered his books and swaggered down the aisle to the seat promptly vacated by a clean-cut, bespectacled boy in a pressed blue shirt. Dom slid down in his seat and cast furtive glances at his paramour across the room, the preppy blonde Carol Ann.

"Shawn, help Ben with the review questions." Mrs. Burger continued, "He's having a lot of trouble. Dominic, sit up straight. Wendy, can you help him with his work, dear?"

The girl with the freshly-scrubbed face beside him leaned close to him, much to Carol Ann's chagrin. Dottie smiled inwardly. Thank you, Mrs. Burger! Cruelty was an art. And privileged teenagers, the finest artisans. Never again would she give a boy the time of day or waste one fleeting thought. She did not feel an attraction to boys. Or girls. She simply had no sexual feelings for anyone. It did not trouble her. Why did others feel the need to meddle? What did it matter? She wished Darnelle had never moved here from John's Bay last year. She wished she had not been stupid enough to reach out to her in friendship upon her arrival. Her foolish, misguided gesture of friendship had been repaid with cruelty.

"Ellen and Patty are saying you're the laughing stock of the whole school, chasing after Ben and making a spectacle of yourself." Hilary had told her one fateful day in late October, "They're saying you're really strange, you can't even go about chasing a boy like a normal person. They're laughing at you. Darnelle and I can't be seen with you. We can't go to the mall or the movies anymore."

Dottie's silence had been undetected by Hilary.

"Ellen and Patty really like Darnelle. And, there's this other girl, Rose who just adores her, too. We all get along so well. We're just simple, ordinary people. Patty doesn't like weird, complicated people. Isn't What's-Her-Name, that obnoxious, bossy girl, Clara, the ugly one, coming back next year when her dad's Sabbatical's over? I'm sure she won't mind hanging around with you. Darnelle says she's a bit of a loser, too. She was ashamed to be seen with you and Clara last year, but she was new, and she hadn't met the popular kids yet. Now that I'm here, she's met everyone I know. When I'm gone next year, she'll have the rest of the gang, so, she wants you and Clara to stay clear of her. She has a reputation to uphold."

"Hilary! Come on!" Darnelle came bouncing behind her, "My stomach's growling! Let's go to lunch! Patty's saving our seats. I brought you some home-made shortbread cookies. I made them myself. My parents are so happy that you're my very best friend!" she beamed complacently, "I just love your new sweater! It looks divine on you!"

"Dottie's sweater's really darling, isn't it?" Hilary cast an uncomfortable glance in her direction, "It's the softest mohair." She patted her like a dog.

"It must be nice to be so rich, and wear real mohair." Darnelle sneered at her, "Some of us have to save our pennies and put something aside for our higher education. Some of us actually have ambition and drive and high aspirations. I'm going to be a doctor while you live on your family's handouts and lounge around doing mindless things. Someday, I'm going to have a lot more money than your family."

Darnelle's large French Canadian family ran a ramshackle rooming house in a seedy part of town. She wore her poverty like a badge of honor. How ironic, she thought. Her elation at having Hilary attend her school had led to the unraveling of her life.

This was Hilary's first year at Beavertown High. She had spent the past year in B.C. with relatives, however, had grown homesick for Beavertown, and felt unhappy about the high school in Vancouver. Dottie had begun the school year by making two fatal mistakes. The first one was introducing Hilary to Darnelle, and the second, feigning an interest in boys. She blinked back her tears, remembering last summer, the three weeks spent at Hilary's house before the start of school. They had requested songs from evening D.J. on the radio station by the wrong titles or wrong artists' names.

"You girls are so stupid! I've never met anybody as stupid as the pair of you! When are you going to get it through your heads? It's Gilbert O'Sullivan who sings "Alone Again Naturally", not Ed Sullivan! It's "The Raspberries", not "The Gooseberries"! It's "The Bells", not "The Dingdongs"! Neil Sedaka sings "Breaking Up Is Hard To Do", not "Cracking Up Is Easy To Do"!"

Now, months following the announcement of her dumping, Hilary seemed to deem it necessary to flag her down when their paths crossed between classes, in order to quiz her as to why she was so unfriendly to her and Darnelle. Darnelle continued to taunt her daily every chance she had.

"Hey, Dorothy, why don't you just click your heels and go back to Kansas? Nobody wants you here."

They were either frighteningly callous, or too feeble-minded to comprehend Dottie might be hurt by the way they had cast her aside. Perhaps, they perceived her as being so inferior, so undeserving of civility that they felt she ought to be grateful for the crumbs they occasionally tossed and accept her lot in life. Dottie had overstepped her boundaries by not accepting abuse from any of them any longer. As an underling, she had broken all the rules. They had discarded her, but still wanted to keep her around for target practice. By removing herself, she had offended them. Much like a childhood disease, once one experienced the full-blown effects of betrayal, one was left with an immunity to its devastation. Dottie had emerged from this dark tunnel more silent, more guarded, and more repulsed by perky conformists with inflexible attitudes, capable of perceiving only a limited range of possible behavior.

The familiar strumming of the liberating guitar sent a wave of excitement through the room. Gathering her books swiftly and thanking Nancy for her help, she ran past the others down the stairs to her locker. Her books landed with a loud thud against its metal floor. She slammed the door shut and locked it. Then, she ran past more malodorous adolescents congregated by the door waiting for their buses. The seventeen block walk to her house was a welcome exertion. She only took the bus in winter, when icy streets, combined with the steep downhill trek rendered the journey much too treacherous for walking. Taking the circuitous route past the university, she was able to avoid heavy traffic. Once she turned the corner of Shore Street onto Waterloo Row, she had a view of her family's imposing three-storey mansion with its multiple turrets, built-on additions, guest house, and multiple-car garage with the apartment over it. In the sunlight, the aged white paint on the clapboard siding was grey and peeling. She let herself in with her key through the side door leading into the kitchen.

"Hello!" she called out into the emptiness.

In the T.V. room with the narrow windows facing the street she deposited her books on the desk. She stealthily took the connecting corridor through the courtyard to the majestic section of the mansion. In the grand foyer, she called out again, only to be greeted by her own echo. She called up the winding staircase, down the hall toward the solarium, into the den, the library, the ballroom, the dining room, and finally the living room. No one. Not a sound. She closed the bevelled French doors of the living room behind her and tiptoed to the liquor cabinet. With quivering hands, she produced the clear liquid in the blue bottle. Unscrewing the cap, she drank breathlessly. The taste, at first antiseptic and repugnant, not unlike rubbing alcohol administered to scrapes, became overwhelmingly warm. She covered it and placed it back in the same spot, behind the brown sherry bottle. She pocketed a handful of green striped Scotch mints in cellophane wrappers from the crystal candy dish on the side table, and tiptoed out of the room. She took the connecting corridor back to the T.V. room and turned on the television set. They were showing soap operas on three of the channels, mindless talk shows on two of them, a cooking show on one, and a re-run of "Gilligan's Island" on the remaining one, by far the best offering. She knelt by the coffee table, where the pieces of a jigsaw puzzle were haphazardly spread over the entire surface. All she had been able to piece together so far was a brown ear. She was scotch-taping the pieces together underneath, once certain they were in correct positions. She wished she, too, could be marooned on Gilligan's Island and never be found.

"Miss Dorothy, honey, when did you get home?"

In the doorway stood Marge in a drab uniform which hugged her stout figure.

"Hi, Marge." Dottie glanced up from her puzzle and flashed her metallic smile.

"Didn't expect you home so early, honey."

"I got all my work done on time."

"I see you're workin' on your deer puzzle."

"I can't wait to see it all finished."

"You and deer. Never seen anybody so crazy for deer. Your cousin sure knew what puzzle to send you."

"I wish Jack didn't have to spend so much time away."

"When he gets married to that one, all of that is goin' to change; mark my words, honey. She'll keep him on a short leash."

"I don't like her. I don't know what he sees in her."

"He's a young man, honey."

"Everyone always goes away, Marge. I don't want him to go away, too. Why doesn't she want to live in this house after they're married?"

"Newlyweds need their privacy. Don't worry, my little lamb, Mr. Jack'll still spend as much time as he can with you." Marge stroked her hair, "I'll bring you some milk and a muffin."

"Last night, I was in the kitchen, scavenging for a snack, and I found some Viva Puffs in the cupboard. I know I can't eat marshmallows with these braces, but I ate the chocolate coating, the jam, and the biscuit part. Do you think I could have some of those now?"

"Sure, honey. I buy them just for the mice. I never thought to serve them as cookies."

"The mice?"

"Gets 'em every time. I've tried cheese, chocolates, peanut butter. They eat the food, but don't get caught in the trap. I tried one of these ones, and they got caught. Been buyin' them since."

"You're the best exterminator, Marge!" Dottie laughed, "I like the boxes you get for the beetles. They go in and get stuck on the sticky stuff. Then, their friends see them and try to join them. I like the way all of them strike up a pose like models."

"Oh, they're models all right. Real beauties. I'll bring you those mouse cookies, honey. You sure you're goin' to be all right here?"

"Sure. I've got my deer puzzle, "Gilligan's Island", my milk and my mouse cookies. Then, later on, "The Gong Show" is on. We're going to be roomies again tomorrow."

"You sure you're not fallin' behind too much at school, honeybunch?"

"There's nothing going on at school. Just exam reviews. I can do that on my own. I've gotta have my regular fix of "Match Game" to keep me going."

"I hope your mama don't get wind of your cuffin'. She don't like you missin' time."

"Don't worry. Aunt Edna writes all my excuses."

"You're a crafty one, you are. I'll get you the mouse cookies, sweetie." She shook her head in amusement, "What a ray of sunshine you are around here. I sure am gonna miss you when you get married and move away."

"Don't worry, Marge. I'm going to be an old maid and stay here forever."

"Now, what kind of a thing is that to say? An old maid, indeed! A pretty lass like you!"

"No one thinks I'm pretty, Marge."

"Rubbish. You'll knock 'em dead, just you wait and see."

"Thanks, Marge."

Two hours later, when Marge came to inform her that her family was shortly being served dinner, she had completed the mesmerizing coal-black eyes of the deer. She discretely raced up the back stairs of the kitchen, past Marge, and her new helper, Pauline, to dress as was expected of her. Her mother would be scandalized to see her at dinner in denim overalls. Promptly, she joined her family in her old stand-by: White pin tucked blouse, black gabardine skirt with box pleats, her Cousin Ella's pearls with the matching earrings. Her fine hair was haphazardly pulled back with an elastic and fastened high with a tortoise-shell clip. On her feet, she wore white bobby socks and black ballet slippers. She awkwardly slid into her chair, attempting to be inconspicuous.

"You're late." her mother chided her.

"I'm sorry." she mumbled.

"Those clothes must reek by now. Don't you ever let Marge wash them?"

"She washes them all the time, Mom." she squirmed in her chair and lowered her eyes.

"It would be easier on our eyes if you would change your outfit once in a while, Dottie. And, your hair! It's a mess. Can't you put a little more effort into doing your hair? Pin it up in a chignon, or a French twist. Honestly, Dottie, you look like something the cat dragged in."

"She looks up-to-date and casually chic." Warren protested.

"Don't encourage her, Warren. She's incorrigible."

Marge entered with the service cart, followed by Pauline. The gleaming solid cherry table seated twenty-four when opened to full capacity, however, these days, it was set to accommodate twelve. With Jack away, and Tony working longer hours, there were only seven of them most evenings.

Being the oldest, Uncle Willy and Aunt Mildred were seated at opposite ends of the table. Her parents sat across from one another on each side of Uncle Willy, while Aunty Audrey and Warren were seated on Aunt Mildred's left. Dottie's seat was beside her mother, with an empty seat between her and Warren, reserved for any lady companions he might invite. Tony's seat was across the table from Dottie, and Jack's, opposite Aunty Audrey, leaving two empty seats between them to accommodate their dates – in Jack's case, his numerous ex-wives in succession. On the rare occasions Dottie's brother, Garrett was presentable enough to eat with the rest of the family he occupied one of the chairs reserved for Tony's or Warren's dates. Garrett's girlfriends were not permitted on the premises, and Dottie's boyfriends consisted strictly of the non-existent variety.

Dottie kept her head lowered during the entire meal, and did not attempt to contribute to the conversation. She paid little attention to its content. She chewed her roast beef robotically, savored her mashed potatoes containing a secret ingredient known only to Frederick, the cook from Austria. She ate her emerald peas, but pushed the orange circles to one side of her plate. After Pauline cleared the plates, it was Peggy who served Frederick's famous black forest cake. He used real rum – no extracts or other shortcuts for him. Peggy winked at her as she served her dessert. Dottie beamed and crinkled her nose.

Once the dessert plates were cleared, the family followed Uncle Willy to the living room for after dinner drinks.

"I'll get the Grand Marnier for us ladies." Dottie's mother gushed like a teenager, "Donald, dear, you can get the cognac for the gentlemen."

Dottie squirmed in her seat and fidgeted with a coaster on the side table. Warren's eyes were on her.

"Donald, dear!" Dottie's mother shrieked, holding up the familiar blue bottle, "I think the servants are dipping into our liquor! Look what I found behind the sherry! We have to start marking all the bottles. You really should speak to them, dear. It's so hard to get good help these days. You treat them like family, give them time off, bonuses at Christmas, and they rob you blind!"

"There's no need for that, Annette." Warren intercepted, "I'm afraid I'm responsible for that. I've been entertaining a new young lady here. Lucy has a fondness for gin and tonic. I'm sorry I've been slack about replenishing the supply. I'll get on it right away."

"Oh, Warren, I didn't realize...I didn't mean..."

"Forget it, Annette. I'll replace it. I think I'll retire to my room and watch television. Care to join me, Dottie? I think there might be "Alice" on one of the channels."

"Warren, I'm sorry."

"It's okay, Annette. Come on, Shortstuff. Let's leave them to their drinking while you and I watch the crazy antics of the gang at Mel's Diner." he motioned her to the stairs.

Once behind the closed door of his room, she looked him straight in the eye.

"Why did you cover for me?"

"What good would it have done to let you get caught and face their wrath? Would that have stopped your drinking? It would have driven you further to drink. I've suspected it for months. There have been wine bottles missing from the wine cellar for quite some time. Now you've graduated to the hard stuff. Your mistake was being so obvious about it. How did you ever manage to smuggle the wine out of the cellar? Did you have an accomplice? Peggy?"

"No. I would never involve Peggy in this. I was alone. I used to sneak down when no one was around. Did anybody else notice them missing?"

"They certainly did. Don't worry: I covered for you. They all think I'm a raging alcoholic."

"I owe you big time, Warren. I promise I'll make it up to you."

"What's going on? Is it experimentation? Are you drinking to escape emotional pain? Has somebody done something to you?"

"Someday, when I can actually talk about it, I'll tell you."

"I'm here when you need me. You know that."

"I do. Thank you." she kissed his cheek.

"In the meantime, we're going to make a deal. I'm going to keep a supply of Tia Maria up here, along with my scotch. You and I are going to be drinking buddies. When you get the urge, you come to me or call me, and we'll drink together. You're not going to drink alone."

"What if I can't get a hold of you?"

"I'll give you numbers where I can be reached. If I'm indisposed, please wait until I'm available. I don't want you to drink alone. Do we have a deal?"

"Yes. Thank you, Warren."

"Booze doesn't make the pain vanish. It just gives the illusion of euphoria for a fleeting moment. When you sober up, all the pain and the problems are still there, still unresolved, looming larger than life. And, they don't go away until you face them head on and deal with them."

"Some things can never go away. No matter what."

"Sharing them with a friend can help. I hope I'm your friend."

"Of course you are, Warren. You're my hero, my shining star."

"I hope I don't let you down, Shortstuff. I hope I can be all that you need me to be, to help you get over this."

"I love you, Warren."

"I love you, Shortstuff."

She buried her head in his chest. And, for that fleeting moment, she was a hapless child again, a child loved and protected from the pain of cruelty, sheltered from the passing of time. This moment was hers. All hers. And, no matter where Fate took her against her will, she would always have the purity of this moment to cherish.

Chapter 8/ At Last

Sydney opened her eyes to be greeted by the sun. Beside her, Brett stirred. She glanced over Brett's shoulder at the clock radio: It was eight A.M.

"Hi, sweetheart." Brett murmured groggily.

"It's too early, Brett. You need your sleep."

"Old folks like me don't need as much sleep." she stretched luxuriously, "Why don't we just lie here and talk for a while?"

"That would be nice."

"It's too nice a day to sleep in." she adjusted both of their pillows.

"I was too nervous to sleep."

"It's understandable. This is your big day. You finally meet your real parents."

"I can hardly believe it. I keep expecting to wake up and find myself back in Sven's clutches, and realize Beavertown and all this has been a dream – a beautiful dream."

"You never have to go through anything like that ever again, sweetheart. Scumbags like Sven can never hurt you again. You have a support system of loving friends and family now. From here on, there's no place to go but up."

"I'm more than willing to sign any papers indicating I have no claim to any family fortune." Sydney stated.

"There's no need for that. Your parents want you to have everything that is theirs – and the Horncastles have no say in it. You are their daughter, the rightful heiress. Besides, they don't have much, anyway, other than the store. The Horncastles like to create high drama."

"I want them to know I came to find them, because I wanted to have a family, not because I had ulterior motives."

"They know that. There isn't going to be a doubt in their minds, sweetheart. They're not Horncastles. Besides, even with the store, they're not exactly affluent. Donald Horncastle has had to bail them out time after time. They fell upon hard times a while back, and never quite recovered. Donald owns the house they live in. Don't look so happy about it."

"I'm sorry. I didn't mean it like that. I'm just relieved they're not loaded like the Horncastles."

"They're nothing like the Horncastles in any way, I assure you. You really are one of a kind." Brett placed an arm across her chest, "Oh, sweetness, you're a treasure. I love you so much."

"I love you, too, Brett."

"Your parents have certainly had their troubles. They don't want for anything, but they're certainly not on Easy Street. His brother Ira in Toronto's the one who ended up with the big chunk of the Goldstein fortune. You're going to have one big interesting clan: Your mother's sister Annette is married to Donald Horncastle, who is Warren's brother and your father's best friend. It's a bit claustrophobic for me."

"Is Donald Tony's father?"

"No. That's Willy, the oldest of the three brothers."

"Is Donald Jack's father, then? Or stepfather?"

"No again. Warren's sister Audrey, who is the second oldest sibling after Willy, is Jack's stepmother. Her late husband was Jack's father. Donald is the third sibling. Then, there's sister Frances, the black sheep of the family, who was banished from the kingdom years ago. Warren is the baby. The spoiled baby."

"Do Annette and Donald have children?"

"Two. Dottie's in high school. Sweet girl. Her brother's almost thirty, and a drug addict. He takes LSD, Speed, Magic Mushrooms, whatever he can get his hands on."

"What are the Goldstein – La Rocque clans like?"

"Much more subdued. Your father only has his brother. Ira and Esther have a son, Jacob, a promising young executive. Your

136

mother has several brothers and sisters all over the country. Big French-Canadian family. Unfortunately, they've cut all ties with your mother and aunt."

"But why?"

"One married a Jew, the other a Protestant."

"That's foolish."

"Religion brings out everyone's foolish side." Brett scratched her left breast, "I must caution you, dear heart: your Aunt Annette is nothing like your mother. As gracious and unaffected as your mother is, your aunt is an obnoxious social climber."

"I may need a little time to digest all of this information. I hope I don't call people by the wrong names."

"It's understandable if you do. How can anyone keep their names straight? Sweetheart, your parents are the most sincere, caring people I've met. It's not at all surprising they'd produce a wonderful daughter like you."

"I don't know what I ever did to deserve this, Brett. You are the patron saint of lonely souls."

"I belong to that club myself, sweetheart."

"I'll clean the house before they get here."

"Don't worry about that. We'll do that together. First, we need to pick out what you are going to wear. We'll go to your place first, pick out an outfit; then, drop by the bakery for some treats, maybe some eclairs. When we get back, we can have a quick bite and give the living room the once-over. After that, we'll get you ready. You have a white dress I'm particularly partial to: it's a gauze, diaphanous number with a lot of lace and ruffles and a full skirt. You look ethereal in it."

Sydney watched Brett tying the sash on her white chenille robe. She wanted to touch her to reassure herself that she was real, and would not vanish if she dared look away.

* * *

137

Brett's eyes filled with tears as Sydney turned to her for approval.

"To risk being clichéd, you are a vision in white. Sometimes, clichés can come in handy, when one is at a loss for words."

"You really think I look okay?"

"Okay? Just take a look in the mirror. Wait a minute. There's one thing missing." Brett reached into her pocketbook and produced a small gift-wrapped box, which she handed to Sydney, "You need this."

Confused, Sydney removed the wrapping to reveal a jeweller's box.

"Brett! When did you get this?"

"Today. When I told you I had to run a quick errand and left you in the book store."

"I thought you were picking up a graduation gift for Laurie."

"I did that, too."

"Brett, I can't believe this! I don't know what to say!"

"Open it, sweetheart."

Sydney's trembling fingers opened the box to reveal a gold heart-shaped locket.

"Brett...this is too nice. I can't accept something this beautiful."

"This is a very special day for you, hon."

"Thank you so much!" she flung her arms around her and kissed her face, "I'll cherish it forever!"

"It has four compartments. You can put your parents, your future husband, and your children in it."

"I'd like to put one of you first."

"Oh, sweetheart."

"It would bring me luck. I'd be honored to carry your photo in the locket you've given me."

"God love you." she squeezed her hand and reached for a photo in a silver frame on the dresser, "I'll give you the one in this frame. You can cut out my face and put it in the locket."

"I don't want to ruin the photo."

"It's a blessing that you asked for a picture. I've been trying to find an excuse to change the photo in this frame for years. Josh is in it. Now, I can cut him out, and put the kids in another frame. I'll save his head in a box for the kids."

They meticulously trimmed the photograph to fit into the locket. As she closed it, Sydney caressed the gleaming metal.

"Come on, sweetheart, let's go down. It's getting close."

Brett put on a record of instrumental wartime songs. Sydney paced the floor in the foyer, peeking through the square window each time she heard a car.

At two-thirty sharp, the forest green Crown Victoria slid into the driveway. From the side window, they could see the uniformed chauffeur producing a wheelchair from the trunk and opening the back door to lift the man from the store on to the chair. Locking the wheelchair brakes diligently, the young man opened the door on the opposite side and re-emerged with a petite brunette in a pink linen suit, a pink pillbox hat, a matching handbag, pink cotton gloves and pink pumps. Brett ran outside to greet them. Sydney took her position out of sight, in the kitchen. She strained her ears to hear their voices.

"We made it up the porch steps, Ryan. Teamwork. Now, we're home free." Brett said.

With no wheelchair ramp, Sydney thought, it would have taken two people to get the wheelchair up the steps.

"When would you like me to come for you, sir?" an unfamiliar male voice was heard.

"Take your time." Brett said, "Go have a coffee. Have fun. You don't have to be back until five."

"Brett, dear, we don't want to impose on you too much." an unfamiliar female voice spoke.

"Nonsense. You're my guests. Ryan, take your time, dear. See you at five."

"Okay, goodbye."

"Thank you, son. Goodbye." the familiar man's voice said.

"Let's go into the living room." Brett could be heard wheeling Sydney's father, "Edna, sweetheart, please have a seat. How have you been?"

"Just fine, dear. How are you and the boys?"

"Terrific. Never a dull moment with those two around. They're having an extended visit with their father and getting spoiled rotten with material things. They'll be impossible to live with when they return."

"Oh, dear."

"You must be wondering why I dragged you here. I'll get right to the point. I don't want to keep you in suspense any longer."

"Goodness Gracious, Brett, dear, is it bad news? Is the club going under? Do you need work?"

"Oh, Edna, no, no. Nothing like that. I'm sorry I alarmed you. It's not bad news at all. In fact, it's very good news."

"You and Tony are getting married?"

"I'm afraid not. But my news is spectacular. You must have heard that Jack hired a new female singer some time ago."

"Oh, yes. A very young girl with an unforgettable name. Greeney mentioned she met her at the store when the two of you went in together." the man said.

"She's not quite as young as you have been led to believe." Brett said, "In fact, Sydney's thirty-seven. She was born on November 11, 1938."

There was dead silence.

"Edna, Sid, there's someone I would like you to meet."

Hearing her cue, Sydney emerged tentatively.

"Meet your daughter, Sydney." Brett announced.

"Mon Dieu...Mon Dieu..." Edna covered her face with her hands and ran across the room to enclose her in her arms.

"Maman..." Sydney murmured in French.

"It really is you...My baby...After all these years, I have you back." She kissed her hair and face.

Arms around each other, they crossed the room to her father, who was waiting with outstretched arms. Sydney knelt beside him and buried her face in his chest. His tears fell on her hair as he stroked her back.

"You've come back to us." he said softly, "We never gave up hope. No matter what the detectives told us, we never gave up hope."

Edna sat on the ottoman beside her husband's wheelchair and placed an arm around their daughter. The three of them remained huddled together, completely at a loss for words, unaware that Brett had slipped out of the room. The phonograph was playing "Long Ago And Far Away".

"Where are you living, my little one?" Edna found her voice.

"In a boarding house on Needham Street."

"Would you like to come home to live with us?"

Sydney glanced up, astonished.

"It's your home, too, darling. We've waited so many years to be reunited with you. Do you think we want to spend one moment away from you?"

"You really want me to move into your house?"

"It's yours, too, just as your mother said, my little one." her father's liquid eyes met hers, "It has three bedrooms, and three bathrooms, so you'll have plenty of space and privacy."

"Thank you...Thank you..." she kissed both their hands.

"Dozens of detectives couldn't find you all those years, but Brett did." her father stroked her hair.

"Sydney..." Edna held her face in her hands, "Our Sydney...We've waited a lifetime for this...You were taken away from me when you were only a baby, by that monster. I kept praying you were safe, wherever you were, and they didn't harm you."

"They didn't." she reassured her promptly.

"Where did they take you? How did you live?"

"They kept moving all the time, to prevent the authorities from finding them. He took menial jobs – whatever he could get. He had friends create false documents. Until I was seventeen, I thought they were my parents. Once I turned eighteen, they said I wasn't their responsibility anymore. Donna gave me all my rightful papers and sent me on my way. I didn't think anybody was looking for me, so I immediately went to Montreal to look for you, Maman. But no one knew where you were. I stayed there all this time, hoping for a lead. I took all sorts of odd jobs to support myself. When I found a job as a singer, they wouldn't allow me to use the name Sydney, because it was a man's name, they said, so, I called myself by my middle name, Valentina."

"Valentina...I called you Valentina when you were a baby, because I did not want anyone to discover your true paternity."

"You've been here all this time, and none of us knew." her father said, "That day at the store...You came so close, but you walked away. I was inches from my daughter, yet, I had no idea. I apologize for Agnes' behavior. I'm sorry she frightened you. I wish Greeney had been working when you went in. She is much more sensitive. You might have been able to tell me who you were."

"I was afraid you might not want me."

"Not want you? How could we not want you?" he pulled her close to his chest.

"I may not be what you hoped for."

"You are much more than we had ever hoped for, my Sydney." She wept in his arms.

"How did you ever find us?" Edna nuzzled in.

"Purely by coincidence. These two women were sitting behind me at the patisserie, talking about former classmates. Then, your name came up, and I listened very closely." Sydney reached under her high-collared dress to pull out her Star of David, its rough dark metal undeniably unattractive in contrast to the gleaming gold locket, "I bought this Star of David when they said your family name was Goldstein."

Tears filled her father's eyes.

"I'm sorry." Sydney blushed, "I hope I haven't offended you."

"No, sweetheart. I feel so honored that you would have pride in your Jewish heritage."

"I was so happy to discover that I'm half Jewish. All my life, I've been inexplicably drawn to all things Jewish. I've been obsessed with George Gershwin ever since I can remember. I sing almost an all Gershwin repertoire at the club. I was so fortunate that Jack loved him, too."

Her parents' eyes grew wide, and both froze.

"Have I said something wrong?"

"No. Not at all, darling." Edna stroked her cheek, "It amazed us that you, too, love George Gershwin. It was our love for him that brought me and your father together."

Brett returned with her silver tea service and placed it on the coffee table.

"Thank you, Brett, for returning our most precious treasure to us." Sid said, "You must have dinner with us tonight at "The Castle"."

"I don't want to horn in on your special time with your daughter. It should be a family celebration."

"It wouldn't be the same without you, Brett." Sydney pleaded, "This reunion is your gift to us. You need to be there."

Brett's eyes met Sydney's and saw the love in them.

"You'll be our guest of honor." Edna said, "That doesn't even begin to come close to showing the depth of our gratitude."

"You're very kind." Brett's gaze remained locked with Sydney's, "Thank you. I would be honored. If you like, I'll call and speak to Tony himself, so we can be guaranteed the best table in the house. What would be the best time?"

"Six? Is that too late? You and Sydney both work tonight, don't you?"

"That would give us plenty of time. I'll go make the call. I also need to call my ex-husband about my sons, so, if you'll excuse me." Brett returned to the kitchen.

"After dinner," Sydney said, "Would you like to come to the lounge for the show? You'd be at the Manager's Table, of course, and all refreshments are free."

"We would be honored to hear you sing."

Sydney visualized them at the club, being served non-alcoholic fruit concoctions, and herself on the stage dedicating a Gershwin song to the two of them: "Our Love Is Here To Stay".

In the kitchen, Brett was dialling the phone for her second phone call.

"Josh Samson." a greying man in beige corduroy answered the black rotary dial telephone on his desk.

"It's me."

"Hi, Brett. Don't worry. I'll return the boys to you in one piece."

"There's been a change of plans. Could you keep them until Shayleigh comes home? I won't be home for supper."

"No problem. I'll take them to Ponderosa."

"Thanks, hon. You're a doll."

"Always glad to oblige." he glanced outside his main floor office window: Students were carrying books between buildings in a lethargic gait, all of them remarkably dressed almost identically, "Hi, Larry, have a seat. I'll be with you in a moment." he waved at a man of similar age with a salt and pepper beard and a fisherman's sweater, "I'm on the phone with my ex-wife."

"I wish my ex-wife looked like yours." he sat across the imposing oak desk, "Then, she wouldn't be an ex. How did you ever let a pin-up girl like Brett get away? Say hello to her for me."

"Larry says hello."

"Hello back. Thank you, Josh. I owe you one."

"Where are you off to for dinner? New beau?"

"Not that it's any of your business, I'm having dinner with the Goldsteins."

"How did you manage to wrangle an invitation like that?"

"We're celebrating together. And, that is all you need to know. I have to go now."

144

"Our talks are always scintillating, Brett." he laughed, "I look forward to them with trepidation."

* * *

"Mr. Goldstein," the Maître D' bowed, "Your table is ready, sir. Please follow me."

Sydney wheeled her father to the table with a stunning view of the river.

"Anything I can get you from the bar, sir?"

"A bottle of your non-alcoholic sparkling white wine, please. And anything the young ladies desire."

"Club soda for me." Brett spoke up promptly.

"Same for me." Sydney echoed.

"You don't have to go alcohol free on our account."

"We want to."

"In that case, please join us in celebrating with mock champagne. Two bottles, please." Sid informed the Maître D' and smiled benevolently at this namesake beside him.

"How did you come to have the surname Bertrand, dear?" Edna asked.

"I took my ex-husband's name when we were married." she said, "I didn't want to carry around the name Roy had passed on. Even after the divorce, I kept Jean-Guy's name."

"I'm sorry about your divorce, dear."

"Oh, don't be, please. It was a long time ago. I was lucky to get out of that marriage. It lasted less than a year."

"Would...Would you like to change your name to Goldstein?"

She was speechless.

"It's your birthright."

"I would be honored to take the Goldstein name."

"That would make us very proud." her father reached over to squeeze her hand, "If you like, I can ask Donald to get started on the process right away."

145

"Nothing could make me happier. Sydney Goldstein...I love the sound of it."

"It touches us deeply that you chose to wear a Star of David. First thing tomorrow, we'll order a gold one for you, so it will match the beautiful locket you are wearing."

"This beautiful locket," she caressed it, "Is Brett's gift. I don't know what I ever did to deserve such a perfect person as a friend."

"Brett is a perfect person." Edna agreed, "She gave you back to us."

Brett placed her hands on Sydney's shoulders as she stood behind her, "I'm going to see if they have a roaming photographer here taking Polaroid pictures of people celebrating a special occasion. I hope we can get a picture of the three of you."

"The four of us." Edna corrected her gently.

"No. It's a family shot. Sydney, hon, if Norma comes to take the orders before I return, do you mind ordering for me? I'll have the surf and turf, medium rare. You three also need to have a toast privately first."

Sydney observed Brett walking toward Bob, the Maître D', and speaking with him. She then disappeared in the direction of the ladies' room. Bob came to their table.

"I'll instruct Jaime to take some Polaroid shots of your family. And, Norma should be here shortly to take your order."

Sydney spotted Tony standing beside a table with two elderly couples, inquiring whether everything was to their satisfaction. Then, as he caught sight of Brett returning from the ladies' room, he froze. At the sight of him, she stumbled and fell against the back of an empty chair. He instinctively reached out to steady her and led her out of the seating area through a door.

"Tony's so smitten with her." Edna mused mournfully.

"And she, with him." Sid said.

"I hate to see her make the same mistake I made so long ago." Edna sighed.

Sid's hand closed on Edna's and the two exchanged tender glances.

"To the future." he held up the glass Bob handed him, "We can't go back to change the past, but we can learn from it and try not to repeat our mistakes. The future is ours. We can mould it whichever way we desire. We have not been given the opportunity to be your parents until now, but we have the rest of our lives together as a family. We hope we can be the parents you deserve."

"I hope I can be the daughter you deserve."

* * *

Tony locked the door of his office and kissed Brett feverishly.

"I can't stand this anymore!" he fumbled with her ruffled bodice, "I want to marry you. No more of this sneaking around! I want to be with you every waking minute."

"Your family..." she stroked his cheek.

"Do you think I give a damn about that? You are all I want!"

"They would make your life a living hell."

"Let them!" he sank to his knees and caressed her calves, "Marry me, and we'll run away! I'll give this all up. Just say the word."

"Tony, sweetheart, you know I can't come between you and your family."

"We'll go to Silverwood tonight after you get off work."

"I can't. The boys would wonder."

"When? Just say when. Tomorrow morning? I'll come to your house after everyone leaves. When do you get the place to yourself?" his fingers crept up her thighs.

"Eight-fifteen, eight-thirty."

"I'll be there at nine." he pulled her skirt over his head like a tent and lowered her underwear.

"Tony..."

His face was buried in her damp, fragrant pubic hair. Her body fell limp and her hands gripped his shoulders for support. She bit

147

her lip to stifle her moans and screams. He pulled her panties back up and re-emerged from the dress cocoon. Kissing her childlike pout, he guided her to her knees. Her fingers fussed feverishly with his fly and let his trousers fall to his ankles. Her mouth found its way instinctively and remained until he relieved himself. Pulling out copious amounts of tissue from the green cardboard dispenser on his desk, she cleaned up both of them.

"Do you have any idea how much I love you?" his eyes were lambent.

She traced his lips with her fingers. He brushed a stray tendril from her forehead. She cleared her throat and swallowed. He opened the liquor cabinet and produced a bottle of Southern Comfort. He filled two lowball glasses halfway and handed one to her.

"Liquid gold." she smiled, taking a sip.

They sat on the uncomfortable loveseat and drank in silence. He then took her arm and led her back to the main seating area.

"I'll be there at nine." he whispered in her ear.

"I'll wear the negligee you bought me." she whispered back.

Norma was serving their meals as Tony walked Brett to her seat.

"The meal's on the house, folks." he said, "Enjoy your dinner."

"Thank you, Tony."

"I'll instruct the staff to provide an all Gershwin musical hour."

"That's very kind of you."

Sydney eyed Brett with tenderness: the sweep of her long eyelashes, the dewy fawn's eyes, and the high arch of her eyebrows...She loved Brett's eyebrows.

"Hi, hon." Brett glanced up and winked at her, "Is your dinner all right?"

"It's fine. Everything's fine. Better than fine." she smiled, filled with love for her, "Nothing can ever be wrong again."

Chapter 9/ The Lost Years

From her third-storey window, Dottie peered out at the beat-up VW Beetle parked in front of the house. An assortment of cardboard boxes and red plastic milk crates dotted the stretch of sidewalk in front of the entire property. Her brother was occupied with cramming as many of these containers as possible into his miniscule vehicle, while a girl with greasy hair was blasting out Rolling Stones songs from a ghetto blaster she had balanced on top of an avocado green laundry hamper on the edge of the lawn. She occasionally ducked her head to join him under the hood of the trunk for drug-infused kisses. Miraculously, every piece of litter managed to find a home in the death trap. Boxes and crates on the back seat were visibly poking one another; a gooseneck lamp was leaning against the back window like a wounded giraffe. Garrett stood back from the clunker momentarily to congratulate himself on his wizardry. His hand rested on his girlfriend's rump. With his unkempt waist-length hair, ripped bell-bottoms, striped Indian tunic and heavy beads, he appeared less menacing than laughable.

She would never have to share the third floor with him, hear his druggie music or the sounds of his animalistic activities with his contraband trash from the other side of the wall. She would never have to endure the horror of catching the two of them in various degrees of undress through the open door, or smell his pungent recreational drugs. She watched the old wreck fade into billows of black smoke, sputtering toxic fumes past the old railroad bridge, toward destinations unknown, into total oblivion.

"Miss Dorothy? You up there, darlin'?" Marge's voice meandered up the stairs.

"Right here, Marge." she called out.

"Why, you look fresh as a daisy, honey." Marge opened the door.

"I feel great, Marge."

"What brought this on?"

"My brother moved out. It's the best thing to happen around here in a long time."

"Maybe he'll get his head together someday, but I'm not holdin' my breath." Marge said, "Honey, the reason I came up is your family's havin' company for dinner, and your mother's asked for you to wear somethin' nice."

"Company? On a Wednesday? Dad bringing business associates or clients home?"

"No, honey. It's a real special occasion. Your Aunt Edna's daughter's turned up."

"Is it true? They've found her?"

"She's found them, as it turns out."

"Jack was right. It was her. I wonder if she's nice. What do you think I should wear, Marge?"

"I reckon anythin' your mother's partial to would serve you well, honey."

"It would be good to have a girl cousin again." she said wistfully, "I hope she's not a crumpet."

"I don't mean no disrespect, Miss, but I think you mean strumpet."

"I'm so dumb!"

"Honey, you're not dumb! Don't you ever say that!" Marge gathered her up in her arms, her reassuring scent of talcum powder intact, "Everythin's gonna sort itself out, you'll see, honey. It'll all work out in time – just be patient."

* * *

Peggy shook off the rain from her umbrella before she entered the mudroom and placed the open umbrella on the rubber mat. She hung her beige trench coat on the wooden rack and stepped out of her comfortable brown loafers. She put on her house loafers and the apron on the hook inside the pantry door.

"Hi, dear." Marge looked up from the work island, "How was your day?"

"Hi, Mom." she kissed her cheek, "I can't believe how quickly the weather turned. I can take over the salad. Here, let me chop the celery. You go and sit over there."

Marge sat at the table in the corner, and placed her swollen, sup-hose clad feet on one of the other chairs.

"Are they having guests for dinner? You've got an awful lot going on here."

"Frederick was all in a huff, havin' to cook an elaborate meal on short notice. I ran down to do the marketin' for 'im, bought his special ingredients. He just complained the whole time in here. Darn near drove me crazy! Talk about your temperamental artistes!"

"Don't pay any attention to him, Mom. He's nothing but a big windbag. What's the big occasion, anyway?"

"Miss Edna's daughter's been found."

"You're pulling my leg!"

"She's gonna be here tonight, in the flesh."

"I can't wait to see what she looks like. I've had this image in my mind for years. I wonder if she's anything like it."

"You'll get to find out tonight. She's the new singer Mr. Jack hired."

Hearing footsteps descending the back stairs, both glanced up to find Dottie in a purple crepe sheath dress, her hair in an impeccable chignon, and her pearls prominently displayed against the dark fabric.

"Oh, honey, you look like a princess!" Peggy said.

"Just like Audrey Hepburn in "Roman Holiday"." Marge said.

"All I need is Gregory Peck."

"You smell like violets." Peggy remarked, "You must be wearing the cologne your Aunt Audrey brought you from The States."

"It's not too strong, is it?"

"No, honey. It's lovely."

151

"I've got my lucky shamrock." Dottie reached inside her bra and pulled out an embroidered handkerchief, lovingly wrapped and tied with a lavender silk ribbon; she deftly removed a blue metal shamrock with both her and Peggy's names engraved on it.

"How old were we when we got those?" Peggy smiled, "Ten and thirteen? We sure had a lot of fun at the Bex!"

"You won me this from the guy who had the big wheel."

"And you won me the green heart. We had both our names engraved on both. I keep mine pinned to my doll's dress on my dresser."

"Remember those boys who kept sneaking up behind us to steal our candy apples?"

"How could I forget? Remember losing our shoes on the Paratrooper?"

The sharp pang of loss seared Dottie's soul. The naiveté of prepubescence, the safe cocoon of childhood, had been dismantled with puberty. All that had been warm and familiar had come to a crashing halt and sent her on an out-of-control Paratrooper ride all alone.

"I'm going to meet my new cousin."

"I know. Mom said. I hope she's nice."

"Me, too. I'm scared."

"We'll get caught up afterwards."

"When I get into my jammies, we'll meet here."

"You bet." Peggy helped her tuck away her shamrock, "Good luck."

Dottie tiptoed self-consciously into the living room. By the front window, seated between Aunt Edna and Uncle Sid was the most beautiful woman she had ever seen.

"There she is." Uncle Sid smiled warmly, "This is our little ray of sunshine: Dorothy Hope. Dottie, meet your cousin, Sydney Goldstein."

"Hello, Dottie." the stranger smiled and extended her hand.

She had dimples when she smiled, and languid brown eyes like a cocker spaniel's when you looked at her this close. Dottie shook her hand in speechless fascination.

"You must be close to the end of the school year." the intoxicatingly fragrant stranger said.

"Our Matrics are coming up. I have Math, History and Biology. Then, as soon as those are over, we have exams."

"It's a terribly stressful time of the year for you."

"Sure is. I hate school."

Her mother's disapproving gaze burned through her.

"I hated school, too." Sydney spoke promptly, "I went to so many different schools, and the material wasn't always similar. I had a very confusing time."

"Sounds dreadful! It's confusing enough when you're in one school. Did they make you read morbid novels, too?"

"Oh, yes."

"We had to read about a bunch of boys who were cannibals. Then, we had to watch an old black and white movie of it, too."

"Dorothy! Not before dinner!" her mother chided.

"We had to read "Romeo and Juliet". Yuck! It made me puke."

"DOROTHY HOPE!" her mother's face was crimson.

"You and I think alike." Sydney laughed.

"Then, we had to read a novel from Nova Scotia about a boy who lived on a farm. He was a real pervert. Total gross-out."

"Dorothy." her mother's icy glare met her from across the room.

"Did you study "Wuthering Heights?"

"Yes, we did. It was a lot better than that other stuff we studied, but I found it a bit too heavy to get into."

"I can see that. Emily Bronte can be too intense."

"I like her sister better. I read something by her once. Can't remember what it was called. I'd like to read more Charlene Bronte."

Everyone was stifling a laugh, except Annette, who was shaking her head in indignation. Sydney leaned closer to whisper in Dottie's ear: "It's Charlotte".

"Who would you recommend for Dorothy to read, dear?" Aunt Audrey spoke up.

"Elizabeth Bowen."

"Who's Elizabeth Bowen? I've never heard of her." Mildred said.

"She's from the Bloomsbury Group. A contemporary of Virginia Woolf's."

"Virginia Woolf. I've heard of her." Dottie said, "Is she any good?"

"She's one of the all-time greats." Aunt Audrey spoke sternly.

"Dorothy, stop pestering Sydney." Annette spoke coldly.

"Dottie and I are kindred spirits." Sydney protested.

Dottie beamed.

"Good evening, everyone. I'm sorry I'm late. Am I holding up dinner?" a handsome dark figure appeared.

Sydney's heart missed a beat.

"Warren, come meet our guest." Annette said.

"Sydney and I have already met." he fixed his gaze on her, "You certainly get around, Miss Bertrand."

"Goldstein now." Annette corrected him matter-of-factly, "Soon, it will be official. Donald's working on it."

"Sydney Goldstein..." Warren smirked.

"We've held dinner long enough. We must adjourn to the dining room before the staff runs out of ideas to keep the food warm." Audrey moved forward in her seat.

"Shall we?" Warren extended one arm each to Sydney and Dottie.

Directed to their seats by Annette, they were served the entrée promptly by Irene, a coquettish new server, and Rose, a veteran. Irene brushed up against Warren and met his gaze. Dottie studied her heavy makeup in disdain, and cast a disapproving glance, unnoticed by the vamp, but not by Warren.

"How do you and Sydney know each other, Warren?" Annette asked.

"From the club."

"I though you refused to frequent the club."

"I changed my mind when I heard about this new songbird." he smiled seductively at Sydney, seated directly across the table.

Dottie had long ago learned to tune out the mundane dinner table discussions her elders engaged in. She kept her focus on her new cousin and dashing uncle. In the corner of her eye, she could see Irene lingering suspiciously around Tony's chair at the far end of the table. Oblivious to her dubious charms, Tony kept his head lowered. Dottie felt Warren's leg accidentally touch her own, and realized he was playing footsies with Sydney.

"Anthony, dear, you haven't contributed to the conversation." Mildred said.

"He's the strong silent type." Audrey remarked.

Dottie eyed Irene with contempt. She knew she did not have to worry about Tony, however, Warren lacked the moral fiber to resist such vulgar temptation. Less than a year ago, Uncle Willy had been compelled to discharge Lucette, yet another nubile young server, who had managed to get Warren into her bed, then claimed to be pregnant with his child. Warren would never learn. He loved women too much. And that love would someday be his undoing.

As Uncle Willy and Aunt Mildred led the group back to the living room, Dottie observed Warren motioning to Sydney to follow him in the opposite direction. Stealthily, she followed them to the solarium and peeked from behind the door. Warren led Sydney through the French doors to the flagstone patio. It was clear and bright once again. Dottie tiptoed into the solarium and crouched behind one of the wicker love seats. Through the open doors, she had an unobstructed view.

"I've missed you." Warren pulled Sydney to himself and kissed her long and hard.

"I've missed you, too." she caught her breath.

155

"Do you fantasize about me the way I do about you?"

"You know I do, Warren."

"I want you to want me, Sydney. I want you to ache for me. I want to be everything to you – your entire universe."

"You are. You never need to doubt that."

"Come here, gorgeous." he pulled her close again, "Show me."

Dottie looked away. She resisted the temptation to look when she heard moans.

"You're full of surprises." she heard Warren, "So, you're the missing heiress. You must be proud of yourself."

"I have been waiting for this moment for twenty years. I'm ecstatic beyond words."

"I'll bet you are."

"You can't imagine what this means to me."

"I'll bet I can."

"Warren, we can't stay out here too long. We'll arouse suspicion."

"Meet me tomorrow."

"Where?"

"I'll pick you up at your parents'." he said, emphasizing the last word, "We'll go out to "The Admiral" on Woodstock Road. You have the early set tomorrow, don't you?"

"Yes."

"Come home when you're done. Make up an excuse for Brett. Be ready for eleven-thirty. Your folks should be in bed by then. We don't want Mommy and Daddy to know what a naughty girl their Princess Sydney is, do we?"

Warren kissed her again, and with an arm around her waist, led her back. Dottie returned to her hiding spot behind the chair when they burst in through the door. She waited for their footsteps to fade before returning to the living room. Sydney, back between her parents, appeared flushed. Warren was not in the room.

"What would you like to drink, Sydney?" Dottie's father asked.

"Ginger ale, please." she took her cue from the glasses in her parents' hands.

Dottie wondered whether she had been told enough of her parents' struggles to know the real reason for their choice of beverages, or she had pieced the basic facts together through observation. Sydney's dress was crumpled, and her hair tousled. She wondered whether the others had become aware of the goings-on.

Warren swaggered in with his air of nonchalance.

"Whatcha been up to, Shortstuff?" he sat beside Dottie and crossed his legs.

"If you break her heart, all hell's going to break loose." she whispered in his ear.

"She's a grown woman. Sydney can take care of herself. She knows the score."

"Warren, be careful. She's not like all the others. She's nice. Please don't hurt Sydney. I know the way you go through women. You could seriously damage someone with her sensibilities."

"I promise I'll be careful, Dr. Horncastle. Cross my heart."

"Do you care about her? I mean, genuinely care about her?"

"Hey – what is this? Don't be trying to tie me down to a commitment."

"Would it really be that bad? Don't you want to settle down and have a family?"

"Perish the thought."

"You're so cynical. Please don't toy with Sydney's emotions. I don't want to see her hurt."

"The blush is off the rose, Shortstuff. She's hardly a virginal slip of thing, a delicate flower unfamiliar with the ways of the world. She's been around."

"Just be careful. Please."

"You're pretty astute for a pipsqueak."

Across the room, Dottie caught a glimpse of Sydney casting a puzzled glance in their direction. She met her gaze, rose, and crossed the room.

"Sydney, would you like to see my room?"

"Don't monopolize your cousin's time, Dorothy." her mother intercepted.

"I would love to see your room." Sydney smiled.

"It's up on the third floor."

"After that big meal, I could use the exercise." she followed her.

"Well, brother, dear," Audrey spoke, once the duo was out of earshot, "You certainly did not waste any time staking your claim on the latest arrival."

"What do you all think of your new niece?" he moved to a seat on their side of the room.

"She's lovely." Annette said, grudgingly.

"Warren promises to behave himself." Audrey reassured Edna, "I think he's quite smitten with your daughter. Don't worry: I'll watch him like a hawk and keep him in line."

* * *

In the third-storey room with the gables, Sydney sat self-consciously on the white wicker sofa. The wallpaper was a sky with frothy clouds. The dormer windows were festooned with wedding-cake layers of white sheer balloon panels peeking through white Priscilla curtains. She removed her pumps and buried her feet in the white shag carpet. The cushions, and the neck rolls on the blue frilly canopy bed were white eyelet. The dresser and armoire were white French Provincial.

"Dottie, this room is a piece of heaven!"

"Now that my brother's out of the house, it will be!" she sat on the edge of her bed, "Garrett's the black sheep of the family."

"Every family has one of those."

"There can be no sheep as black as Garrett."

"Sounds like there's no love lost between the two of you."

"You got that right. You can't imagine how I loathe him. I had to share the attic with him since I was six. Being the youngest two, we got the undesirable space. I wouldn't have minded, had there been someone other than my brother to share it with. His room was right next door, so I could hear everything. I got more than I bargained for – way more."

"Where did he go?"

"Who knows? Who cares?"

"Your family's very interesting, Dottie."

"Now, it's your family, too. Complete with skeletons in the closets."

"I've never had a family before."

"I hope you'll like the one you ended up with."

"I know I will."

"I'm glad you and I are cousins, Sydney. I have no other relatives from my mother's side of the family. Our mothers had a lot of brothers and sisters, but none of them remained in touch."

"Isn't that highly unusual for a French Canadian family?"

"Everything about this family's unusual, as you'll soon find out."

"I'm glad we're cousins, too, Dottie."

"You might change your mind once you get to know me."

"Dottie, no. Why would you say that?"

"Everyone else does. Kids my age think I'm too hard to understand, so they don't want to have anything to do with me."

"You deserve much better than that lot. You're a sensitive, complex human being. When you stand for something, you don't win any popularity contests. Conformists are more venomous than hardened criminals. They do far more psychological damage."

"You sound like you've been there."

"I've been an outcast all my life."

"Talking to you is really nice. You understand things."

"Any time you want to talk about anything, you know where to find me."

"Are you ladies ready to call it a night yet?" Tony's voice could be heard from the landing, "I think Edna and Sid want to go home."

"We're coming, Tony!" Dottie called out.

"We'll talk again, very soon." Sydney squeezed her hand, "I'm right across the yard, any time you need me."

In the grand foyer, Dottie stood aside as good-nights were exchanged. Sydney made deliberate eye contact with her before she dissolved into the night. Tony shut the door and the remaining members of the group returned to the living room.

"She's an imposter." Annette announced with gusto.

"I thought we had settled all that." Audrey peered at her with enormous eyes behind large framed bifocals, "I don't know why you keep harping on this."

"I'm certain of it. Something about the girl just doesn't add up. She's keeping secrets. There's something she's holding back."

"She's a perfectly charming young woman." Audrey stated, "Besides, she has all the legal papers in order."

"She could have stolen them from the real Sydney in order to impersonate her. The real Sydney could have been a friend who died. She could have stolen her identity to stake a claim to her inheritance."

"Don't let your imagination get the best of you, dear." Audrey shook her head.

"She might have a point, you know." Mildred piped in, "For Heavens' Sake, she could rob them blind and disappear. She could murder them in their sleep."

"Mildred's right." Annette said, "She could have a criminal record. She's all sweetness and light, but she could well be a con artist."

"I've got to hand it to her: She's good." Warren remarked, "I haven't quite determined yet whether or not she's the genuine article, but I'll stay on the case until I do."

"This would not have anything to do with the fringe benefits, would it?" Audrey uncrossed her legs.

"She doesn't look like either one of them." Annette said, "Edna's petite and small-boned. Sid's tall and lanky. This girl is tall, big-boned and full-figured."

"She's curvaceous. It hasn't escaped my brother's eye." Audrey glanced at Warren.

"I think you folks are overly paranoid." Tony said, "Just look at her eyes: They're not the eyes of a con artist; they're thoroughly earnest."

"My son the poet." Mildred laughed.

"Her blood type matches Sid's." Tony added.

"Do you know how many people have O+ blood?" Annette shot back at him, "Roy had the same blood type, too. That's how Edna was initially able to convince him that Sydney was his child."

"Edna and Sid are happy." Audrey sighed, "Isn't that what matters most? Whether or not this young woman is their daughter, they are contented with accepting things at face value. Their daughter could well be dead, or addicted to heroin. She may never be found. She may not be a very nice person. After all, she has never known her parents. If she's destitute, she could well be the one to pose a danger to them. If this young woman is providing some comfort for them, who are we to interfere? Perhaps she is a harmless imposter, not out for material gain, but lonely. Perhaps, she, too, is looking for the family life she never had. She might well be better for them than their own daughter. There are some things we have to accept on faith. There's little else we can do."

"All the same, we'll have to keep a close eye on her." Annette said.

"Sid wants their wills changed. I told them not to rush things, but he was adamant." Donald said, "He also wants her surname legally changed to Goldstein."

"She's too fat to be theirs." Annette persisted.

"Sid had some aunts who were heavy set." Donald said, "We don't know anything for certain at this point. I haven't told Sid, but

I've hired Hank to investigate her background. I think it's absolutely necessary."

"She could be trouble." Mildred sighed, "She's much too attractive."

"She is rather decorative." Audrey agreed.

"I don't see anything wrong with that." Willy smiled, "Not a thing. We can always use a pretty face around here to brighten things up."

Audrey cast a sympathetic glance at Mildred, who was shaking her head in disdain.

"Time will tell." Donald said, "In the meantime, all this speculation is not doing any good. Let's just wait and see."

"Don is right." Audrey agreed, "I wonder whose investigation is going to be more thorough: Hank's or Warren's?"

* * *

Sydney stood stirring the saucepan of warm milk and sugar. She was home...Home: What a soothing sound it had. She had called other places "home" only out of a lack of more appropriate names, but all those places had never been home. Never a warm, welcoming, safe place like this. Never a place she belonged. She needed to hold on to this, no matter what the cost. Turning off the electric burner, she poured the warm beverage into the two brown ceramic mugs on the white counter. What did the Horncastles think of her? Were they shocked by her humble existence in Montreal? Did they disapprove of her? She prayed they would never learn about Sven and the dives she had been forced to work in. She carried the mugs into the living room and placed them on coasters beside her parents.

"Thank you, sweetheart." her father kissed her forehead, his eyes glowing with pride.

"Sit beside me, darling girl." her mother motioned beside her on the sofa.

Sydney obeyed her. Edna guided her head to rest on her shoulder. The past was buried. She was finally where she belonged. And she would not allow anyone to take this away from her. Ever.

Chapter 10/ Tender Saplings

The taxi sped off down the tree-lined road. On the sidewalk, the two women stood, surrounded by red luggage.

"Is this where you live now?" the younger one with the expressively full eyebrows surveyed her surroundings, "Quite a step down from Sunshine Gardens and Skyline Acres."

"It's homey."

"More like homely." she scoffed, tossing back her long straight golden-brown hair, "It's a dump."

"Thank you." she picked up the largest suitcase and headed up the porch steps.

"Good thing I'm only here for a week." the younger woman picked up the smaller suitcase and the cosmetic case, following her reluctantly, "When you said a Victorian house, I imagined one of those palatial mansions on Waterloo Row, or, at least in that part of town. God, when was the last time this place was painted or renovated? I hope you have indoor plumbing."

"Very funny." she unlocked the door tentatively and placed the suitcase in the foyer.

"Wouldn't this make a great location to shoot a movie about the Civil War?" she dropped her luggage with a loud thud.

"It's not a three star hotel, but we call it home."

"Where are the two village idiots, anyway?"

"That's no way to speak about your brothers, Laurel Rose."

"I can speak any way I please. Where are they?"

"With Dad. He's bringing them around later."

"Where do I sleep? You've got only three bedrooms. You've got one, the old maid's got one, and the idiots share the third one. Who do I bunk with?"

"Me, of course."

"Wouldn't that cramp your style? What about your boyfriends? Or are they into threesomes?"

"Laurie!"

"Just kidding. Don't have a coronary. I have to pee. Where's your outhouse? Out back in that little shed?"

"It's up the stairs, first door on your left."

"I need a shower. I'm all grimy from the trip."

"There is no shower. We take baths."

"Are you pulling my leg? No shower? How do you exist?"

"We're used to it."

"How do you wash your hair?"

"There's a yellow pail in the bathroom. You put it in the tub, under the faucet. There's a little plastic measuring cup in it. You fill the pail with water, and use the cup to pour water over your hair."

"You're kidding me, right?"

"Don't look so horrified. You just kneel down in the tub."

"The only time I want to be down on my knees is when I'm giving a blowjob! I had no idea you were living is such squalor! Does Dad have any idea the boys are living in substandard housing?"

"He's well aware of our living conditions."

"Why hasn't he fought for custody of the boys?"

"He doesn't want them. The arrangement we have now suits him fine."

"This is 1976! Not 1876! People take showers these days. God, I hate to see what the rest of the place looks like!"

"Believe it or not, I actually have a twentieth century electric stove, a refrigerator, and an oil furnace."

"Wow, Mom, you're really living the high life, aren't you?"

"I'm sure you can rough it for one week, Laurie. Pretend you're camping."

"I don't do camping." she glared at her with contempt, "Are there any decent clubs around here? I'm not talking about old fogies' cocktail lounge places like the one you work in. I mean a modern disco."

"You're under age."

"I'm eighteen."

"Nineteen is the legal age."

"When did you turn into such a prude? The one decent thing I could always say about you was that you weren't as prissy as the other mothers. Now, you don't even have that going for you."

"Sorry to disappoint you."

"You might be able to fool other people with your high and mighty act, but I was there when you were the laughing stock of Beavertown. I was the one who had to scrape you off the floor. Remember those days, Mom?"

She was painfully silent.

"I remember them." Laurie said, "Only too well. I was taunted at school every day because I was the daughter of the town whore. You were out, cruising the bars every night, picking up younger men. Most nights, you didn't even bother coming home. And when you did manage to stagger in, it was in the wee hours of the morning."

Brett turned her face away from her and blinked away her tears.

"I was only eleven, then. I couldn't even understand the stuff they were saying about you. I stuck up for you because you were my mother."

Brett crossed her arms across her chest and pressed her chin into her chest like a building prepared for an implosion.

"You didn't even care about us. If it hadn't been for Mrs. McNichol, the landlady upstairs, the boys and I would've perished in that dingy basement apartment. When we walked home from the bus stop after school, Mrs. McNichol invited us in for milk and cookies with Judy and Meg. She kept us there until you got home from your job at the book store, so we wouldn't have to go into a cold empty apartment. Yes, Mom, we were the kids everybody felt sorry for. All the other mothers forced their kids to invite us to their birthday parties, because we were underprivileged."

"Laurie, I am so sorry that you had to go through all of that. If there were some way to go back and change it, you know I would, in a heartbeat. There's nothing I'd like to do more. But I can't. I know there's nothing I can do to make it up to you for those times, but I would really like to try."

"Do you remember Mrs. Barker, the busybody who called Social Services to report you for leaving us alone at nights? You started coming home after that, and bringing those men with you. I had to endure that life for four years. Then, I finally made my getaway and got Dad to send me to boarding school far, far, away from here, so I would never have to look at you! It was glorious to be away. Why the hell did I agree to this visit? I must've been really stoned."

"Laurie, I never wanted you kids to suffer. I know you are too young to understand this, but I did those things because I could not allow myself to be vulnerable. Had I moped, tried to be good and stuffed my emotions in, I would have cracked up. I would have either become a nagging, screeching discontent, or a catatonic. I had three kids to raise; I couldn't afford to fall apart. And, I didn't want to take it out on you kids. I did what I had to do, in order to remain intact. I took comfort where I could find it. I'm sorry that I was an embarrassment to you, and I hurt you. But, you and the boys were always my first priority. I loved all of you fiercely and I always will."

"You're not providing a decent home for the boys. Dad pays child support and alimony. What do you do with it all? Spend it on young boyfriends?"

"Laurie, the boys don't want for anything."

"All that aside, where am I going to get a shower and wash my hair?"

"I can wash your hair in the kitchen sink if you like."

"Do you have decent shampoo, or are we going to use lye soap?"

"You'll find everything you need in the bathroom."

"I still haven't peed!" she ran up the stairs.

Brett washed her face with cold water in the kitchen sink. Laurie returned with towels, a blue and yellow striped bottle of Breck shampoo, and pink Adrienne conditioner.

"What kind of junk is this? Discount store rejects?" Laurie held up the cylindrical bottle of conditioner.

"It's our drug store's own brand. Shayleigh likes it."

"She's obviously not hip. And, what's with the Breck? It's got no scent."

"It smells clean, fresh, and natural."

"Didn't they stop making it two years ago? What did you do, buy out the entire stock of every store in town?"

"Something like that."

"I only use professional quality products. I care about my hair."

"No one's hair has been damaged from using it."

"Well, I suppose I have no choice." she slid off her tank top over her head and flung it on a kitchen chair.

Massaging Laurie's scalp, she remembered another time and place...Bathing a very young Laurie in their apartment on West 42'nd Street, the one with the black and white linoleum, black and white ceramic wall tiles, the narrow toilet with the high-mounted flush requiring one to pull a chain, the white sink with its metal intestines on display...the radiator which never seemed to get warm enough...No doubt, Laurie had only vague memories of their early years in New York, and, most likely, no memories from that apartment. Laurie did not know that she had once loved her mother, never wanted to leave her side, spent countless hours helping her in the kitchen, playing and singing with her. Only Brett carried the distant memory of Laurie's adoring little-girl eyes, the whipped cream texture of her arms, the nectarine taste of her round cheeks, the squishy soft nose like cooked pasta, the golden corkscrew curls. She had failed her as a mother. Her tears fell, mingling with the freshly-scented shampoo.

"How's Sexy Jack?" Laurie suddenly spoke, her voice muffled by the sound of the water.

"He's on tour."

"Sorry I missed him. I'd love to get in his pants."

Brett bit her tongue and remained silent.

"I'm sure you've already beat me to it." Laurie's hair appeared like a wet seal as her mother rinsed out the shampoo with deliberate thoroughness under the faucet, "Tell me, then, is he wild in bed? Come on, fess up!"

"I wouldn't know."

"Do you expect me to believe you would let a tenderloin like Jack get away?"

"It's true."

"You must be losing your touch, Mom. Blew you off, didn't he? Heh, heh. Didn't even dish out for a sympathy fuck."

"That's enough about Jack. He and I are just friends, nothing more."

"Hit a nerve, didn't I? You must be fading fast, Mom. Better get some Geritol. I just love it that you couldn't get Jack into bed! Heh, heh. I bet I can."

"He doesn't sleep with girls your age."

"Want a bet? No man is immune to the charms of a firm, nubile body. They get tired of wrinkled old prunes like you after a while. Dad did."

Brett wrapped a towel around Laurie's head and rubbed gently. The clean scent of Breck filled the air.

"My mother, the town whore." Laurie laughed, "Other moms bake cookies and knit sweaters. Mine guzzles booze and seduces boys. Are Keir's friends afraid to come over here because his old bag of a mother tries to catch them in dark corners to try to kiss them? I couldn't go to high school here, because I knew you'd make a play for all my boyfriends. It's been three years since I saw you last, and I hope it's at least another three before I see you again."

"You can unpack in my room." Brett was wiping the counter, with her back turned to Laurie, "It's the third door on the left. Help yourself to facecloths, towels, soap, powder, bath oil, and anything else you need. If you have dirty clothes, just put them in the hamper. I'll take care of them."

169

As Laurie ran up the stairs without a word, Brett sank into the overstuffed chair and buried her face in her hands. There had been a time when making love with Josh had sustained her. She revelled in her role as wife and mother. Then, Josh's indiscretions had extinguished the spark. She had come face to face with the demon existing just beneath the surface of her consciousness, a demon she had been powerless to conquer. The demon had dominated her life and destroyed everything in its path.

Laurie returned, dressed in a fresh pair of jeans and a white cotton peasant blouse with red embroidery, her long hair gleaming, her face freshly made up. Brett's heart stirred. Her daughter was such a beautiful young woman.

"Do you have any records I can play?"

"They're all over there in that cabinet." she motioned wearily.

Laurie rifled through them impatiently.

"Don't you have anything good? I've never even heard of some of these people!"

"You know Dionne Warwick."

"She's for senior citizens. Don't you have any "Fleetwood Mac"?"

"That name sounds backwards. Shouldn't it be Mac Fleetwood?"

"It's a group, not a person! You're so out of touch with modern society! Do you have Peter Frampton? The Bee Gees? Bay City Rollers? You don't even have ABBA! Most old people like ABBA. Don't Keir and Toby have any records?"

"Up in their room. When they come home, they can take you up and play them on their phonograph for you."

"Hell, I'm not standing around waiting for them to come home! I'll go up and see what they've got!"

"I don't think that's a good idea, Laurie. They wouldn't want anyone to go into their room without their permission."

"I'm their big sister, whom they haven't seen in three years."

"All the same, I think you should wait."

"Then, you go up, and bring me their records."

"Not without their permission."

"Don't tell me you don't go in their room to snoop around and look for telltale signs of sexual activity, porn mags, condoms and stuff!"

"Laurie, they're only little boys!"

"Yeah, right. Well, I might as well phone Sharon and see if there's any action at her place. I wrote to tell her I'd be here for a week." she padded into the kitchen.

Brett shut her eyes and sighed.

"Hi, Shar..." Laurie could be heard, "Yeh, it's me, in the flesh!...What's shaking?...Cool...Can't wait to hear about it...Yeh, I just got in today, a little while ago...Really?...I can't really talk now...No, you can't come here. My mother lives in Little House On The Prairie. She's on some religious kick or something...Yeh, it must be the change of life...They get funny when they get to be a certain age...So, what's going down tonight?...Cool...I'll come to your place. We'll talk then. See ya."

Laurie ran up the stairs and returned with her cosmetic case.

"I'll be back for my stuff later. Got some money for my cab and a night out on the town?" she held out her outstretched palm.

"All I have is a twenty." Brett opened her handbag and produced a crumpled bill with trembling fingers.

"Big spender. I suppose it'll have to do." Laurie snatched it away and stuffed it into her back pocket.

Brett could hear Laurie muttering profanities under her breath in the kitchen, turning pages, and dialling the phone.

"Send a cab to...just a sec. What's the number here?" she bellowed.

"360 Odell Avenue."

"360 Odell Avenue...Yeh. Going to 457 Montgomery Street." she hung up.

"Is there a number where I can reach you?"

"I said I'd come for my things when I get around to it."

"The boys are going to be very hurt."

"They'll get over it."

"Laurie, you can stay with Dad, if you like. His house is modern."

"I'd rather stay with Sharon until I leave town. I don't want to see any of you – now or ever!" Laurie stormed out and slammed the door behind her.

In the icy silence, Brett went into the kitchen. On the counter by the wall phone, the telephone book was left open to the yellow pages. She closed it and placed it back in the drawer. She opened the cupboard to the left of the sink and produced a juice glass with the suits from a deck of cards. The hearts were fading to a coral pink from repeated washing. Filling it from the tap, she removed three small tablets from a prescription bottle on the counter. Throwing her head back, she swallowed them and washed them down with the water. She heard a key in the lock, and the creaking of the door.

"Hello? Anybody home?" Shayleigh's voice echoed in the foyer.

"Oh, honey, am I glad to have you back home!" Brett ran to her arms.

"Brett, what's wrong?" Shayleigh stroked her hair.

"Laurie." she wept.

"Is Laurie here?" she asked sheepishly, "When did the two of you get home from the airport?"

"She's already left."

"Left? Where did she go?"

"Her friend's house."

"Brett, what's wrong?"

"She hates me! Shayleigh, she hates me!" she wiped her tears on her sleeve.

"What happened?" Shayleigh hung up her pocketbook and trench coat on the hall rack, and placing an arm around Brett, led her to the living room.

"She's never forgiven me. She was at a young impressionable age and I've damaged her permanently."

"No, you haven't."

"I'm unfit to be a mother."

"Don't say that! Don't ever say that!" she pulled her closer, "I would have given anything to have a mother like you!"

"No!"

"Yes! Brett, you're the ideal mother! All my life, I've dreamed of a mother like you."

"I'm not what you think I am. I did things...horrible things."

"What things?"

"After the divorce, I started drinking heavily. I slept with a lot of men. I neglected my children."

"You were lonely. You were hurting. Laurie has no right to throw that back at you now and keep punishing you for imagined hurts against herself. She's an immature, selfish brat! And, you mustn't listen to her."

"She's right, hon. I did mess up her life. She's been through things no one should have to go through."

"I'd much rather get messed up that way than the way my mother messed me up. I'd gladly trade places with Laurie any day."

"You are so good to me."

"I think you're a terrific mother, and I wish you could have been mine."

"I can't begin to tell you how much that means to me. You're family to me. I think of you as my daughter."

"Meeting you was the one saving grace in my sorry existence, Brett."

"Oh, honey, I love you." Brett kissed her cheek and took her hands in her own.

"I'm going to call Sam and cancel for tonight."

"Oh, sweetheart, I can't let you do that! You've finally met a nice guy. I can't go messing that up for you."

"You wouldn't be. If you like, I can ask him to come here, if you're up to it."

"That's a great idea, hon. I hope he doesn't mind."

"Not at all. He's very down to earth. Besides, when the boys come back and find out Laurie's gone, they'll need the distraction. We'll all have take-out pizza. We can watch "The Rockford Files" at eight, "The Love Boat" at ten, play board games, charades..."

"That sounds wonderful." she pressed her hand to her cheek.

"I'll go call him."

Brett shut her eyes and felt the moisture of her tears trickling down her cheeks.

* * *

"Brett, you haven't stepped outside that door for two days, just in case Laurie might return. You haven't slept a wink. You can't let her control your life." Sydney said.

"What if she comes back and no one's here?"

"Somehow, I think she'll survive. Don't let her manipulate you with her guilt trips."

"I have to go to work tonight. I have the early set, too. What if she comes before the boys are back from the pool?"

"I'll wait for the boys, don't worry." she gathered her up in her arms, "Why don't you have a warm bath? I'll make you a light lunch, okay?"

"I can't eat."

"Please try."

"Just for you."

"Oh, honey..." she pressed her close, "It'll be all right."

"Thank you, sweetheart."

Sydney waited for the sound of running water to stop before turning on the faucet and filling a saucepan with water, expertly gauging the amount from previous experience. From the pantry, she removed the familiar envelope of chicken soup mix and opened it over the pan. The sound of the doorbell prevented her from turning on the burner. Covering the pan with its lid, she went to the door and peered through the glass at the unfamiliar young woman's face.

"Who the fuck are you?" she shot at Sydney, who tentatively opened the door.

"Are you Laurie?"

"Where's my mom?" she barged in, "Are you the Shelley chick?"

"No. I'm Sydney."

"Why do you have a guy's name? You a dyke or something? Is my mom into chicks now?"

"You're Laurie all right. Your mother's been worried sick about you, though I don't know why."

"Now it makes sense. She's into chicks, isn't she? Otherwise, she would have fucked Jack."

"I'm sure there is some logic in there, somehow."

"Where's Mom?"

"She's upstairs, taking a bath."

"I came to pick up my stuff. I don't want her in my hair."

"Just let her know you're here. Go in and talk to her."

"What for? What do you care?"

"I don't. But, for some reason, your mother does."

"Saint Bernadette doesn't care about anyone except herself."

"You're wrong! She cares very deeply about you."

"Yea, sure. I'm going up to get my stuff. Sharon's waiting for me in the car. Her mom drove us here. Once I pick up the last of my things, I never want to have any more dealings with my mom." she stomped her feet on her way up the stairs.

Sydney returned to preparing the soup, listening to the muffled voices from the second floor. Laurie's harsh and shrill, Brett's soft and tearful, barely audible. It was impossible to make out any words.

"You go to hell!" Laurie was heard clearly as she came bounding down the stairs, suitcases in tow.

"Laurie!" Brett emerged suddenly, barefoot and dripping water, her tattered lavender robe falling open as she leaned over the dark banister, "Laurie, please come back!"

Without turning around, Laurie burst through the heavy wooden door, allowing in a gust of wind in her wake.

"Let her go, honey." Sydney ran to Brett and held her close.

"She's gone..." Brett's thin frame seemed to be melting under Sydney's touch, her flesh and bones disintegrating.

"She's quite a piece of work, your daughter."

"It's my fault. I deserve this, can't you see? All my chickens are coming home to roost."

"Brett, how can you say that?"

"Please hold me. I need you." Brett nuzzled into her with the ease of a small child.

Sydney pressed her tightly into herself and caressed her.

"Sweetheart, please have some soup. But, first, let's get you into some dry clothes. Let me turn off the stove."

Brett obeyed her. Upstairs, Sydney dressed her in dark dress pants, a blue T-shirt, and a dark knee-length cardigan with enormous flat buttons. She brushed her hair and patiently applied her make-up.

"Is your gown at the club?"

"I left it there."

"Do you have everything you need in the dressing room? Your shoes? Spare nylons?"

"It's all there."

"Then, let's get some soup into your stomach."

They sat at the chrome kitchen table across from one another. Sydney served the soup in white Corelle bowls with olive green daisy trim. They drank ice-tea in tall glasses with a blue floral motif fading in places.

"The boys were very upset when they didn't find Laurie here. I had to tell them something unexpected came up and she got called away. Good thing Shayleigh and Sam were here, too. Sam distracted them with sports talk. Sam's very stable and reliable. I hope he marries Shayleigh and provides a stable home for her. What she needs most in life is stability."

"I'm sure he'll take good care of her. Can I get you anything else?"

"No, thanks, hon. This was perfect. I need to get going."

"Are you sure you're going to be all right?"

"I'll be fine. Thanks for staying here to wait for the boys."

"I'll be here until Shayleigh comes back, so they won't be alone. I have the late set, anyway. I don't have to be at work until ten-thirty. Shayleigh never stays out past ten on a weeknight."

"Thank you, sweetheart." she rose, "I'd better get going."

"Want me to call you a cab?"

"No, I'll walk. It'll help me clear my head."

"Are you all right?" she reached out to her.

Brett took both of her hands in her own.

"My Sydney, do you have any idea how much I treasure you?"

"I'm so lucky that I met you, Brett."

Brett kissed her forehead and blew her a kiss from the door.

She walked her familiar path to the liquor store on Queen Street. She did not speak to the clerks as she paid for her Prince Igor Vodka and slid the paper bag into her crocheted tote bag. Accustomed to her exuberance, the clerks observed her in astonishment as she walked out in silence.

At Willow Place, The Castle was a beehive of activity, however, Chandler's Lounge was not yet open for business. Young employees were diligently placing crystal candle holders on the blue table cloths.

"Brett, what are you doing here so early?" Johnny-O, the Maitre D', who was behind the bar with a group of waiters, came around to meet her.

"Hi, Johnny. Can you be a doll and let me borrow Andy for a while?"

The baby-faced young blond came around the corner.

"Go ahead." the middle-aged man motioned to him, "I don't need you yet."

"Andy, sweetheart, I need you to run an errand for me." Brett took Andy's arm and led him to a corner, "I have a throbbing headache, and my prescription's run out. Could you renew it for me, baby doll?" she pressed the empty bottle into his palm, "It's Ross drugs, just down the street a little ways. Please?"

"Okay." he glanced at the label.

"Here's some money." she handed him a mess of crumpled small bills, "This should cover it. Could you bring it down to the dressing room?"

"Sure."

"Thanks, hon." she blew him a kiss on his way out and took the public stairs down to the dressing room, instead of the staff stairs through the club.

Shutting the door behind her, she removed the vodka from her tote bag, opened and poured some of it into the Styrofoam cup on the vanity. She guzzled it in one breath. Then, she slipped out of her sandals and wiggled her toes. She tossed her cardigan on a chair, unzipped her pants, let them fall at her feet, and then stepped out of them. Her T-shirt came off. Humming "It Never Entered My Mind", she wrapped the black chiffon negligee, from the hook behind the door around her slender frame. The Marabou feather trim danced with her every move. She poured herself another drink and sat on the curved white enamel vanity chair, crossing her long slender legs.

There was a tentative knock on the door.

"Brett?" Andy's youthful voice was on the other side.

"Come on in, baby doll." she cooed.

"Here you are." he stood stiffly by the door, stretching out his hand toward her, making a conscious attempt to avert his gaze from her exposed legs.

"Bring it over, hon." she tossed her hair back and took a swig from her Styrofoam cup.

He approached her reluctantly and stood in front of her. She let the front of her negligee fall open, revealing her firm breasts and black satin panties.

"Thank you, sweetheart. Would you like a drink?"

"Um...um...no...thanks..." the horrified youth began backing away.

"Come a little closer, Andy." she motioned with her index finger. He obeyed sheepishly.

"Kiss me!" she commanded.

"I...er...um..."

"Kiss me!" she repeated, seizing him by the elbows and attempting to pull him down, "I don't bite."

His face was now down at her level. Her slender arms encircled his neck and her mouth sought his, her tongue searching in hunger. He stumbled and fell to his knees. She fumbled with his bow tie.

"You have the softest lips." she purred, "You know, there are a lot of advantages to being with an older woman. We don't have the unrealistic expectations that younger women have. We don't make unreasonable demands. We're not as self-involved. And, we know how to satisfy a man. You don't have to worry about getting us pregnant, either."

"I...I have to go." he made a feeble attempt to pull away.

"I can tell you're nervous. Don't worry, I'll make it easy for you, Andy." she caressed his shoulders, "How old are you, Andy?"

"Um...Twenty-one."

"You're just a baby. Do you have a girlfriend?"

"Um...Yes."

"Is she very pretty?"

"Yes."

"Do you think I'm pretty, Andy?"

"You're real pretty, Brett."

"Did you know that I used to be a model in New York?"

"No."

"Do you like tall women?"

"Sure."

"Do you know tall I am, Andy?"

"No."

"Six foot one. I took after my daddy."

"That's nice."

"You're a fine-looking young man. There must be a lot of girls interested in you."

"I don't know."

"Have you made love with a lot of girls?"

"Um...not really."

"With your girlfriend?"

"Um...not really."

"Would you like to know what it's like to be with a woman, Andy?"

"Um...I don't know."

"I can show you things you never imagined possible. Kiss me!"

He bent down reluctantly and planted a quick peck on her lips. She wound her arms around him ravenously and pulled herself up to her feet, tugging at his now loosened bow tie.

"I...can't get my uniform mussed up."

"I'll be very careful with it." she removed his tie, placed it on the vanity, and began unbuttoning his shirt with frenzied fingers. She hung it with care around the back of the chair in the corner. She then unzipped his trousers and eased them off. She folded them with precision, paying particular attention to the crease, and placed them on the seat of the same chair.

"Did your mother iron the crease on your trousers, Andy?" she asked.

"Um...yes."

"I can do it for you, if you like. I would like to take care of you. Would you like that, Andy?"

"I don't know."

"I would like you to take care of me, too. I would like you to come over here and show me that you desire me."

180

"You're really pretty, Brett."

"Do you find me desirable? Do you want to ravage me? Do you want to live out your wildest fantasies with me?"

He stood trembling as she removed her panties. She let her negligee fall to her feet and slithered over to him, allowing her fingers to dance up and down his body in a tantalizing pas de deux. Her tongue explored every part of him. Intoxicated by his desire for her, he leapt toward her. His youthful arms crushed her fragile frame, his perspiration-soaked peach-fuzz burning against her musky satin skin, his hardness urgently searching for her harbor. She gently pushed him down on the cot and mounted him, guiding him inside her. As he lifted his eyes to her face, her sultry doe eyes appeared larger than life. The sagging mattress creaked with her rhythm. In the sticky early summer heat of Beavertown, in this unlikely subterranean paradise, Andy's youthful naiveté dissolved into the humid night. When he was reduced to nothing but a heap of steaming flesh, she dismounted him, and gathered up her crumpled negligee. She poured herself another drink and opened the pill bottle. She emptied it into her palm and stared down at the cold white oval tablets like dead fish caught in a net.

"Mmm..." Andy stirred, "Come back here."

"You'd better go, Andy."

"What's wrong? You said you wanted to take care of me."

"You're a nice kid, Andy. You shouldn't let anyone ruin you. Go home to your mother. Go back to your little girlfriend and forget this ever happened."

"I can't forget it happened." he sat up.

She closed her fist with the pills in it and concealed the empty bottle behind a perfume atomizer.

"Please go, Andy."

"Okay, but I'll be back for more." he struggled with his underwear discarded like a wilted cabbage on the floor.

She kept her back to him as he dressed.

"Later." he kissed her neck on his way out.

She sat before the vanity mirror and glanced at herself staring back in disapproval. Her left index finger traced the fine lines on her face. She would be forty-nine in only three more days. Aware of the wetness on her inner thighs, she pressed her legs together. She opened her palm and was about to shove the pills into her mouth when she heard voices on the stairs.

"She should be downstairs, Syd."

"Thanks, Johnny." Brett frantically spit out the pills into her palm and returned the rest into the prescription bottle. She placed the vodka bottle back in the tote bag under the vanity table.

"Brett? Honey, are you in there?" Sydney knocked on the door.

"Sure, hon. Come on in." she smoothed her hair and tied her sash around her waist.

"Are you all right?" Sydney closed the door behind her.

"Sure, sweetheart." she forced a smile.

"Don't worry about the boys. Shayleigh came home early."

"Bless her little heart."

"Brett, honey, are you sure you're all right?"

Sydney surveyed the room and caught glimpse of Brett's crumpled panties on the floor. Her eyes returned to Brett and detected the stream trickling down her legs. Her wet pubic hair gleamed and curled like the freshly-groomed fur on a long-haired kitten. Casualties of the careless tryst, stray marabou feathers lay lifeless on the floor. The subtle starchy scent of lovemaking hung heavy in the stale basement air.

"I'll help you get ready." Sydney said.

She could not venture a guess regarding the identity of Brett's lover. And, perhaps that was a blessing. Some things were better not exposed. She removed Brett's strapless black gown from the wall hook, and peeling the ribbon loops from the pink satin hanger, placed it on the ironing board.

"I must be a mess." Brett murmured.

"I'll brush your hair and re-do your make-up."

"I'll freshen up first." Brett picked up her panties from the floor before disappearing into the adjoining bathroom.

When she returned, Sydney silently helped her step into the form-fitting gown with rigid whalebone supporting its bodice. She brushed Brett's luxuriant wavy hair. Sydney loved brushing Brett's hair, feeling an extension of Brett at her fingertips, touching her, yet, not quite touching her. She re-applied warm beige foundation to Brett's freshly-scrubbed face. Once her task was completed, she stood back to check for flaws.

"There. All done. You look gorgeous."

"Thank you, sweetheart."

"Knock 'em dead." she reached for Brett's perfume atomizer, only to knock down the pill bottle. She picked it up and read the label, "Brett, did you take any of these?"

"No."

"Are you sure?"

"I'm sure."

"Honey, please be careful with them."

"I'm careful."

"I want to know you're okay."

"I know." Brett kissed her cheek, leaving behind a perfectly formed imprint of her chocolate cherry lips.

Sydney took her arm, and led her out to the hallway, locking the door behind them. Upstairs, once Brett took her position behind the curtain and the drumroll sounded, Sydney released her touch and stroked her shoulder in support before the curtain opened.

"Ladies and gentlemen, everyone's favorite chanteuse: Miss Brett Morrow!" Richard announced.

Sydney inconspicuously made her way to the floor and sat at the manager's table. Brett possessed that elusive quality which made all men fall to their knees. All her life, Sydney had been mystified by such women. A certain look, a certain way of moving, a certain way of speaking could entrance any man. Sydney had always been too awkward around men, and completely illiterate in the language of flirting. Perhaps it was for this reason she had been shunned not only by men, but by women, as well.

"Can I take your order, Syd?" Andy, appearing dishevelled and flustered, stood beside her.

"A martini, please, Andy."

He did not hear her.

She was at once struck aware of the carnal familiarity in Andy's eyes as they became diverted in Brett's direction. How old was he? Barely over legal age, she observed, judging by his full, smooth cheeks. Had he even been with other women before this? Behind her, she heard two regular female customers chuckling.

"Look at Andy. Does he ever have the biggest crush on Brett!" one said.

"It's adorable!" the other said.

There was nothing adorable about it, Sydney thought. It was all tawdry and perverse. It was not surprising that a young man with raging hormones would be captivated by Brett's allure. Why wouldn't he become infatuated with the woman who had shown him the ways of the world?

"Huh? What?" Andy was staring at her with a dim-witted expression.

"A martini, please."

"Yea right. Coming right up."

She would not hold her breath. Her thoughts wandered to Warren. He had only initiated an affair with her in order to obtain information about her identity. The only reason he was still with her was to disprove her claim as a legitimate Goldstein. She knew only too well nothing positive could ever come out of their union. She knew she had to play by his rules. It was just that, having to be on her toes at all times to please him, not being able to relax or be spontaneous out of her overwhelming fear of callous treatment drained all of her energy. Physical intimacy and companionship came with a high price. She knew he would soon tire of her and bored with the issue of her identity and move on to his next conquest, granting her freedom, and, along with that freedom, her deep, aching loneliness. He did not want her, or care for her. He would not have given her the time of day, had there not been a question about her authenticity. For all the hype surrounding it, the Sexual Revolution was nothing more than a cruel slap in the face for women like her. It was based on the naïve assumption that men and women were wired the same way. While exciting for a certain type of woman, it was nothing more than a false promise of pseudo-equality for some, and a tragic letdown for others. Men were the only ones to benefit from it. They received more sex with less effort. Women now begged to be exploited and disrespected. And, women like her, who still possessed self-respect, were the casualties in the fallout from the sick joke that was "The Sexual Revolution". Looking at Brett crooning, she could see that Brett, too, was a victim. She followed its rules blindly, embodied the idealized liberated woman, but was not shallow enough to pull it off. Both of them were victims of social change, victims of a modern, uncaring society that mocked and isolated women, valued them only on their sexual prowess.

Brett was stepping off the stage for her break and approaching the table when she was accosted by the starry-eyed Andy. It was apparent he was not prepared to take no for an answer now that his libido had been aroused. The altercation had begun to take on a volatile tone. Sydney approached them cautiously.

"Andy, could you please be a dear and freshen my drink?" she took Brett's arm, "Could you also bring a Club Soda please?"

Scowling, Andy obeyed her grudgingly. Sydney led a dazed Brett to the table.

"Can you stay with me tonight, sweetheart?" Brett looked at her with pleading eyes.

"Of course I can." she patted her hand.

Gene, the conductor of "Gene And The Matchmakers", a congenial man with youthful features, was making his way toward them.

"Are you ladies all right?"

"It's under control now. Thanks for coming over, Gene." Sydney said, "Please join us."

"Don't mind if I do." he gave Brett a brotherly kiss on the cheek.

"Hi, sweetheart. You look so spiffy in your suit."

"Excuse me for a moment." Sydney said.

On her way to the staff ladies' room, she paused upon hearing muffled male voices from the back corridor.

"Way to go, Stud Muffin." someone snickered.

"Mr. Big Stuff." another said.

"Is she good? Go on, you can tell us. What did she teach you?"

"Shut up, will ya!"

"Andy got laid." one repeated over and over in a sing-song.

"Shut up, I told ya!"

"Andy's got a Sugar Mama!"

"Cut it out!"

"He's got it bad for her."

"Nah I'm just using her for experience."

"Yeah sure."

"Want a knuckle sandwich?"

"Must be love."

"Come on, you loafers. Get back to work." Johnny appeared suddenly and admonished them.

She slid, unnoticed, into the bathroom and turned on the faucet. An antique wash stand was in the corner, with a white enamel basin and porcelain pitcher, a bejewelled brass tissue holder and an old copper kettle filled with peach and white silk cabbage roses. A rust-colored vinyl chair from the 1960's was in the corner, its seat ripped and roughly patched up, its headrest stained with Brylcreem. She wondered who had sat in this tired chair before. Had it been in someone's home?" A waiting room in a medical office? What tears had been shed by its occupants? What laughter had it heard? Her tears began falling like a torrent. In this protected tiny cell, she allowed herself to give into the pain.

* * *

She lay on her back, her eyes wide open, feeling the soft rhythm of Brett's breathing and the warmth of her head against her chest. The scent of her Chanel # 5 mingled with her perspiration, and the stale boozy air in the stuffy room. The sliver of light from the street light creeping in through the gap between the curtains cast a mournful light across Brett's back. She was creating a mental home movie of all of this, to be re-lived some day when it would be taken away from her. She wanted to remember everything exactly as it was on this night.

Brett nuzzled in closer and threw one leg across hers. She wished she could make all of them go away and let Brett be, give her breathing room to do much needed soul-searching and discover her own strength. She knew Brett was better than the way she was being perceived by others. Her life seemed to be a warped record being played on a broken down phonograph, its needle stuck on the same song. Brett had it in her to get the needle unstuck.

"Sydney?" Brett murmured in her stupor.

"Yes, honey, I'm here."

"Stay with me."

"I'm not going anywhere."

"Thank you for being here. I need you."

"Thank you for needing me."

For this fleeting moment, all was well with the world. Until sunrise. Then, reality would creep in through the back door and shatter all illusions, destroy all joy.

Chapter 11/ Emerald's Child

The real estate sign was strategically planted on the narrow strip of grass between the long narrow living room windows and the cracked sidewalk. She stepped back in disbelief.

"Is there anything I can do for you?"

A tanned, buff young man with a bare chest and straight dark hair emerged from the side of the house and glared menacingly.

"I was looking for Mrs. Parker."

"Whatever you're selling, we're not interested."

"I'm not selling anything."

"We don't want religious propaganda, either."

"I'm not from a church."

"You're one of those Jehovah's Witnesses, aren't you?"

"No. I'm not here for business. I used to live here."

"In that case," he scrutinized her with icy grey eyes, paying particularly close attention to the golden Star of David around her neck her parents had given her, hanging slightly above the locket, which had been Brett's gift, "Come in."

He opened the front door and bellowed into the dark interior.

"Gran! There's a woman here to see you!"

Daisy emerged from the depths of the dwelling, her face pale, and her eyes devoid of their sparkle.

"Sydney, dear, how nice to see you!" she embraced her.

"Mrs. Parker, I had no idea you were planning to sell your house. You didn't mention it at Brett's birthday party."

"I didn't know it myself then, dear."

A young woman with wild, unkempt, black hair to her waist, and bushy eyebrows emerged from the inner recesses of the house and glared at Sydney. Her eyes lingered on the Star of David.

"Are you a land developer?" she demanded to know.

"No, dear. Sydney's my friend. Sydney, dear, meet my grandson Billy, and his wife Lucy." Daisy beamed, "They're visiting from British Columbia."

The couple continued to glare.

"Billy's a physicist." Daisy said, "They have the most darling little girl, Deandra. She's taking a nap right now."

"Grandma's moving out to Victoria with us." Billy said,"This place is getting too big to manage, and the cold climate is bad for her health. We're helping her sell the house. Gran's busy now. You'll have to excuse us." he directed her to the door.

"When will you be moving?" Sydney asked sheepishly.

"At the end of the month." Lucy stated matter-of-factly, "Whether or not the house sells by then, once Billy's holidays are over, we're shipping everything off to B.C. and moving lock, stock and barrel. Then, it's up to the real estate agent."

"This is so sudden. I'm going to miss you." Sydney turned to Daisy again to embrace her.

"I'm going to miss you, too, Sydney. I had such a lovely time at your new house. Your parents are lovely people and your house is beautiful. I'm very happy for you."

"Thank you, Mrs. Parker. I came to ask you to have dinner with me and Brett at The Castle. I had no idea it would be a send-off."

"Gran doesn't have the time." Lucy folded her arms across her chest.

"It's only a little dinner."

"No. It's not possible. You'd better leave now."

She met Lucy's stern, unflinching eyes.

"Sydney, dear, have some tea." Daisy tugged at her sleeve like a small child.

"Now, Gran, we have an appointment. Don't you remember?" Billy said.

"What appointment?"

"Have you already forgotten? Really, Gran, you're getting terribly forgetful lately."

"You didn't tell me anything about an appointment, Billy, dear."

"You can't remember. Just like you couldn't remember you left the stove on this morning."

"But I know I turned it off."

"You thought you did. Good thing Lucy went in there to heat up Deandra's bottle, or the whole house would have gone up like a tinder box. You had the pot holders next to the burner on the counter. A few more minutes, and they would have caught fire."

"I really did turn it off. I'm very careful with those things. I could have sworn I turned off the stove, put the stew pot on the counter, and hung up the pot holders."

"Well, you didn't, Gran. Your mind's going. At your age, you can't expect any different."

"We all forget things." Sydney intercepted, tears welling up in her eyes.

"This doesn't concern you." Lucy glared at her.

"Face it: You can't be trusted to live alone anymore, Gran." Billy said.

"I was fine just last week."

"These things can sneak up on you unexpectedly."

"I was just fine at the birthday party...Happy and gay."

"Don't use the word "gay", Gran. It means something different now."

"What does it mean, dear?"

"Homosexual."

"My, my." she laughed, once again her old self, "I'm too old to learn how to be gay, then."

"Gran, you're talking foolish." Lucy chided her.

"You frown too much, Lucy, dear. If you open your heart and learn tolerance, you'll feel so much better. That yippie religion from B.C. doesn't seem to be serving you too well. You're filled with hate, tension, and intolerance. Why don't you move here? It'll do you good."

"We've been through all this before, Gran." Billy said, "It's all settled. You'd better say good-bye to your friend now, because she's not welcome here anymore. And," he pointed a finger at Sydney, "If you try meddling again, you'll be very sorry."

"You take care of yourself, Mrs. Parker." Sydney embraced her tearfully and felt Daisy's fingers sinking into the flesh of her arms in despair.

"I wonder what's become of Acacia." Daisy murmured.

"Acacia?" Sydney stood back in astonishment.

"She's talking rubbish again." Lucy said.

"The little girl." Daisy whispered, squeezing Sydney's elbow, "Please find her, Sydney."

"Gran, that's enough nonsense."

"The little girl from the apartment building?" Sydney asked.

"Yes. I remember her name now. She went to Saint Peter's School on Regent Street around the corner. Please find her, Sydney, and make sure she's all right. It seems to me, it was a double name...Acacia Ann? Acacia Sue? Acacia Lynn? She wanted to be called just Acacia. She thought it sounded too country, too Southern with the double name."

"Mrs. Parker, I think I can bring Acacia here to see you before you go."

"You are amazing, Sydney, dear. I knew I could count on you."

"The two of you have already been reacquainted."

"Time to go." Lucy took Sydney's arm and clamped down on it, "We're pressed for time."

Lucy was scowling so hard, she had the appearance of a Rottweiler. Billy ushered Sydney outside as she turned around to wave at Daisy. Billy stood on the curb to ensure she made her way

191

down the street. He glared menacingly at her each time she turned around to look. Only after she crossed Carleton Street, did he return to the house. Voices could be heard from the house, even on the final block of Needham Street: Billy's reprimanding tone and Lucy's shrill screeches. Sydney quickened her steps and maintained her pace until she reached The Green. She found an empty bench under a weeping willow. What could she do to keep Daisy in Beavertown? She had less than a month to come up with a miracle. She turned toward the road to see the cars coming from Queen Street. It was around this time each day that Warren came home from work through a circuitous route (for reasons she would most likely never know). If she could flag him down, she could ask for his help privately. And, not too long later, the impeccable sheen of the onyx Mercedes Benz was gliding through the overpass. She waved wildly to attract his attention, though she was doubtful he would glance in the direction of The Green. To her astonishment, he parked his car by the curb and crossed the road.

"What's up, Stormy? What are you up to now?"

"Warren, I have to talk to you. It's important."

"I'd say it must be important if you're flailing your arms about like that." He placed his foot on the edge of the bench and leaned on his knee.

"What can a person do if she suspects someone she cares about is being abused?"

"Whoa! Wait! What are we talking about here? Child abuse? Wife beating?"

"Elder abuse."

"You're always involved in intrigue, aren't you?"

"I'm serious, Warren."

"What's going on?"

"Daisy Parker, my former landlady. Her grandson and his wife have come for a visit from B.C. and they've coerced her into putting her house up for sale."

"Wait a minute. How do you know she has been coerced? It's a pretty harsh word. Persuaded, perhaps?"

"No. I'm absolutely certain. I know her. She would never willingly give up the life she has, no matter how persuasive someone might be. Warren, I saw how frightened she was. They're gruff and intimidating, and, they seemed extremely paranoid. They couldn't get rid of me fast enough. Billy, the grandson, threatened me. At the end of the month, they're clearing out of here with Mrs. Parker and shipping all her belongings to Victoria."

"What does this clown do for a living there?"

"He's a physicist."

"Is his surname Parker?"

"No. Mrs. Parker only had daughters."

"Where are these daughters when she needs them?"

"I wish I knew. Billy and Lucy kept insisting she was getting forgetful and could not live alone anymore."

"They obviously want to have her declared mentally incompetent."

"She's as lucid as you or I. Can they really do that?"

"It's done every day."

"Warren, this is frightening." she shuddered, "What can I do?"

"I'm not a lawyer. Tony's the one you should be talking to."

"I don't know him that well."

"I have an idea. I can't promise anything, mind you, but I have a friend who is a social worker. I can tell him what you've told me, and see if anything can be done. They might send a social worker to the house to investigate."

"But Social Services are always backed up. By the time they send someone, she'll be long gone."

"Never fear. Ken owes me a favor, so he'll give this priority. He'll also contact Social Services in B.C. Where in B.C. do they live?"

"I think it's Victoria."

"They can investigate what's happening to her, if she's been moved there. Hopefully, we can get a surname and have the asshole investigated there."

"Warren, thank you."

"You and I can pay a visit to Daisy together. The asshole might think he's a big shot, intimidating a woman, but let him try to intimidate Warren Horncastle. He's a coward. I'll get him to spill his name, rank, and serial number."

"Are you sure?"

"Watch me. I'll talk to Tony, and see if he can offer some legal counsel."

"You can't imagine how grateful I am, Warren. You are a terrific person."

"Don't let it get around, or you'll destroy my reputation." he winked, "Come on. Hop in. I'll give you a ride home."

* * *

Brett leaned back and shut her eyes as the phonograph played ABBA's "My Love, My Life", a haunting love ballad unlike the usual upbeat disco numbers typical of the group.

"I'm too old for this, hon."

"You're a fabulous dancer, Brett! You disco a lot better than all the university kids!" Shayleigh protested.

"My whole body hurts! At my age, when you have any fun, you always pays for it the next day. But we sure did have fun, didn't we, hon? What a terrific way to spend my night off."

"It was great fun."

"I can't believe you'd want to spend your evening with an old fogie like me."

"You're not an old fogie! I love being with you."

"Thank you, sweetheart. I hope Sam didn't mind me tagging along."

"You made the evening."

Brett straightened herself at the urgent ringing of the telephone.

"I can get it." Shayleigh said.

"It's probably Richard. He said he was going to call about a change in the schedule for next week." she rose and started toward the kitchen.

Shayleigh turned off the phonograph as Brett picked up the receiver.

"Hello, Brett, dear. How are you?" an affected female voice was on the other end, "This is Emerald Wallace."

"Oh, hello, Emerald." she winked at Shayleigh, who was standing in the hallway, "I'm great. You?"

"Not so good, dear. I'm getting chest pains all the time. Is my Leigh driving you crazy?"

"Why would you say that? I would be lost without her. She's a treasure."

"You must have the patience of a saint, Brett. I don't know how you put up with her."

"Emerald, your daughter's a lovely, sensitive, intelligent, young woman, and you ought to feel honored she's yours."

"I can tell she's hoodwinked you. She must be on her best behavior around you, but you don't really know her the way I do."

"I don't think it's right for you to be saying such things."

"You can't believe a word she tells you about us, you know. She spins a good yarn, but it's all lies. She's emotionally unstable. It's just a matter of time before she needs to be committed. She couldn't function on her own."

"I think she's a strong, reliable young woman. My boys and I adore her."

"She's mentally deficient. Henry wanted her out of the house, so we could finally get our own lives back, but I can see we've passed our problem on to you. She would be very difficult to deal with for someone as gracious as you. At least, I knew how to keep her in line. She'll take too many liberties if you don't put your foot down."

"Emerald, I don't know where you're getting these ideas, but you're totally out of line."

"You'll understand in time. Don't say I didn't warn you. By the way, the reason I called you is: You and I must stop this wedding! I just hope it's not too late. She's not pregnant, is she?"

"Emerald, I'm afraid I cannot support you in this. I think they make a lovely couple and they have my blessings. Sam is the best thing to happen to that little girl, and I am not going to allow anyone to mess that up for her."

"Sam's mother, Lynn, agrees with me."

"Well, I don't, and I am not going to allow you or Lynn to cause any heartache for those kids."

"When he sees her for what she is, he'll leave her. Then, she'll be even more difficult to put up with."

"I'm sure the two of them are going to have a long, happy life together."

"Henry and I certainly don't plan to waste our hard-earned money on a sham of a wedding for that ingrate."

"Don't worry, Emerald. You keep your cash. I plan to give them a wedding."

"I suppose that's your way of trying to show us up. I'm not falling for that guilt trip."

"I don't expect anything from you, Emerald."

"Do what you want. Just don't expect any handouts from us. Leigh belongs here under our watchful eyes. Not in your den of inequity, and not playing house."

"You're upset because you can't dominate and control her anymore. You just want an unpaid servant chained to the house, dressed in rags, lonely and depressed. You'd love that, wouldn't you, you sadistic old bag. I'm glad she's building a life for herself and declaring her independence from you! She finally has a chance, now that you're not around strangling the life out of her!"

"How dare you speak to me that way, you cheap trollop! I know what kind of woman you are! Leigh was pure as the driven snow

196

until you introduced her to the seedy side of life: your orgies, liquor, drugs, and, who knows what else! You're trying to buy her friendship, because no one else wants to be your friend. People have reported to me that they've seen you consorting with homosexual men. And you have two young sons at home!"

"At least, I don't bully my children until they break. I'm glad Shayleigh's moving to John's Bay after she's married."

"She'll come crawling back when he breaks her heart. You mark my words. I give it a year, tops."

"Don't hold your breath, Emerald. What those two kids have is for keeps. And nothing can come between them. Not you, not the other meddling mother. Those kids are going to make it."

"Your own daughter doesn't live with you. In fact, she wants nothing to do with you. You're not exactly "Mother Of The Year" material."

"This is Shayleigh's home. This where she is loved and wanted and appreciated. When you care about someone, it's natural to want them to have the things they need and enjoy. It's not natural to begrudge them a few measly toys and presentable clothes when they're children. I'm not surprised, now that she's all grown up, you begrudge dishing out a cent of your precious money to contribute to her wedding."

"At least, I didn't spoil her rotten and create a monster like your daughter."

"No one could ever accuse you of spoiling your daughter, Emerald."

"If you don't let them know who's boss from the start, and enforce your authority, they'll run roughshod over you. If you praise them or encourage them, they'll get a swelled head. You've got to keep them on your toes at all times, tell them what to do, monitor their every move, and point out how they can improve themselves. It's called responsible parenting. If you buy them toys and clothes, they'll become selfish and vain."

"I can't take this anymore. I have to go." Brett slammed down the receiver and burst into tears.

"Thank you for sticking up for me." Shayleigh said.

"What a piece of work your mother is! How did you ever stand it? I can't even take a phone conversation with that witch. I don't know how you lived there for twenty-two years and did not go stark raving mad or die!"

"Maybe because a part of me knew that, some day I would meet someone like you to show me what a real mother is like. You're the only reason I'm here in one piece."

The telephone rang again.

"Let's ignore it." Shayleigh said.

"It might be Richard."

"I'll answer it." Shayleigh ran to the kitchen and reached for the receiver.

"Brett?" Richard queried on the other end.

"It's Shayleigh, Richard."

"I tried before, but your line was busy."

"Sorry. That was my fault. Could I take a message for her?"

"Tell her Sydney's volunteered to do the late sets on both of the nights Danny's away. Is that clear?"

"Yes it is. I'll tell her."

"Good enough."

Shayleigh hung up the phone and returned to Brett's side.

"Sydney's doing both late sets while Danny's away." she told her.

"Bless her heart. She's always covering for me."

"That's what friends are for."

"I'll make sure Tony drives her home when she works late."

The telephone rang again.

"If it's Mom again, let me handle it." Shayleigh returned to the phone and spoke reluctantly.

"Shayleigh, your mom's on a rampage." Mindy's voice was on the other end, "She phoned here in a tizzy and said she was having chest pains, and you had to call her. She's mad at Brett or something. She was having a heart attack and it was your fault or something like that. Maybe you should phone her."

"I'm sorry she involved you in this foolishness."

"She tried to get me on her side again the way she always does when she's mad at you."

"I'll call her."

"Good luck."

"Never ceases to amaze me!" Brett laughed, "Between Emerald and your future mother-in-law, Lynn, you and Sam have a tough climb uphill."

"I'll call Mom before she calls everybody in town." Shayleigh dialled the number, "Hi, Dad."

"Don't "Hi, Dad" me. Your mother's critically ill. She waited for you to call and apologize after that woman upset her. When you didn't, she nearly had a heart attack. Now she's too weak to come to the phone. You nearly killed your mother! Don't come around here playing families again. You're no longer our daughter. You're dead to us. I don't know why we waited so long. We're disowning you before you cause one of us to die of a heart attack!"

"Just tell her I called."

"Wait a minute. She's saying something. She's getting up in her condition, so she can hear your voice before she dies."

"I hope you're satisfied!" Emerald was on the other end now, "You've been telling that nasty woman all sorts of lies about me. I've given birth to a snake who bites her own mother's hand. Anyone who allows trash like Brett Morrow to speak to me with such disrespect is no daughter of mine! When I die, my blood will be on your hands. You'll be banging your head against the walls. If I had the strength, I'd go over there and give you the beating you deserve!"

"Mom."

"Don't "Mom" me. I'm not your mother anymore. You've always been a big disappointment to us. Other people's children turned out so well-adjusted, and went on to establish prestigious careers. Not you. Always falling apart, pathetic, useless, mentally deficient, and unstable. Other people had children who were helpful and pleasant, children who did things for them. Dora's daughter Doreen is your age. She and her husband are both engineers. They paid for Dora's gold treatments for her arthritis. All I get from you are those God-awful lockets and perfumes and sweaters I only end up having to give away, anyway."

"Mom, listen."

"I wasted my life taking care of a useless idiot like you, when I could've had a real life. I could've travelled more, gone to more parties. Instead, I cooked supper and did laundry. What appreciation do I get for all the sacrifices I made? Defiance and disobedience. Other mothers get devoted daughters. I get stuck with the likes of you. Some day, I hope you get what you deserve. I hope you'll be all alone for the rest of your life. Your precious Brett's going to toss you out when she gets tired of you. It's just a matter of time. Sam's going to leave you for a real woman. No one can tolerate you for long. Some day, I hope you learn firsthand how painful it is to have an ingrate for a child."

"Mom."

"Your mother is gravely ill." her father came on the line, "I hope you're proud of yourself. I have to go take care of her now. She needs me. You're no longer our daughter." he hung up.

Shayleigh sank to the kitchen floor, pulled her knees up to her chin, and stared into space vacuously. Brett knelt beside her and placed a protective arm around her. They sat there on the cold linoleum in silence for an eternity, Brett massaging Shayleigh's shoulders and neck, and kissing her temples.

* * *

Maggie observed the sun freckles on Brett's cleavage when the younger woman bent down to offer her hot hors d'oeuvres from a silver tray.

"These cheese puffs are frightfully good, Brett." she popped one of the tiny pastries into her mouth, "I hope there'll be some left for the Dragon Lady." she spoke in a muffled voice as she gobbled up the treat.

"Oh, Maggie, I don't know what to do."

Placing the serving tray on the coffee table, Brett sat beside her on the sofa and folded her long legs under her.

"You're doing everything that is humanly possible, Brett."

"Nothing can undo all those years of damage they did to her, not to mention the ongoing damage."

"You've provided a buffer, so that the impact of the mistreatment is not as profound."

"Maggie, all I'm providing is a temporary respite, not a miraculous solution."

"You're a safe haven for her, something she's never had before."

"I hope Sam can keep her safe and happy. He is the key player in this."

"He's a steady, dependable boy. I'm betting my money on him."

"Shayleigh's got troubles ahead with that mother of his. That woman has the eyes of a killer. I hope Sam's strong enough to protect Shayleigh from the triumvirate of evil. I'll bet it's their diabolical presence in her life that caused her recent illness."

"Oh, I know all about the power of evil."

"This illness is far more serious than her bouts with viral infections in the past. It zapped all her energy. Nothing's showed up on tests, but I'll bet this is a new virus no one knows about yet."

"I could've sworn she had mononucleosis."

"It could be a new strain of it. Whatever she has, it's very real and debilitating. I hope John Myers can figure it out. He's young and smart as a whip. I had to do a lot of pleading with Jeannie, his receptionist, to get her in to see him. I'm going with her when she goes in."

"I hope he can help her."

"John's a terrific doctor and a caring, compassionate human being."

"That is certainly rare in this day and age. Health care is becoming so impersonal." Maggie glanced at the antique clock on the wall, "I certainly hope Shayleigh and Sydney get here before Mama Bear does."

"I'm happy to see the budding friendship between them. I think Sydney's good for her."

"I like Sydney. She's an honest, dependable girl."

"She has a lot in common with Shayleigh. Both of them have broken spirits, but they have emerged from the trenches with their inner beauty intact."

"I hope they get here soon, or Her Majesty's going to arrive before they do."

"Let her. We're ready for her, aren't we?"

"I don't know why you even agreed to meet with her to talk about the wedding in the first place."

"I want to keep a close eye on her and her husband to make sure they behave themselves at the wedding. I don't want anyone to ruin Shayleigh's special day. Why women compete with their own daughters, I'll never understand." Brett repositioned her deer legs, "Emerald is driven to break her spirit, to prevent her from having any happiness. Imagine despising and envying your own child so intensely, trying to prove how much better you are at everything she has talent for. It's sick! Shayleigh is so much better at everything than Emerald is. It must drive her crazy."

"Emerald's certainly knows how to turn on the charm when she wants something."

"She's the ultimate narcissist. People exist for the sole purpose of meeting her needs. She wanted Shayleigh sentenced to a life of servitude. She was not entitled to her own identity or dreams."

"What a horrendous life that child has had."

"Both of her parents were sadistic and vile. There was constant abuse. They resented Shayleigh for being born. She was an inconvenience, a financial burden, an obstacle to their soulless, hedonistic lifestyle. Henry is more quiet and smooth, but you can tell he is seething inside, filled with ill will. He's a sneaky one, most likely even more dangerous than Emerald."

"At least, Emerald and Lynn are out in the open, not duplicitous like Henry."

"Poor Shayleigh insists on trying to see some good in them. She keeps making excuses, telling herself their phony, manipulative words of affection are genuine. Maybe, if she faced the truth head on, she would not be able to deal with the weight of such a burden."

"You may want to follow your own advice, Brett, my dear. Doesn't it sound all too familiar? Making excuses for the other person, blaming yourself?"

"It's different with Laurie. I'm the reason she's so...so..."

"Obnoxious."

"Had I been the kind of mother she needed..."

"Rubbish!"

"No, Maggie."

"Laurie needs therapy to find out why she blames you for all her troubles and shortcomings."

"Laurie's justified in feeling the way she does about me."

"Brett, one of these days, I swear I'm going to put you across my knee."

They heard a key in the lock, and Sydney's voice from the porch.

"Thank you, Ryan. Bye."

"Hello!" this was Shayleigh in the foyer.

Brett sprang to her feet and ran to greet them.

"I'm sorry we took so long." Shayleigh said, "I found some shoes, finally! They're medium-heeled, kind of squashed, retro style. And, they've got a pearlized finish."

"They sound lovely, hon." Brett embraced her.

"I'll show them to both you and Maggie." she cast a warm glance at Sydney, "Sydney helped pick them out."

"I didn't do anything."

"Yes you did." she stepped into the living room to exchange greetings with Maggie.

"They're like the shoes I wore when I was young." Maggie said as Shayleigh unveiled her treasure, "Everything comes back in style."

"How are things going with that situation?" Brett whispered to Sydney.

"Not well at all. Warren's run into all kinds of roadblocks. There is absolutely nothing we can do to prevent them from taking her to B.C. She's willing to go with them and relinquish all her rights and worldly possessions to them."

"I must say, I'm impressed with Warren. I didn't think he was capable of caring this much about anyone other than himself and going out on a limb to help anyone."

"I told you he wasn't that bad."

"I hope I don't live long enough to find out what it's like to be in Daisy's predicament."

"Brett, don't say that!"

"I don't want to be dependent on others. That would be degrading and frightening."

"Don't worry. As long as I'm alive, I'll take care of you. Besides, you're going to be youthful and vibrant and beautiful at a hundred! We'll celebrate your hundredth birthday together and you'll blow out all the candles."

"I love you, sweetheart." she kissed her cheek.

"I love you, too." she squeezed her hand and led her to the room.

"I'll take these upstairs to my room, and work on the refreshments." Shayleigh gathered up her shopping bag.

"I'll go up with you, hon." Brett said.

"I can get the coffee started." Sydney offered.

"No, sweetheart, we'll do all that together. You and Maggie take it easy. There's no hurry. Let Emerald wait." Brett followed Shayleigh upstairs.

Shayleigh deposited her pocketbook and shopping bag on her burgundy ruffled bedspread. The late afternoon sun cast a rosy glow through the blush pink Priscilla sheers.

"I wish I had kept in touch. Now, it may be too late."

"It's not too late, hon."

"I was too embarrassed to keep in touch with anyone from that time. Too ashamed. I didn't want anyone to know how badly I turned out."

"Don't talk like that, hon. You should be very proud of the way you turned out. I know I am."

"Thank you, Brett."

"Come on. Let's go down. We'll talk a lot more later." she took her arm.

The doorbell rang. As Sydney opened the door to Sam, Shayleigh called out from the landing.

"Hi, honey!"

"Hi, sweetie!" he smiled up at her, and waited for her to come downstairs and gave her a shy peck on the lips, "I'll help you in the kitchen."

"You're definitely good husband material." Brett patted him on the back, "Don't let him get away."

When the doorbell rang again, Brett floated in her magenta and cream abstract print silk Mumu. A striking blonde stood in the doorway, shimmering in aquamarine silk.

"Hello, Emerald. So glad you could make it." Brett greeted her cordially.

"You have a lovely home."

"Thank you."

"Hello, Mom." Shayleigh joined Brett.

"What have you done to your eyebrows?" Emerald lunged at her daughter, "Did you pluck them? You look dreadful."

"Why don't we go in and sit down?" Brett made an attempt to lead her into the living room.

"You've put on weight, Leigh." Emerald continued to glare at her daughter, "If you were home, I wouldn't allow you to indulge your appetites like an animal. You have no self-discipline."

"Emerald, you must remember my friend, Maggie." Brett pulled her by the arm.

"Of course. How nice to see you again, Mrs. Cheeseman."

"Charmed, I'm sure." Maggie said.

"I think it's poor manners to call one's elders by their first names."

"And, this is a very dear friend of mine, Sydney Goldstein."

"Goldstein is a Jewish name. I'll have to avoid having business transactions with you, won't I?"

"Hello, Mrs. Wallace." Sam broke in.

"Hello, dear. What's this I hear about Leigh losing her job at the library?"

"Her only connection and reference, Miss Evans, retired. They won't keep her on without a connection. That's how elitist Beavertown businesses operate."

"Nonsense. Young lady, you march right up to that fat German boss of yours and demand your job back!"

"It won't do any good, Mom. They only hire professors' daughters or other well-connected girls. I was lucky to get the last three years because I knew Miss Evans."

"You have no spine. You can't even speak up for yourself."

"No one messes with Heike Dietrich." Sam said, "Not even Mr. Dietrich. She's a foot taller, and weighs a hundred pounds more than him. Don't worry, Mrs. Wallace. We'll be married soon and I'll be supporting her."

"I don't want her sitting around all day, watching soaps."

"Mrs. Wallace, Shayleigh's too ill to be working, anyway."

"She'll be better soon. Then, she'll have to go out to work and be self-sufficient. No woman can stay at home and stagnate. I always had my art."

"She has her writing."

"She's no good at it. She'll never be successful enough to make money."

"She's a wonderful dress designer."

"That's for stupid women with no education."

"With her intellect, Shayleigh can find her way. She'll never stagnate." Sam persisted.

"Let's have some tea, shall we?" Sydney poured tea from the silver teapot into pansy-patterned china cups.

"That dress looks absolutely hideous on you, Leigh." Emerald tugged at her, "With those enormous hips of yours, you ought to be wearing loose, baggy tops and sweaters to hide your figure."

"Shayleigh's got a beautiful hourglass figure." Brett protested, "Just like my favorite actress, Sophia Loren."

"Sophia Loren's a vulgar tart. Why don't you give those clothes to me? I'll put them to good use." she smirked, eyes twinkling demonically, "I have the figure for them. I haven't let myself go. If you don't shape up, Sam won't stick around for long. A handsome young man like him is not going to waste his time with a slovenly wife."

"Here you are, Mrs. Wallace." Sydney handed her a teacup, "One sugar, the way you like it."

"Why in the world would you want to marry my daughter, anyway?" Emerald took the cup, "She's lazy, stupid, and socially inept. She's not a good cook. She's not good-looking. She doesn't even have money."

"I think I'll take my chances." Sam placed an arm around Shayleigh.

"Don't say I didn't warn you."

"Have some hors d'oeuvres." Brett stuck a tray under Emerald's nose.

"I hope there's no ham in these." Emerald inspected a pinwheel, "I never eat ham. It's too fatty."

"It's chicken."

"Don't assume our money's going to be Shayleigh's when we're gone, or that we're going to be helping you financially in any way." Emerald continued.

"I plan to support her."

"You know, Leigh, if you're not working, you ought to be doing graduate work and establishing a career. Too bad you weren't smart enough to major in Psychology. What future is there in Sociology? It was the easiest thing they offered. When my friends tell me how their daughters are successful doctors, dentists, business women, administrators and such, I feel too ashamed to tell them mine never got past her B.A. Now, you want to live a lower-class life in an industrial city. Your husband's just starting out as a teacher and isn't going to make enough to afford rent for even the worst dump on his own."

"Just because something isn't right for you, it doesn't mean it can't be right for me."

"How can you possibly know what's right for you? Living here in this depravity has distorted your values. You've even lost your manners. You'd never have dared speak to me in that tone before you took up with these questionable people."

At the sound of the telephone, Brett ran into the kitchen. Her voice could be heard from the room.

"Hello...Yes, Stan...Of course...How about tomorrow afternoon?...Two o'clock?...Okay...See you then."

"New boyfriend, no doubt." Emerald scoffed, "This phone number must be in every men's room in Beavertown. People are gossiping, you know. They know Leigh lives here. I'm ashamed to show my face."

"Your friends must think less of you now." Maggie piped up, "Your daughter's consorting with women of easy virtue, marrying a lowly teacher from John's Bay, not pursuing a graduate degree! They're inviting Charles, and openly gay man and Georgia, my lesbian friend, to the wedding, too. You really ought to cover your face, so no one can recognize you. My Arab friend Jamila can loan you a head cover."

"Well!" Emerald stormed out of the room in indignation, "I don't intend to stay here and get insulted this way!"

"You must stay for the Matzah balls!" Maggie called out.

"As for you, Leigh," Emerald was in her daughter's face, "I refuse to associate myself with you any longer! If I am to save face in this community, I can't appear to be in accord with the choices you've made."

"I'll escort you to the door." Sam took her arm.

"You know I don't drive. I have to call my husband."

"I'll drive you home myself." he offered, waving at the others as he led her outside.

Shayleigh scurried to the kitchen. The others heard the slamming of the back door. Sydney ran after her and caught up with her.

"Why don't we go to Jim's Steakhouse for some coffee?"

"I don't have my purse."

"It's okay. I've got my wallet in my skirt's back pocket."

"Brett might worry."

"I'll call her from there. Come on. It's only fifteen minutes away."

"Okay. Thank you, Sydney."

From the living room window, unseen by both, Brett watched, silent and dewy-eyed.

"I guess it's just you and me again, Maggie." she turned from the window once they were no longer visible.

"Come, sit with me. I'm sure Sydney'll take good care of her." she motioned to the seat beside her.

"I know she will."

"We can have more goodies, now that we don't have to share them with the Dragon Lady." Maggie popped a pinwheel and a spinach pastry into her mouth together.

"It's going to get ugly." Brett sat beside her, "She's going to lay a guilt trip on Shay. That little girl's all twisted up in knots inside. Sometimes I think she's fighting a losing battle." she bit her fingernails, "I hope Stan has the answers I'm looking for."

"There's nothing you can do right now. She's with Sydney and she's all right."

"Oh, Maggie, I must drive you crazy with my fretting."

"It's all right, my darling. Sharing your experiences makes my life more interesting."

"Maggie, you're a Godsend." she patted her hand.

"Have some of these pastries before I polish them off." Maggie popped two cheese pastries into her mouth.

"I think I hear Sam." Brett sprang up, "He must be very upset."

"Emerald's an expert at making enemies and alienating people."

"No doubt, she's a tortured woman, but that doesn't give her the right to destroy her daughter's life. Shay didn't ask to be born. She doesn't want Shay to be happy, because she's not happy...Hello, Sam." she opened the door, "I'm so sorry about all of that."

"It's okay, Brett. Shay's mom complained the whole time. She's not a big fan of yours."

They laughed.

"I'll just see Shay for a minute and go back to my dorm. I have to finish packing my meager possessions, so I can drive down to John's Bay on Saturday in Dave's truck and deposit them at my mom's house."

"Shay was upset, so, Sydney took her out some place."

"That's okay. I'll call her tonight. Thanks for everything, Brett. See you later. Take care."

"You, too, Sam."

"Such a polite boy." Maggie remarked when Brett returned to the room, "You'd better hide the rest of these, or I'll eat them all."

"That's all right, Maggie. Help yourself. Sydney would be very happy to know that you were the one who ate her creations."

"You draw a lot of strength from Sydney, don't you?" Maggie took two pinwheels and a spinach pastry.

"She's my rock."

"You have a true friend in her."

"She's other-worldly. Sometimes I look at her, Maggie, and she just glows. There's a special aura about her. When I'm with her, I feel so grounded, so safe and protected."

"I can see you never take off those pearls she gave you."

"I want to be buried in them. I feel a part of her is always with me when I'm wearing them." she fingered them with tenderness, "Maggie, if I ever lost her friendship, I think my life would come to an end."

"I don't think anything could come between you. Not even a man. That's the true test of a friendship between two women."

"It seems most female friendships remain superficial. They talk about their children, husbands, homes, jobs, recipes, daily activities. At best, they are sympathetic and helpful, but they don't share deep, intimate things."

"It's all kept prim and proper, within defined parameters. No emotional outbursts, nothing outside of what is deemed socially appropriate. They're hung up and paranoid about sharing too deeply, feeling too much emotional intensity, touching each other too much. But, since they're too uptight to have self-awareness, that satisfies them."

"Not us. We don't follow the herd. Here. It's all gone now." she held out the empty tray.

"Couldn't think of a better stomach to hold them." Brett kissed her cheek.

"I've made quite a pig of myself, I'm afraid. It's going to wreak havoc with my blood pressure and cholesterol."

"It's not every day you have such delicacies before you."

"I'll have to deprive myself the rest of the week."

"Oh, Maggie, what would I ever do without you?" Brett placed her head on her shoulder.

"Likewise, my dear." she patted her knee.

They remained there in silence: two women, searching, aching, one with each other's pain.

Chapter 12/ Fractured

The stark white real estate sign could no longer be seen displayed in its prominent position. Dandelions once again frolicked on the tiny patch of green, young and oblivious.

"Has it already been sold?" Shayleigh peered out the back window of Warren's car.

"Wouldn't there be a "Sold" sign?" Brett leaned over Shayleigh's shoulder to catch a better glimpse.

"Maybe it's been taken off the market." Warren remarked.

"I can't see them backing down." Sydney mused, "Something's up."

"Let's find out." Warren parked in front of the green house.

The four of them stepped out of the car and walked tentatively toward the front door. Sydney rang the doorbell. Daisy's smiling face appeared promptly.

"Hello, dear. How nice to see all of you."

"Mrs. Parker, are you alone?"

"Why, yes, I am, dear." she stood aside as they sheepishly stepped into the foyer.

"Where are Billy and Lucy?" Brett glanced around her.

"They're on their way back to Victoria."

"I don't understand."

"It seems they've changed their minds."

"What prompted this sudden change of heart?"

"I don't understand it myself, dear. There was a man in here yesterday, appraising my antiques. Then, later, he had a private talk with Billy. After the man left, there were two phone calls for Billy, which seemed to upset him. He called the real estate agent to take the house off the market and changed their plane reservations. He cancelled mine. They packed up and left without a word. I don't understand what happened."

"It doesn't matter." Sydney embraced her, "All that matters is that you're here, in your own house."

"It's wonderful to be able to stay here. Let's have some tea, shall we?"

"Daisy, Shayleigh has a surprise for you." Brett said, "The rest of us are going to wait outside while the two of you have a chat. Then, we'll all have a celebration of your not going to B.C."

"Is it all right if I freshen up?" Sydney said, "I'll join you outside in a few minutes."

"Sure, hon." Brett followed Warren outside, to the backyard separated from the neighboring one by a white picket fence. The grass was uncut, a task normally undertaken by a teenaged boy from one of the neighboring houses.

"I'm impressed with the way you've handled this entire situation with Daisy's grandson." Brett sat on the edge of the picnic table, "I saw a whole different side to you, Warren."

"I always knew you were carrying a torch for me." he smirked, perching on top of the table, "There are a lot of things you don't know about me, Brett."

"I'm finding out. You showed genuine compassion."

"I am human, after all. What a shocker."

"I'm serious."

"Does this mean you're no longer upset your Sydney's dating an ogre?"

"I've never called you an ogre, Warren. I'm just very protective of Sydney. She's vulnerable."

"How noble."

"Don't break her heart."

"You don't have much faith in me, do you?"

"Take care of her heart. I beg of you."

"Sydney's a grown woman, Brett. She doesn't need mollycoddling."

"She's not like all your conquests. She's sensitive."

"Are you sure your feelings for her are just friendship? Maybe you just want her for yourself. I wouldn't want to get in the middle of a love triangle here. I know it's every man's dream to get two chicks in the sack, but, no offense: I don't find you attractive, Brett."

"Can't you stop being an asshole long enough to take things seriously?"

"I'm afraid I must decline on the threesome. Thanks for the offer, though."

"You're disgusting. Just when I start thinking you have some redeeming qualities and let down my guard to give you the benefit of the doubt, you go and spoil it."

"I love you, too, Brett."

"I don't know what my Sydney sees in you."

"YOUR Sydney! You really are jealous! Methinks there's much more to this desperate plea than you're letting on. I might be willing to make an arrangement with you: You could have her Tuesdays and Thursdays."

"You're vile and repulsive!"

"If you try to badmouth me to her, you'll alienate her. You don't want any man to have her. You want her all to yourself."

"Sydney needs a reliable, trustworthy man to anchor her."

"Methinks the lady doth protest too much."

Sydney emerged from the back door and struggled through the tall grass as she came toward them.

"They're having a wonderful reunion. I'm glad Shayleigh was able to confront her painful childhood memories and re-connect with someone from her past who was a healing force."

"I found it very difficult to be left alone with Brett all this time." Warren said, "I had to keep fighting off her advances."

"He wishes." Brett rolled her eyes.

"I was hoping the two of you were getting along better."

"For your sake, I gave it my best shot, hon, but he certainly didn't make it easy." Brett said, casting a cold glance at him.

215

"Your Aunt Annette was having a great chat with Emerald after the symphony concert the other night." Warren remarked to Sydney, pulling her closer.

"That Emerald knows anyone who's influential in Beavertown." Brett said, "She arrived here sixteen years ago as an artist and wife of a lowly civil servant. After three years in that apartment next door, they bought an old house in disrepair. As soon as Shayleigh moved out, they sold it and bought the showplace they've got now. They even begrudged her a decent roof over her head."

"They're quite a pair, Shayleigh's parents." Sydney said, "They're bitter and frustrated because their lives didn't work out the way they had hoped. They don't want Shayleigh to be happy, either. Hurting her and depriving her provides relief from their own pain. They get a sick pleasure out of seeing her suffer."

The rickety kitchen door opened and Shayleigh peeked out.

"Sorry to keep you guys waiting so long."

"It's okay, hon. I'm glad you had this time with Daisy." Brett said.

"Let's go back in." Shayleigh led them to the kitchen.

Daisy was humming to herself as she prepared tea.

"What a lovely surprise this has been! Imagine, after all these years, finding little Acacia! Not so little Acacia. You've grown into a beautiful young lady."

"I hope you're not upset with me for not coming forward sooner."

"No, dear. I'm just so pleased to see that you're all right. Promise me you'll come and visit me again."

"I promise."

"Sydney, dear, thank you for finding her."

"I'm afraid I deserve no credit for that, Mrs. Parker. When you said "Acacia", I had a strong feeling it had to be Shayleigh. There aren't very many Acacia Leighs out there."

Shayleigh drifted off as their voices faded into the inaudible hum of the warm evening air. She wondered what would have happened had she not met Brett that fateful night of the Sociology party at the Faculty Club...

...It was 1969, two weeks before Christmas. Ornate glass decorations in fuchsia and plum hung from the tree placed between the two adjoining rooms. Steeped in tradition, this corner of the campus had resisted relinquishing its formal elegance in the face of overwhelming pop culture. The rich dark wood, the claret velvet, chocolate leather, and jade marble bore testament to the generations of young minds who had stepped through the doors of the institution. Shayleigh did not know that many people at the party, but recognized familiar faces from her classes and exchanged greetings with those who appeared benign. She deliberately avoided eye contact with the promiscuous girls who carried themselves with an air of superiority. The steady flow of martinis kept her discomfort under control and concealed from other people. On her fifth visit to the bar, she heard a deep, throaty female voice behind her.

"Another martini drinker. We must be kindred spirits."

She turned around to find a deer-like woman in a black beaded gown. She was tall and slender, with enormous dark eyes. Her lustrous brown hair was in an elaborate up-do.

"I'll get yours." she placed a hand over Shayleigh's to prevent her from paying, "Frank, dear, put this young lady's drink on my tab and please give me another extra dry vodka martini."

"Yes, Mrs. Samson."

"Tell me, are you a Sociology major?"

"Yes I am."

"Are you alone?"

"Yes. I'm not good around people."

"Everyone's probably jealous because you're so stylish and beautiful."

"Me?"

"Of course you. Your dress is lovely. I'm sure you didn't get it around here."

"Thank you. I was visiting my Aunt Della in Arkansas last summer and she bought it for me."

"A Southerner!"

She nodded shyly.

"Nice to meet another ex-pat. I'm from Vermont myself but spent eighteen years in New York."

"I can't believe this! I spent my school years in New York and my summer holidays in Arkansas with my grandmother and aunt until I was ten."

"A fellow New Yorker! This gets better all the time!"

Frank served their drinks and the woman tipped him generously. The tall man grinned broadly.

"Let's find a quiet little corner and get better acquainted." she led Shayleigh to the lounge adjoining the bar, "It's too noisy in the main area."

They sat by the Palladian windows with a view of the river. The lights from the North side of Beavertown reflected on the water. It would be a matter of days before the river would turn to ice.

"I'm Bernadette Samson." the woman said, "My husband teaches at this madhouse."

"I'm Leigh. It's really Acacia Leigh Wallace."

"Acacia. What a pretty name!"

"Thank you. People have always made fun of it, so I just go by Leigh."

"Have you ever thought about combining the two to create a new nickname? How about Shayleigh?"

"I love it! Thank you!"

"I shall call you Shayleigh, then."

"Thank you, Mrs. Samson."

"Please call me Brett."

"Brett. I like that."

"I didn't like any of the nicknames for Bernadette, so I named myself Brett. Tell me, Shayleigh, what is a nice Southern Belle like you doing in a dreadful place like this?"

"You don't like it here, either?"

"Honey, I'm so homesick for New York, I can taste it! It's in my blood. The noise, the filth, the colorful characters, the glamor...My husband, Josh, decided some time ago he wanted to commune with nature in the Canadian wilderness. We packed up and came here. But my heart belongs in New York."

"I'm so glad I met you. And, to think I almost didn't come to this party!"

"I'm very happy that you did."

An ungainly man in a tweed blazer with brown corduroy elbow patches appeared to have spotted them from the far end of the hallway and began making his way toward them. He came around behind Brett and placed his arms seductively around her neck.

"Come on, gorgeous. The Wilsons are waiting. They have to get back soon. Their babysitter has to go home."

"I was just starting to enjoy myself. Oh, Josh, this is my new friend, Shayleigh. She's a New Yorker, too."

He nodded coldly.

"This grouch is my husband, Josh."

"Will you excuse us for a few minutes, please?" he pulled Brett away.

"Josh, that is not very nice. Shayleigh and I were just having a lovely chat."

"It's our obligation to make new graduate students feel at home."

"Why don't you ask Abe and Lois to arrange rides for some of them and drop you and whoever else can fit into their car off at the Hillside Pub? I'll drive Shayleigh home and join you there later."

"You drive a hard bargain. If you weren't so beautiful, I would never let you twist me around your finger like this, Brett Samson." he kissed her.

Brett returned to her seat.

"Is everything okay? Do you have to leave? Am I disrupting your plans?" Shayleigh asked.

"No, sweetheart. Everything's fine now. He's leaving with his friends. We can stay as long as we want."...

...After that evening, Brett disappeared without a trace. Shayleigh crossed paths with Josh Samson at all the university functions, always with a different woman at his arm. He avoided her glance uncomfortably. While babysitting for Clara, the Wilsons' young daughter, Shayleigh inquired about Brett when Mrs. Wilson was out of her husband's earshot.

"Brett and Josh are separated, dear. She went off to do her own thing. Being a faculty wife just wasn't her cup of tea."

The next time Shayleigh saw Brett was four years later, at the jewellery counter of the Five and Ten.

"Brett?" she tapped her on the shoulder.

"Shayleigh!" she glanced up and smiled, "You're a sight for sore eyes! How have you been?"

"Fine. How about you?"

"I'm all right. You look so thin, sweetheart. Have you been eating well lately?"

"I lost this weight last summer after a long bout with one of those pesky summer flus."

"It sure was a cold, damp summer. You poor treasure. Why don't you come out to my house for a meal tonight? It's nothing fancy, but I would love to get caught up with you and hear about your life."

"That would be wonderful. You look so beautiful, Brett. How are your kids?"

"Driving me crazy, as always. But I love them to pieces."

"Are you still living on Parkhurst Drive?"

"Josh and I aren't together anymore, hon."

"Mrs. Wilson said...I thought you might have stayed in the house."

"Not with those uptight neighbors. They were ready to tar and feather me. They didn't want a loose woman on her own within a close proximity of their husbands. Perish the thought! I might lure them away from their wives and destroy their families! That stodgy suburban prison wasn't for me, sweetheart. The boys and I are renting a Victorian house on Odell Avenue. Laurie's at boarding school."

"Oh, Brett, I'm sorry I was so insensitive."

"You're never insensitive, hon. The boys and I are all right. We get by. I give piano and vocal lessons to supplement my income from my job at the new club. Josh is not good with the alimony and child support cheques. He's got the house, and the sympathy of all the neighbors. He's living the life of Riley. Things are beginning to look up for me and the boys, at last. We had some pretty rough years for a while. This new residence is going to be lucky for us. I just feel it."

"It really has been a very long time, hasn't it? I wish I had been there for you when things weren't going well. I wish I could've done something to help."

"What a thoughtful thing to say. Those lean years are behind us now. Seeing you again is a very good omen."

"For me, too. I can't wait to see your house. I've always loved Odell Avenue. It's so pretty, with the park right across the street."

"I love it. We spent some time in the basement apartment of a bungalow in Skyline Acres. Those were dark days. Now, my Laurie wants nothing to do with me."

"She'll come around."

"I hope so."

"Of course she will. Where's this new club, Brett? I'm not up to date on the local night life."

"Chandler's. It's a jazz age style lounge. A real class act. Unusual for this neck of the woods. You must come and see it."

"I'd love to. I don't get out much. There isn't a whole lot to do on your own."

"You're not on your own anymore, hon. I'm here now. I'll bring you with me."

"I'd love that."

"Why don't we pick up a few groceries from the supermarket down the street before we go to my house? I'm afraid we'll have to walk, though. My old car gave up the ghost last year. I can't afford a new one. But I can't honestly say I'm upset. I hated driving."

"I can't drive to save my life!"

"We're a pair, aren't we? They say it's a sign of great intelligence, even though everyone treats non-drivers like half-wits."

"I'm so happy to see you again, Brett."

"So am I, sweetheart. Where are you living now?"

"Still at home. I don't make enough money at my library job to afford a decent apartment. Besides, my mother would never let me have a moment's peace if I were to live alone."

"Oh, hon, I've got a third bedroom at my place! Why don't you move in with us?"

"Are you sure? I can really rent a room from you?"

"We could be roomies. It would be so much fun."

"It would be fabulous! You've got yourself a lodger!"

"What about your parents?"

"I won't be living alone, so they won't start imagining all sorts of wild scenarios."

"It's a done deal. Let's celebrate. The boys will be thrilled."...

..."Shayleigh, hon, where did you go?" Brett was waving her hand in front of her face, "You've been off in your own thoughts for a long time."

"I'm sorry." she blinked in confusion.

"You're about to be married. You're allowed to be dreamy." she winked.

"You must be nervous, dear." Daisy said, "I remember my wedding night. I got into bed first and pretended to be asleep, but my husband was too clever."

Shayleigh smiled. She had survived the shipwreck. Would she survive the rescue? Would her life raft sink under her weight?

Chapter 13/ Promise Of Hope

Brett stood behind Shayleigh, her hands on her shoulders. The scorching August sun was pouring in the rows of casement windows on two of the walls and casting abstract shapes on the sumptuous hand-crocheted bedspread. The younger woman peered at her own image in the oval vanity mirror.

"Nervous?"

"I've never been calmer." she reached out to close one hand over Brett's.

"Not even...?"

She shook her head and turned to face her.

"Thank you for the talk, Brett. If there was ever a woman green enough to really need that classic mother-daughter talk, you're looking at her. I appreciate it more than you'll ever know."

"You'll always be my daughter." Brett kissed the top of her veil softly.

"I owe everything to you, Brett. You're the only real mother I've ever known. I owe you my sanity."

"You have your own strength to thank for that, hon."

"You are the source of that strength, Brett."

"You give me too much credit, and yourself too little."

"So do you. Brett, you deserve so much more credit than you give yourself."

"Thank you, sweetheart. You look so beautiful in my grandmother's dress. She would've been very proud to see it on a lovely young woman like you. You have her coloring, the true redhead's porcelain skin."

"This is the most exquisite dress I've ever seen."

"I'm happy to see it find the right home."

"Thank you so much, Brett. This was the perfect wedding."

"And the location is perfect, too. This is the one place I know you've always felt safe as a child and a teenager. Mindy's parents offering the house is a good omen. You and Sam are going to have a strong marriage. Honey, you stick to Sam like glue and never let go. Mindy's parents' marriage has lasted forty-three years and it's still going strong."

"Today was perfect. No one, not even my mother-in-law could ruin it."

"She sure is no shrinking violet. Did you see the way she pushed people out of the way to catch the bouquet?"

"She fancies herself a femme fatale."

"She wishes. She's not fooling anyone with her ostrich plumes and theatrical displays. She's just a girl from the wrong side of the tracks who likes to put on airs. Don't let her get to you. Keep her at arms' length. That sanctimonious bitch is not good enough to kiss your feet."

"You're so wonderful to me."

"I love you, sweetheart."

"I love you, too, Brett." she fell into her open arms, "I hope your ex-husband didn't mind driving out here to pick up the boys."

"He loved it, no doubt. Josh is so nosy, he'd do anything to see other people's houses. He must be green with envy after seeing this estate." she unzipped Shayleigh's gown and guided her out of it deftly.

Shayleigh changed into the long crisp cotton print circle skirt and white eyelet blouse for their honeymoon drive to Halifax. Brett wrapped the wedding gown in tissue paper and placed it back in its box as Shayleigh changed into white sandals and placed her wedding shoes in the original box and plastic store bag. Brett tucked the flat box under her arm and took the bag from her. They descended the stairs from the fifth to the fourth level of the contemporary-style mansion. Shayleigh joined Sam and stood uncomfortably in the living room. Emerald was laughing with the Cloutiers and the LeClercs, Henry's colleagues and their wives.

"They're leaving." a voice cried out.

All eyes were averted to the young couple. Shayleigh and Sam embraced Brett, Mindy's parents, Maggie, Daisy, and Sydney. Emerald pulled Shayleigh close and squeezed her elbow hard. The couple shook hands with the other guests and waved good-bye on their way to their rental car, followed by Mindy. The guests resumed their former positions, as though on cue. Emerald picked up the thread of her conversation with the slender, elegant Francophone women. Henry, who had not moved from his position by the picture window, glanced at his watch impatiently, which he had been doing every ten minutes since his arrival. Senator Marion Magnusson, a gentle elderly woman and her friend, Bessie McKillop, the sister of the former Governor General, joined him in the corner and attempted to engage him in polite conversation. Fidgeting with his serviette, he smiled uncomfortably and exchanged empty platitudes while his eyes darted around the room, resting occasionally on Sydney's ample curves accentuated by the bias cut of her blue polyester dress. Spying her crossing the room, he swiftly approached her and offered to bring the hors d'oeuvres tray in her hand to his companions. He brushed up against Sydney, mumbled an apology and let his hand rest momentarily on her hip. She crossed the room hastily to where Brett was standing.

"You've been on your feet all day."

"She looks beautiful, doesn't she?" Brett said brightly.

"Absolutely. Your grandmother's dress fits her perfectly."

"You'd think it was made for her. Didn't even need alterations. My mother and my sister Polly were also married in that dress. None of my nieces wanted it, so it was passed on to me for Laurie. I knew Laurie would want no part of it. If she ever does tie the knot, I'm sure it'll be in a bikini."

"Shayleigh is the fourth generation to wear it. You did her hair and make-up like a pro."

"Thank you, hon. Don't turn around, but that old pervert, Henry is checking you out."

"He's a creep."

"What a crew Shayleigh has to deal with. Look at Lynn Cullen over there."

A woman in a sequined dress was gesturing dramatically before her stoic audience consisting of three middle-aged women.

"Hobos living under her cellar and in her chimney." Brett rolled her eyes.

"I just hope Shayleigh's health improves."

"I knew John would come through for her. He says it is definitely a virus, and it's very real. He's referred her to a colleague in John's Bay. He gave her a prescription for a tonic."

"She has good color in her cheeks. Do you want me to help with those?" she motioned to the box and the bag Brett was carrying.

"I'm going to put them in the trunk of Tony's car."

"I'll do that." this was Tony.

"Where did you come from?"

"I'm never too far." he took them from her.

"You two go and get some fresh air." Sydney suggested.

"Thanks, hon."

Sydney returned to the room. Lynn was still holding court with her cousins Eleanor and Theresa, and her late husband's sister-in-law, Louise. Mindy, her mother Marjorie, and her friends Betsy and Kathleen were on clean-up duty. Betsy and Kathleen (or Kath, as she liked to be called) were both naturally slender like Mindy. Shayleigh did not know them well, but she was accustomed to Mindy's ever-changing, ever-growing circle of normal friends from normal homes that Shayleigh could not relate to. Sydney remembered Shayleigh talking about this sense of never quite belonging, something she herself understood well. Mindy's father, Bob was engaged in a conversation with Daisy and Maggie. Sydney began to make her way through the crowd, when Lynn Cullen's voice stopped her dead in her tracks.

"I give this marriage a year, three years at the most. I know my Sam is going to leave her when he comes to his senses. He's going to find a nice Catholic girl to settle down with. I tried to fix him up with so many nice girls, but he found fault with all of them. He told me he was going to marry a colored girl, if he got married at all."

"He was just trying to get your goat, Lynn. He knows how much you hate colored folk." Louise patted her on the shoulder.

"Them colored people never had nothing. Now they're making so much noise, demanding things they don't deserve. I don't want my Sam to be mixed up with them colored girls. They all have babies by the time they're fifteen. I don't want my Sam raising a bastard child. I want him to marry a good Catholic girl and live with me. That one refuses to live in my house. Wants a modern apartment. My house isn't good enough for her. She's making Sam pay rent to strangers. She's not even working or contributing to the household expenses. She's a moocher. This is the darkest day of my life. The day he told me he wanted to marry that one, my heart just broke in two."

"There, Lynn. Have some more tea, dear." Theresa reached for the teapot on the dining table and refilled her cup, "Don't worry. Marriages don't last long these days. You said so yourself. You'll have Sam to yourself again soon."

"They're not married in the eyes of God. A Justice of the Peace can't marry people. Without a church wedding, they're not really married. They're going to be living in sin. Oh, this is a dark, dark day, indeed."

"Don't work yourself up, Lynn, dear. You know you have to watch your blood pressure."

"Thank you, Theresa, dear."

Lynn caught a glimpse of Sydney glaring at her. Meeting her gaze with ice-blue eyes, she whispered to her companions:

"That nosy Jew's been eavesdropping on us. Have to keep my eye on her. She's trouble. That beanpole's trouble, too."

"You've got your work cut out for you, Lynn."

"Them people don't scare me. Them people in my cellar don't scare me, either. They send electric shocks through the floors. They want to kill me. Sam and that one don't care."

Sydney lifted her chin and brushed past them with a forced air of nonchalance. She smiled inwardly at the innocent image of the newlyweds setting out on their honeymoon, Sam with his arm around Shayleigh, smiling with boyish self-consciousness.

Brett and Tony were returning from his car. As they caught a glimpse of Emerald glaring at Brett, Tony pulled Brett nearer and kissed her cheek. Sydney smiled warmly at this image of devotion.

The crowd was thinning. Women were exchanging embraces; men were shaking hands. A steady flow of guests headed outdoors. Sydney felt Henry's eyes on herself and a chill shot through her. She ran outside, where Warren was ogling a girl with long raven hair.

"She's too young for you." Tony remarked to Warren.

Brett joined Sydney by the lamppost.

"Men..." Sydney shook her head in disgust.

"That smarmy pervert, Henry, still bothering you?"

"He gives me the creeps."

"What a cesspool Shayleigh grew up in."

"They're a miserable bunch. Emerald, Henry, Lynn. They don't want anyone to be happy."

"Speaking of the devil." she gestured discreetly in the direction of Lynn and her entourage approaching them. Lynn's tall, stylish friend Gerda and her husband walked briskly ahead of the others to the side of the road where their navy blue Crown Victoria was parked. The remaining members of the group stood in a circle, cackling until a middle-aged couple with two adult daughters emerged from the house. Sydney remembered them being introduced as Emerald and Henry's friends from John's Bay. Lynn's followers split into two cars, with Lynn settling into Theresa's car.

"Maggie and Daisy must be wondering where we are." Warren was behind Sydney, massaging her shoulders.

"Bob might have to light dynamite under some of the folks to get rid of them." Tony said, slipping an arm around Brett.

"We'd better get them home." Sydney said to Warren, "Excuse us."

Tony led Brett to a secluded corner of the garden.

"Stan is the best in the business. That's why I recommended him."

"I don't know what to do now that all my suspicions have been confirmed beyond a doubt."

"Have you decided whether or not you're going to tell her?"

"I've been staying awake every night since Stan contacted me. I don't want her to be hurt as a result of the fallout."

"That might be inevitable. When this hits the fan, there's going to be a lot of drama. I'll be right beside you when that happens."

They stood hand in hand, observing the departing guests in silence. The blazing afternoon sun frolicked relentlessly, showing no signs of cooling down despite the advanced hour. Laughter spilled out from the foyer through the open door. They were perfectly content to remain there until Marjorie and Bob bade their remaining guests good-bye and shut the door. The day had come to a close.

Chapter 14/ Science Fiction

A childlike voice echoed through the spacious marble foyer. Marge responded promptly.

"Hello, Miss. I'll tell Miss Dorothy you're here." she glanced around in search of the staff member assigned to opening the door to visitors, who had fled too soon, "Miss Dorothy, dear! You have a visitor." she called up the stairs, straining to be heard from the third floor.

"Thanks, Marge!"

"You can go up to her room." Marge said, observing the youthful visitor climb the stairs.

"I'm back!" the tall blonde skipped up the last few steps.

Dottie stood on the third storey landing watching the other girl's twin ponytails bobbing up and down in a dizzying motion, and her face growing larger with every step.

"Well, aren't you ecstatic to see me, Dormouse?" she twirled around in her green kilt, once she reached the top of the stairs.

"Hi, Clara. It's good to see you." she smiled warmly.

"So, what's new around here? Anything exciting since your last letter in May?" she flung herself on the bed.

"Nothing much. I'm sorry about the gap between letters. I'm terrible at that stuff."

"I'm here now. You can tell me everything in person."

"I wish there were something to tell. Nothing's really happened since that last letter. Same old boring stuff."

"My year was boring, too. A whole year in London, and I didn't meet any cute boys! Can you believe it? They were all scrawny and yucky. No meat on their bones."

"All the boys around here are the same, with nasty personalities to match."

"We should go check out some university guys. Hey, I'm glad your loser brother moved out. I didn't like him at all. He was even worse than my brother, if that's possible. Where is he now?"

"I don't know and I couldn't care less."

"Way to go, Dormouse. Now I can stay in his old room when I come over for weekends. I hope your maids wash the linens! Ugh! I don't want his diseases!"

They laughed.

"I was really shocked about Darnelle."

"Don't even mention her name."

"Maybe it was the other girl's fault, what's her name…Valerie?"

"Hilary. I've known Hil since kindergarten. She wouldn't be deliberately cruel. She's more of a follower, not an instigator."

"Darnelle seemed like such a nice girl in grade ten."

"I guess we didn't really know her."

"What an ingrate! After you took her under your wing when she was new, she turned around and stabbed you in the back like that! Who needs her sort, anyway? You've got me."

"Thanks, Clara."

"Last year must've been a bummer. Isn't Hilary going to be away in Taiwan or some place this year?"

"She left last week. Her dad's on Sabbatical. I'm glad your dad's Sabbatical was last year, not this year. Darnelle would have a field day with me."

"We'll just watch and see what she does without Hilary."

"She won't have any trouble finding new people to twist around her little finger. She's a master manipulator. All the teachers are under her spell, too."

"She's a show-off. Her family's dirt poor. None of them got through grade six. They think she's a genius and spoil her rotten. The arrogant bitch."

"Hilary didn't even say good-bye to me when she left. I'm sure she and Darnelle had a mushy farewell."

"They're stupid. Forget about them. Maybe they're in love."

"They like boys."

"Maybe they're bicycles."

"What does that mean?"

"It's when people are straight and gay at the same time. I was eavesdropping on my brother's girlfriend with her friends, and she said someone she knew was a bicycle, because she was in a gay relationship even though she had a boyfriend."

"How can someone be both? I thought you could only be one or the other?"

"I thought so, too, but Gwen knows a lot. She's been around. I'm sure she's right. She's a lot more experienced than all the experts."

"You're lucky. You know so much stuff."

"Naturally. No one else can be as captivating and brilliant as Yours Truly, Aralc, the ruler of Planet Zarik!"

"How's your writing?"

"Great. I've had plenty of time to work on it. The weather wasn't exactly conducive to outdoor activities. Oh, I've put you in it, too: Eittod, a visitor from the planet Tumra."

"That sounds really nice."

"Where do you want to go? "

"It doesn't matter."

"Let's get a sundae at "The Jade Palace"."

"Sure. I'll get a sweater." Dottie opened her closet to look for an appropriate sweater.

Clara picked up a record album from the top of the brass record rack and studied Jack's face on the cover.

"Now, there's a dreamboat." she sighed, "Don't you think?"

"Clara! He's my cousin!"

"Step cousin. So? You can still appreciate his looks."

"That's perverted."

"Dormouse, you're still a prude."

"He's family."

"I wouldn't mind having him in MY family!" she jumped off the bed, "Can you fix me up with him?"

"He's too old for you."

"I don't mind."

"Besides, he's engaged." she put on a loose off-white cardigan and pushed the closet door forcefully.

"Again? Doesn't he ever take a breather between floozies? Who is she this time?"

"A dancer named Linda."

"Eww."

"She's really snooty."

"I've got to find a way to break them up."

"She's got a mean streak. I wouldn't mess with her if I were you."

"Shucks! All the cute ones are taken."

"So are all the nice ones." Dottie pulled down the sleeves of her cardigan to cover her hands.

"Are you going like that? No make-up, your hair in a ponytail, your old jeans?"

"It's comfortable."

"You've got a lot to learn, Dormouse. Come on, let's go."

They bounded down the stairs, laughing.

"Is Brett Morrow still working at Jack's club?"

"She sure is." Dottie paused before a neighboring mansion to re-tie her shoelaces, propping up her left foot on the rung of an iron fence.

"Her ex-husband works with my dad, you know. I just adored Brett when I was a little kid. They used to come over to our house for dinner all the time. When they returned the invitation, Brett always included me. She treated me like an adult. I haven't seen her in ages, not since she and her husband split up. All the faculty wives say she has loose morals."

"They must be jealous because she's so pretty."

"When the ladies go into the living room after dinner, the men retire to the den to play cards and have a few after-dinner drinks. You wouldn't believe what they have to say about her."

"Must be really gross."

"They use words I've never heard before. I've got a secret listening post: the air duct in my room leads directly down to the one in the den. I can hear everything they're saying. They all want to sleep with Brett."

"Perverts!"

"It must be so nice to be beautiful and desirable, to have so many men lusting after you."

"You'll find someone, Clara."

"What's this about your Aunt Edna's daughter turning up after all this time? I read your letter three times to make sure I didn't imagine it."

"It's true. Sydney's really nice. She's dating Warren."

"Boy, it sure must be nice. All these older women have it made. Why can't we get dates?"

"They must have something we don't."

"Old age. We have to wait until we're on Geritol before we get boyfriends."

"You'll get someone soon, I'm sure, Clara."

"I go away for one year, and I miss all the juicy stuff!"

"That was the highlight of the year."

"And the Darnelle saga. If I'd been here, I would've given those two a piece of my mind."

"I appreciate that, Clara, but they would've turned people against you, too. It's best to stay away from people like Darnelle. They're poison."

"Nasty bitches. My mom says: 'What goes around comes around'. Something bad will happen to Darnelle one of these days."

"Don't hold your breath. Bad people are protected from suffering. They only have good stuff happen to them."

"You're too young to be so jaded, Dormouse. Those two really did a number on you."

"Their perfect lives will go on being perfect."

"If I could go out with Jack, my life would be perfect, too." Clara pushed open the door of Jade Palace; the interior was dark and empty.

"Are you sure they're open?" Dottie whispered.

"The door was open."

"Maybe they accidentally left it unlocked. We should tell them."

"Sh...h... I hear something. It's coming from behind that door."

"It's all in Chinese."

"Sounds like they're fighting."

"Clara, let's just leave. Something's not right. They've got no lights on, no music playing. There's nobody here except us."

"Business must be slow."

"Why don't we go over to Mimosa Gardens? It's a lot nicer."

"That place is for old people. These guys have the best hot fudge sundaes in town."

"Clara, this place gives me the creeps."

"Sh...h... The old guy's coming over."

The enormous black door at the back of the restaurant was pushed open and a scowling Asian man approached them.

"Yes? What you want?"

"We would like two hot fudge sundaes." Clara stated.

"Sorry. No sundaes."

"What about eggrolls?"

"No eggrolls." the man glanced furtively at the three young men who had entered the restaurant without making a sound.

The swinging door to the kitchen was opened again and a woman who appeared to be the same age as the older man exchanged meaningful glances with the young men.

"How about fortune cookies, then?" Clara persisted despite Dottie's nudging.

"No fortune cookies. You go now." he shot back coldly.

"Well, if that's the way you're going to be! Come on, Dormouse, let's get out of here! We'll take our business elsewhere!" she pulled Dottie by the hand and led her outside.

235

"What was going on in there?"

"They've got hookers working out back." Clara stated matter-of-factly.

"Clara, hookers? This is Beavertown, not Halifax!"

"Wake up and smell the coffee, Snow White. They've got hookers working out of a lot of businesses around here. Go to any out of the way, back street stores in old, run-down buildings run by immigrant families, and you'll find a lucrative escort service. Pizza places, convenience stores, repair shops, second-hand stores, any place run by Asian, Middle-Eastern, and East European immigrants. All have hookers."

"Do the cops know about this?"

"Of course they do. They're some of their best customers. They turn a blind eye to it. There's illegal gambling and drugs in the back of most Asian restaurants. And they have bookies, cock-fighters and all sorts in Greek and Lebanese businesses. A lot of insurance fraud, too. They burn down their own businesses and the firemen play along and don't put out the fires."

"Clara, are you sure someone wasn't pulling your leg when they told you this stuff?"

"My brother got it from a really reliable source, a cop. At Jade Palace, the password is "The Five Dollar Coke". Why do you think those guys were in there and didn't get kicked out? The old geezer knew what they were after."

"Clara, this is really gross."

"Do you remember that big fire down the street back when we were in grade nine?"

"How could I forget? It wiped out more than twenty businesses and an entire block. You could see the flames all the way from the other end of town."

"Remember how it took them a whole week to put it out? That's because the fire department was in on it and helped it spread to buildings that normally wouldn't have been touched by it."

"Why would they do that?"

"The same guy owned every single building that was destroyed, except for Marvin's. He bribed the fire department. It was insurance fraud."

"Clara, this makes me sick! There were so many people left homeless! All because of a rich guy's greed! I wish they could run him out of town."

"He owns everything your family doesn't. No one can touch him. Unless your family buys him out."

"I can't see them buying a bunch of seedy businesses and tenements with exorbitant rents. My family has some scruples. I hope people don't think my family's anything like that scum bucket."

"Don't worry about that, Dormouse. No one's that stupid."

"I lost my appetite, Clara. I still remember all the tenants of that apartment building, who were left out on the street. They were like one big happy family. They looked out for one another. I saved the newspaper article about it. One man went missing. He went in to save some of the others and never came out. They never found a body. He's technically still a missing person. He had a family, people who cared about him. People are disposable to that evil, greedy business man. I'm going to boycott every business he owns."

"That might be harder than you realize. He owns just about every business and rental property in town."

"I hope he goes bankrupt. I hope someone rips him off."

"Come on. Let's go to Zeeman's and get our sundaes there." Clara nudged her, "Don't be such a Gloomy Gus."

"I'll check to see if Sydney's working at the record shop, so I can introduce you."

"I'm really curious to check her out, and find out if she really is as nice as you say."

"She is. I wish there were more Jewish businesses in Beavertown."

"In a small town, you don't find too many Jewish families. They congregate in big cities like Toronto."

"It's a shame. I hope Uncle Sid, Aunt Edna and Sydney don't move to Toronto. Uncle Sid's relatives are all there."

"Don't worry: Warren'll keep Sydney here, and her parents'll stay for her."

"I'd better make sure Warren marries her."

"Don't get your hopes up. That's a pipe dream."

"Here we are." Dottie pressed her nose against the display window and strained her eyes to discern the figure obscured by the two tall customers. "It's Greeney." She stepped backwards, to collide with a plump, bespectacled woman with fine black hair, "Oops, I'm sorry! Oh, hi, Lea." she smiled upon glancing up.

"Hi, Dottie." the woman smiled warmly, "You look lovely. How are you doing?"

"Just fine, thanks. How are you?"

"I'm fine, too. Are you girls enjoying this gorgeous weather?"

"Oops, again. Where are my manners? Lea, this is my friend Clara Wilson. She spent the past year in London. Her dad was on Sabbatical."

"How wonderful."

"Clara, this is Lea Norbert, a family friend."

"I'm very pleased to meet you, Clara." Lea shook her hand.

"Nice to meet you." Clara muttered.

"Where are you two young ladies off to? Someplace romantic to meet your boyfriends?"

"We wish." Clara grumbled.

"By the way, Dottie, I saw Tony at Chandler's the other night." Lea said, "He was talking to a very beautiful brunette, one of the singers there."

"It must be Brett." Clara said.

"No, it must've been my new cousin, Sydney." Dottie nudged Clara, "She's new there. He's showing her the ropes, what with Jack being away and all. Sydney is Warren's girlfriend. They're practically engaged. Sydney and Warren, that is."

"What's Tony doing these days?" Lea continued, dewy-eyed under her horn-rimmed glasses.

"Busy. Real busy. He's taking care of both businesses, as well as his law practice. It keeps him very very busy."

"Yea, real busy." Clara echoed.

"It's all work, work, work, for poor old Tony." Dottie said.

"Will you please tell him I said hello?"

"Sure. I'll be sure and tell him."

"Thanks. It was good to see you, Dottie. You and I should get together some time, you know, for girl talk."

"That would be nice."

"I'll give you my number. Call me any time, okay?" she reached into her oversized brown handbag and produced a small notepad and a purple Bic Banana felt tip marker; she proceeded to scribble on the pad and tore out the top sheet which she handed to Dottie.

"Thank you." Dottie tucked it into her right front jean pocket.

"Bye, Dottie. Nice to meet you, Clara."

"Bye, Lea."

They watched Lea until she entered a new and cramped china shop.

"Nouveau chic." Clara said.

"What?"

"That new place she just went into. She's got the hots for Tony." she giggled.

"I feel terrible about that. She's such a nice person, and I like her so much, but my cousin hasn't been a good citizen as far as Lea's concerned, I'm afraid. He's pretty well used her, dated her on and off, more or less out of convenience. Men can be so stupid when it comes to matters of the heart."

"How did they ever meet, anyway?"

"Warren fixed them up. Everyone in my family was going on about Tony not meeting any nice women and still pining away for Brett, Warren picked out someone the family would approve of,

239

even though she wasn't Tony's type. Tony dated her just to get them off his back."

"What does she do?"

"She teaches at the French school. Warren knew her from teachers' conferences and stuff. I think Lea really got a bum deal. They all used her. I'm ashamed of the way my family uses people."

"Everybody uses people! Come on, let's get our sundaes."

At the lunch counter of Zeeman's, a young blonde about their age with blue eyeshadow took their order.

"Talk about tacky." Clara whispered to Dottie once the waitress was out of earshot.

"She seemed nice enough."

"Who wears blue eyeshadow anymore? It looks so sleazy. She must have a boyfriend. Doesn't everybody, except us?"

The blonde returned with their sundaes and smiled.

"A dollar sixty-five each."

Dottie removed the exact change from her back pocket. Clara avoided eye contact and grumbled unintelligibly as she fished out a five dollar bill from her tan disco bag. She counted the change that was returned to her and dropped it into her bag, almost disappointed that no mistake had been made.

"It's good." Dottie remarked, tasting her sundae.

"It's a rip-off." Clara sulked.

"She's back!" a shrill voice, eerily familiar to them, startled Dottie.

They turned around to find Darnelle settling into the bar stool on the other side of Clara.

"Clara!" she gushed, "You're back!"

"Hi, Darnelle."

"How was London?"

"It was great."

"We'll have to get together so you can tell me all about it."

"Sure." Clara played with her spoon.

"Why don't we take in a movie tomorrow night?"

"I'm busy. Maybe another time."

"We're starting our final year of high school. Can you believe it? What universities are you applying to?"

"I'm going to University of Toronto."

"I expect to get a sizable scholarship, no matter where I go. I may join you there." she jovially punched her in the arm, "I'm saving my money, because living expenses are going to be awfully high, but, hey, it sure beats staying around here!"

"Sure."

"My best friend in the world, Hilary, wants me to stay here and go to E.C.U. But she's going into Business and I'm going into Science, so I can go to medical school. What are you going into?"

"Arts." Clara said.

"You're smart enough to go into Science, Clara. Don't waste your time with Arts. Any dummy can get into Arts. Of course," she turned to Dottie, "Some of us have to actually work hard and try to get good grades, so we can get accepted and win scholarships. We don't have a family name to use as a ticket into E.C.U."

Dottie looked away.

"Listen, Clara." Darnelle placed an arm around Clara's shoulder, "I would really like your advice about something."

"What is it?"

"I'm looking for a birthday present for my sister."

"The one you'd like to kill?"

"I'm trying to decide between one of those leather ponytail holders with a pencil through them, or a set of sterling silver barrettes like the ones Sybil wears."

"Who the hell is Sybil?"

"She's this beautiful girl in the Spanish Club, who looks like Sylvia Plath."

"Don't know her."

"Please, Clara, can you come over and help me choose?"

"Come on, Dor, we might as well."

"Um...I meant just you, Clara."

"You two go ahead. I have to buy some stuff, anyway. I'll meet up with you at the checkout later, Clara."

"You sure?"

She nodded.

"Okay. See you in a bit." Clara followed Darnelle.

"Can I get you anything else?" the waitress returned to clear the sundae dishes.

"Maybe a coke." she pulled out the right change.

"Coming right up."

Dottie savored her chocolate colored sweet beverage in the tall curvaceous glass. The blonde waitress smiled each time they made eye contact. She smiled back warmly.

"Nasty piece of work, that girl who took off with your friend."

"Darnelle's something else."

"One of the popular girls, eh?"

A pretty and outgoing girl like this was not among the ranks of the popular girls? Dottie glanced at her name tag and saw "Laynie" in thin, black block letters.

"She sure is." Dottie responded, "Her favorite hobbies are stealing other people's friends and spreading malicious gossip."

"Stuck-up bitch. I hate her sort. I find girls in the Academic wing are all full of it. I'm so glad I'm in Commercial. All the girls get along. No one tries that one-upmanship stuff. You should switch. I know all the girls would love to hang out with you. We could have a lot of fun."

"Thank you. I wish I could. I would love it. But my family would never let me."

"That's a bummer. I'll see you at lunchtime, at school, then. Maybe we can eat together. My locker's in the first group of lockers on the first floor of the Commercial wing. I'll introduce you to the others."

"Thanks. I'd like that. I'm Dottie."

"I'm Laynie. See you at school. I'll get your change. You paid me for a large coke, but you got a medium."

"Don't bother."

"We're not allowed tips here. If there's extra cash in the till, Helen keeps it. I'll get your change." she laughed, "If you knew Helen, you wouldn't even want to eat here."

"I don't like Academic studies at all. Commercial would be so much more fun."

"Maybe you could take one elective from our wing."

"I hope the guidance counsellors allow me to."

"They're dinosaurs. They hate modern technology. Hope to see you at school, Dottie."

"Me, too, Laynie. Thanks."

They exchanged waves as Laynie approached a new customer to take her order. Dottie would have to make a purchase, as she had told Clara. The cosmetic department was nearby. A tube of lipstick would be a practical item. She had only been permitted to wear it since last summer, and even so, only beiges and pinks. A new color would be a welcome change. She did not know what to choose. Reds and burgundies were too vampy for her. Peaches and corals were too orangey for her taste. Could she wear sultry chocolate the way Sydney did? No, she was not sultry. She needed something fresh and original. Then, she saw it before her, beckoning her. Lilac! A frosted, creamy, almost mocha-kissed lilac. She smiled to herself as she carried it to the health and beauty aisle to select a box of extra absorbent sanitary napkins. A swift glance at the stationary aisle gave her an idea: She could buy markers like Lea's and use them for taking notes in university. They didn't care what kind of pens or markers you used once you were in university. She could take notes in pink, purple, green, turquoise, brown, orange and red. Until then, she could use them for writing letters to Jack.

By the time she found her way to the only checkout which was open, Darnelle and Clara were standing on the other side, their purchases paid for.

"Magic markers!" Darnelle shrieked, "Dottie, aren't you too old for magic markers? My ten year old brother has them."

"They're not magic markers." she stated proudly, "They're Bic Banana markers for writing. My cousin's girlfriend who's a teacher uses them. Charles Nelson Reilly does the commercial. I thought everybody knew that."

"Some of us have better things to do to occupy our time. You won't be allowed to use anything like that at school, anyway."

"It's for university."

Darnelle burst out laughing. Clara bit her nails and looked away.

"Purple lipstick?" Darnelle shrieked again, observing her purchases being placed in a plastic bag, "How wasteful! When would you ever get to wear purple lipstick? You'd look like you were dead and turning blue. It must be nice to have so much money to squander away on dumb things like gaudy make-up."

"It's not purple. It's lilac." Dottie corrected her.

"You're still using sanitary napkins, little girl? Haven't you graduated to tampons yet?"

"You'd better start saving your money for plastic surgery, Darnelle." a voice behind Dottie piped up, "There isn't enough make-up in the world to help your ugly face!"

Dottie turned around to find a girl from her English class she had only had occasion to exchange hellos with until today.

"Well, I never!" Darnelle tossed her long raven hair and turned on her heels, followed outside by a sheepish Clara.

"Thank you, Minette." Dottie smiled congenially at her new-found ally, tears of gratitude and warmth welling in her eyes.

"It's okay. I wasn't about to let her get away with that abuse. You're too nice to stand up for yourself, but I'm not."

"I appreciate that."

"See you at school, Dottie." the tiny bundle walked through the aisle for those without purchases and waved on her way out.

Dottie paid the cashier and tied her bag at the top to keep it closed. The ends of the knot resembled bunny ears. Outside, she found Clara alone, pacing.

"Ready to go?" she pounced on Dottie.

"I'm surprised Darnelle didn't spirit you away."

"I came with you and I'm leaving with you. Darnelle really isn't all that bad, you know. I think you should give her a second chance."

"Fat chance."

"I was going to ask you to go to her sister's birthday party with me tomorrow, but I guess you're not interested."

"I wasn't invited."

"You can come as my guest."

"I'd rather take a bath in a vat of acid. You go ahead and have a good time."

"She chose the doo-hickey with the pencil."

"That's nice. Dorelda's a nice girl. She's nothing like Darnelle. That's why they don't get along."

"I saw you talking to Minette."

"Yes, she's really nice."

Dottie was suddenly drained of all energy, and felt a migraine creeping up on her. She wanted to get away from Clara and go home to watch T.V. She just wanted to be left alone, in peace.

Chapter 15/ Discarded Lives

"Goldstein's Music Shop. Sydney speaking."

"Hi. I have to cancel again for tonight." Warren announced coldly, "I have a board meeting."

"That's okay."

"Well, see you around."

He hung up before she was able to get the words out. Blinking back tears, she hung up and turned on the phonograph in the corner. Jack was singing "We Were Lovers" in his boyish, sensitive style. It was not meant to happen this way. People who were engaged in relationships without commitments or emotional entanglements were meant to walk away unscathed, as she had observed. They were meant to collide and come apart without injury. Perhaps it was nothing more than a bruised ego for having been discarded callously. Perhaps Brett's warning had been more accurate than she had been willing to admit. Perhaps she was not sufficiently shallow to qualify for the status of modern womanhood. She had blindly thrust herself into a game whose rules had been unfamiliar to her. A change of scenery was what she needed. This upcoming trip to Toronto for Yom Kippur would be uplifting, nourishing for the soul. She was finally going to meet her father's side of the family. She was going to learn more about her Jewish heritage and be introduced to new people.

She heard the jingle of the bell over the door and turned around to find Dottie, her eyes strangely sunken.

"Dottie! It's good to see you. I haven't seen much of you lately."

"Hi, Sydney. Grade twelve is really demanding. I hate it."

"You'll find university much more enjoyable."

"I hope so. Are you guys leaving on Monday?"

"As far as I know, honey."

"I wish I were going with you. No doubt, Aunt Ethel's got some eligible bachelors lined up for you. I wish she would find some for me, too. If you don't like them, can you send them to me?"

"Oh, sweetheart!" she hugged her, "What would a young girl like you want with a bunch of boring middle-aged men?"

"I'm hard up."

"You're priceless."

"Sydney, did you and Warren have a falling out?"

"No, sweetheart."

"Aer you guys breaking up?"

"We're taking a break for a while."

"Are you going to get back together?"

"It's too early to tell yet, sweetheart."

"Do you want to get back together with him?"

"I'm not sure, honey."

"I thought you'd be the one to tame him."

"I don't think anyone can do that, Dottie."

...She remembered his solemn face across the dinner table three weeks earlier...

"I need more space. It's getting too claustrophobic. We need to start seeing other people and chill out for a while."

"Fine. All right."

"Don't look at me with those eyes, Stormy. I thought we had decided to keep things loose."

"I know. We did."

"Then, why the eyes?"

"I don't know what you mean."

"I told you not to fall in love with me, not to get too emotionally involved and clingy with me."

"I haven't."

"You can't fool me, Stormy. I can see right through a woman."

"You're wrong. I haven't made any demands from you, or asked for you to commit to a monogamous relationship."

"You're too smart to be that obvious, but you're smothering me, Stormy. I can't breathe. You're emotionally intense. You can't help the way you are. But, frankly, it scares the hell out of me."

"I'm sorry. I didn't realize there was something wrong with being oneself." she rose abruptly, banging her knee against the side of the table.

"Where are you going? Sit down. Don't create a scene. People are looking."

"I don't really care." she winced.

"Come on. You're being childish."

She ran out to the street, a small part of her hoping against hope he might follow her, however, ended up walking home alone...

...His subsequent calls, allegedly to talk things over, seemed to dissolve into predictable cancellations...

"Sydney, if you marry one of the men you get fixed up with, it means you'll move to Toronto."

"Oh, Dottie, I haven't even met them yet, and you've got me married off!" she laughed unexpectedly.

"I don't want you to leave. You just got here."

"Sweetheart, there's no chance of my meeting anyone suitable. Besides, my family's here. I've got a job I love, friends I care about. I wouldn't give up all of this."

"You're not going to let Warren drive you away?"

"Of course not."

"It's going to be uncomfortable to bump into him at family functions."

"I think we can get past it. We're adults. There's no need for this to be messy, and affect other people."

"Being away might help. You know, to lessen the impact."

"You're right. We'll get past this."

"Toronto will be fun. You'll meet all your relatives."

"I really am looking forward to spending Yom Kippur with extended family. Discovering my heritage is quite exciting."

"You'll get to know Jacob. He's your first cousin. I haven't seen him in at least six years. I wish I could go, too, and visit Jacob. Mom and Dad never let me go anywhere. They go off to Europe and leave me behind. The only time they took me with them was to London once. It rained the whole time. Mom came down with the flu, so we never left the hotel."

"Oh, Dottie!"

"I amused myself by imagining I was in an Agatha Christie novel and a murder was about to take place."

"You're remarkable."

"Jacob's a big business executive now. I'm sure he wouldn't have time for little old me."

"I'm sure he'd love to see you."

"He hasn't written for months. We used to confide in each other about all kinds of stuff. Now that he's engaged to Mimi, he has no time."

"Dottie, sweetheart, Jacob's never going to stop being your friend, no matter what. I'm sure there's a very good reason for his tardiness in writing."

"I have a present for him. Would you mind giving it to him?"

"I'd love to."

"It's a rare two-record album of "Porgy And Bess" with Cleo Laine. Greeney had to pull a lot of strings to get it for me."

"I'll make sure he gets it."

"Living in Toronto, he can get all the rare recordings he wants. He might even already have this one."

"Even so, coming from you, this will mean a great deal to him."

"Thanks, Sydney. I'd better get going. See you tonight at dinner."

"See you tonight, sweetheart."

Once alone, she realized that Jack's record had long since grown silent. Placing the needle back on the same side of the record, she returned to the counter and the new catalogues of sheet music. Her temporary insanity had ended. Her life had returned to its lacklustre familiarity. She wondered what Toronto had in store for her.

* * *

Sydney leaned against the metal railing of the balcony with the sweeping view of the city. At this height, she felt embraced by the clouds. Toronto was exceptionally warm for early autumn.

"What would you like to drink?" a male voice called out from inside.

"Whatever you're having." she called back.

"Martinis all right?"

"I'd love it."

"Coming right up."

The sounds of the city below them were muffled. Buses and cars scurried past like industrious insects. Other high-rise buildings surrounded them, sturdy, reliable denizens of concrete and steel, indestructible, yet softened by glass and stucco.

"Here we are." a thin, dark-haired young man emerged through the sliding patio doors with two martini glasses, and handed one to her.

"Thank you." she smiled.

"I'm very sorry about the fiasco. Mom feels absolutely dreadful."

"It's not her fault."

"When word got out that she was looking for eligible bachelors for a Jewish girl from a nice family, all the nut jobs started coming out of the woodwork. They thought this might be a chance to marry off their sons."

"No doubt, those with nice sons made sure to keep them away from the likes of me. Who would want them to fall into the clutches of a woman with a sordid past? And a lounge singer, to boot."

"This entire matchmaking custom is pretty ludicrous in the first place. It's totally humiliating for both men and women. Why do they continue putting people through such torture, generation after generation?"

"Old traditions die hard."

"I couldn't believe Mrs. Weiss would actually send Milt as a candidate." he shook his head.

"Thank you for rescuing me from him, Jacob."

"When I saw him sneaking into the kitchen after you, I knew what he had in mind. Then, there was that pretty boy Marty Kovacs."

"Talk about cold as ice. He made it clear from the moment he walked in that he couldn't wait to get out of there. When his mother asked him to dance with me, he was horrified. He sulked the entire time we danced."

"He's a fool. With his disposition, he'll never get a date with a real woman. He couldn't appreciate a special woman like you."

"Thank you."

"Marty has a standing appointment at the massage parlor every Friday. His mother's telling people he's going to Hollywood to seek his fortune. With his winning personality, the only parts he's qualified to play are characters in a wax museum."

"Who knows? There might be a big demand for those parts."

"You never know. Let's not forget Isaac Steinberg, the amorous one." he placed his drink on the green patio table, "He's a neurotic. His brother says he draws up a strict schedule to follow around the clock, and carries it around in his pocket all day. Pity the woman he marries. Can you imagine what he'd be like? "It's precisely eleven-o-five, dear. We must make love now, because this is when I scheduled it in.". Any woman who's had one date with him avoids him like the plague. He sure seemed to be sweet on you."

"They were all interesting characters." she sipped her drink, "I didn't have high expectations, anyway. No one would want their sons to marry a thirty-seven year old lounge singer. I'm not anybody's idea of a good catch."

"Sydney, don't speak that way. You are a very classy lady and any man should feel honored to have you as his wife."

"Thank you." she lowered her eyes.

He leaned over to kiss her cheek. His sporty, green aftershave lingered in her nostrils.

"I feel I've known you all my life, Sydney."

"I feel the same way, Jacob."

"I can talk to you about anything."

"Likewise."

"I'll refresh the drinks." he gathered the glasses.

She returned to the view of rooftops and chimneys of other balcony people like them, sunbathing alone, or gathered around tables with friends, couples stealing kisses, all miniature dolls in pre-fabricated doll condos.

"You have such a lovely view from this balcony, Jacob." she said, hearing his footsteps behind her.

"It's very relaxing to come out here on warm days, and watch the hustle and bustle of the city. It's calming at night, too." he placed the drinks on the table and joined her by the railing.

"Jacob, did you just touch my shoulder?"

"No." he smiled, perplexed.

"It must have been a spirit friend, then." she smiled.

"Spirit friend? You mean ghost?"

"I guess that's how they're sometimes referred to."

"You're so calm about it."

"I feel very comfortable around spirit visitors. More so than the living."

"What about evil spirits?"

"We meet just as many, or more evil spirits among the living each time we venture out and meet new people at social gatherings. We have more to fear from the living than we do from the spirit world. Our society frowns so much upon communication with the dead, but social gatherings are revered, though they represent a far greater danger."

"This is absolutely fascinating. Can you actually hear or see these spirits?"

"I'm not that evolved. I can only hear or see them in a dream, when they have a message for me."

"How do you know it's not just a regular dream?"

"You just know."

"How can you tell if they're around when you're awake?"

"I can feel their touch, smell their cologne, feel a vibration, and have an awareness of a presence."

"Can you summon them when you want?"

"They come to me when they choose. They sense when they're needed. But when I feel I really need their help, I do call out to them. They respond with reassurance and support."

"Doesn't it feel like you're being watched?"

"They try to be as unobtrusive as possible. They co-exist with us very peacefully. That's why most people aren't even aware of their presence."

"This is incredible."

"I realize it's all too far out there. I did not consciously seek this out. It's been this way all my life. For the longest time, I didn't even realize other people did not have spirit friends or excursions to the other side. I find it all quite comforting."

"This blows me away."

"We all have the power of Astral Projection at our fingertips. We just need to develop it. We all send out a certain energy into the universe. There are bound to be collisions."

"I've always wondered about spirits and angels, especially after...But I never knew anyone I could talk to about this before."

"I smell flowers...Gardenia...Do you smell it?"

He sniffed and shook his head.

"Jacob, we are not alone."

"Gardenia. That was the perfume she always wore."

"She's here."

"But I can't see her! I can't feel her!"

"It's okay." she took his hands in her own, "She's watching over you, Jacob."

He sought comfort in her arms. She enclosed him with protection. The warmth of his body was soothing. She did not want to let him go just yet. She shut her eyes and pulled him nearer. The truth was too frightening in the glaring afternoon sun.

* * *

Orange fingers climbed up the faded green curtains with a sinister crackle. Long-haired reptiles in garish costumes were brushing hot wax from tin cans on to squares of cotton before them in complete oblivion. A mustachioed bandit strolled leisurely up and down the aisles, critiquing each masterpiece. Dottie glanced up to find herself face to face with the orange intruder.

"Mr. Sawyer! The curtains are on fire!" she screeched.

The bandit averted his gaze to the dancing dragon above the hotplate where a large pot of melting wax spewed out lava angrily.

"Everyone out! Now!" he commanded.

Dottie gathered up her portfolio and followed the others outside to the lobby.

"Hey, Dorky, where're you going?" a voice from the other side of the maze of acid orange lockers called out, "Why aren't you in class?" Clara peeked her head between metal rows of identical metallic monstrosities.

"There's a fire in the Art Room."

"Why aren't they sounding an alarm or evacuating the building or something?" she was beside her now, clutching her clarinet.

"Mr. Macho Sawyer wants to be a hero and put it out all by himself. And he doesn't want to get into trouble for his negligence. They never evacuate, anyway. There were three fires in Chem labs last year. We only found out because of the putrid smell.

There was no alarm or anything. They don't want to set three thousand inmates loose on Beavertown Mall across the road and lose track of them."

"All the fire doors are padlocked. If a fire ever got out of hand, none of us would make it out alive. We'd be barbecued."

"That's the idea."

"Eww...I smell it now. It's gross!"

"Burning wax."

"Disgusting. What were you guys doing with wax, anyway? Having a séance?"

"Batik."

"You mean that hippie stuff? How tacky."

"Are you on your way to Music class?"

"I was. The Music Room's next door to your nuclear waste site. I don't think we have class now."

"Clara!" a tall, gangly boy with dark-rimmed glasses ran toward them, carrying a beat-up trumpet, "Music's cancelled. Mr. Hall said it stinks in the Music Room. They had a fire in the Art Room, those dope heads."

"Dottie here was in that fire, you know."

"Oh, I see." he cast a hostile glance in Dottie's direction, "Hey, Clara, why don't we go the Caf for a sticky bun?"

"Well...Uh...Sure." Clara turned to Dottie uncomfortably, "See you later Dor."

"Sure. Bye." she started toward her locker.

Girls with long hair were smooching with their boyfriends and exchanging hushed obscenities. Everyone except her appeared to be one half of a couple. Opening her combination lock, she tossed her portfolio into her locker. Gathering up her books for her next class, she locked up again.

"Hi, Dottie!" she heard a cheerful voice behind her.

"Minette!" she beamed.

"Darnelle pestering you again?"

"I haven't seen her today. I'd like to keep it that way."

255

"Let's keep our fingers crossed. I didn't know you had a free period now."

"I normally have Art right now. But the Art Room just burnt down."

"My stars! Are you okay?"

"No one was hurt, but the room's going to need a lot of work before we can use it again."

"I'm sorry."

"Everybody in that class is stoned. By tomorrow, they won't even remember what happened. Neither will Mr. Sawyer. He doesn't spend much time on this planet himself."

"This means you'll have a free period for a while. We can hang out. I have a free period now."

"That's wonderful!"

"Since we don't have the same lunch, we don't get that much time to hang out at school. This'll be a treat."

Dottie was aware of a warmth, much like hot chocolate, a secure and contented feeling.

Past the final cluster of lockers around the corner, Dawn emerged out of the shadows and came waddling toward them in yet another grease-stained T-shirt.

"Hey, Dopey, you got yer French homework done? Gimme it!" she held out her hand.

"Her name is Dottie and she is not going to do your work for you anymore! Go away and crawl back under your rock, and leave Dottie alone!"

"Yeah? Sez who?"

"Says Minette. Remember that. If you mess with her, you answer to me. Capiche? You dig? Tu comprends?"

Dawn scowled, eyeing Minette with narrow eyes.

"Scram!" Minette motioned to her, "Beat it! Sayonara! Arrividerci! Adios! Au Revoir! Get lost!"

Dawn walked away, casting occasional glances over her shoulder.

"Thank you, Minette. I really admire the way you stand up to people."

"This place is toxic. I can't wait to graduate."

"Me, too."

"School's no place for the sensitive. It breaks the spirit. It's life-destroying. You've got to be tough on the outside, no matter how much it hurts on the inside."

"I wish I could be more like you."

"You're perfect the way you are, Dottie. Outside this prison is a world aching for a gentle, nurturing soul to bring sunshine into people's lives, to heal the sick and the poor."

"I wish I were more assertive. When Cathy was threatening my life last year for no reason, I just walked away and said nothing."

"That was just as well. That little tart is criminally insane. She didn't even know you and tried to kill you. It's best not to tangle with her sort."

"Minette, what are you doing after school?"

"I usually just walk home alone."

"So do I. Why don't we walk together?"

"Let's meet here by your locker and stop by that greasy spoon "Joe's" on the way for a pogo."

"What's a pogo?"

"It's a hot dog fried in batter and served on a stick. It's delicious. When I have a bad day at school, I usually grab one on the way home to cheer myself up."

"Sounds yummy."

"You're sure Clara won't mind?"

"When she's not walking home with Darnelle and her cronies, she's stalking Edgar and any other boys she finds "cute" in her Music class."

"Has a thing for musicians."

"Has a thing for all members of the opposite sex."

"I see her in action at lunch time. I keep an eye out for all those guys since I have their lunch hour. I'm glad Laynie has your lunch hour. She's a nice girl."

"It's going to be fun you and me walking home together."

"I didn't know you walked, too."

"I didn't know you did."

Both laughed.

Dottie smiled inwardly. Her world was safe and filled with sunshine once again. Having this wise, unconditionally accepting friend was a soothing, healing breeze. She only wished she could hold on to her, and navigate the ocean of adolescence together with her. She wished their friendship would remain solid into old age, no matter what choices both of them made along the way.

Chapter 16/ Unspoken

Their laughter rang out in the hallway of the high-rise, unnoticed by blasé city dwellers. A trail of small puddles behind them darkened the cocoa-colored floor tiles in the corridor. He unlocked the burnished wood door and shook out his umbrella into the hallway once she was inside.

"I'm so sorry about all this! I had no idea the weather was going to turn. I thought we could just take a nice leisurely walk over to Simpson's."

"It's okay, really. It was fun." she stood, drenched and shivering, her hair dripping, her jersey dress clinging to her, revealing her undergarments.

"The umbrella was useless." he said, his own hair and face dripping, his green polo shirt clinging. He stepped effortlessly out of his loosely-tied sneakers and placed them beside the open umbrella.

"Why don't you get out of those wet clothes, Sydney?" he attempted to look away from her breasts molded in green jersey, "You can get changed in the bathroom. I'll give you a bathrobe. I can take your clothes to the laundry room and put them in the dryer later."

From the linen closet down the corridor, he produced two white terry cloth robes and handed one to her.

"Help yourself to the clothes hangers in the bathroom. I'll get changed in the kitchen. If you need anything, give me a shout."

She hung her dress from the shower rod, however, hesitated when it came to her undergarments. She rolled them up into a tiny bundle and tucked them into a towel. She concealed the inconspicuous roll in the back of the basket of face cloths on the vanity. Tightening the sash of her robe, she emerged from the

259

bathroom to find Jacob in the matching robe, holding up a soggy bundle of his own.

"Make yourself at home." he smiled, "I'll hang these in the bathroom and get us some brandy."

"That sounds delightful." she tucked her feet under her on the love seat and picked up a thin book on modern architecture from the coffee table. She could hear Jacob singing "How Long Has This Been Going On?" from the bathroom.

"We never did make it to the left-wing book store." he said when he returned, "But there's always tomorrow."

"Jacob, are you sure you want to waste another day of your vacation with your old cousin when you could be out having fun with your friends?"

"You're much better company." he handed her a brandy snifter, "I can see them any time, but how often does my beautiful cousin visit?"

At this unexpected declaration, she blushed. He put on a jazz record and sat on the floor by her feet.

"Your mom says you're engaged to a lovely girl." she said.

"Mimi and I are going through a rough patch right now."

"I'm sure you'll work things out."

"Meems and I barely know one another. Our parents arranged our engagement. I certainly have a great deal of respect for her. She's twenty-eight, has a successful career in Public Relations. She's bright, ambitious, and vibrant. Our ages and careers are similar, as are our family backgrounds. But these is no spark, no deep connection."

"Like the one you had with Ella."

"You can never replace something as perfect as that."

"It's not replacing. Ella is always going to be a deep part of you, but she would want you to share yourself and your life and experience a caring relationship again with the right person. Ella would want you to move on and be happy again."

"I don't know if that is possible."

"Dottie was telling me that Tony Horncastle experienced that type of pain when his wife, Adele passed away. It took him years, but he did move on. He fell in love again, with my friend Brett."

"I remember Dottie writing about them. Apparently, the family doesn't approve of Brett."

"Brett has pulled away and refuses to commit because of that. I think it's totally out of line for his family to interfere. No one has the right to stand in the way of love."

"I agree with you. From what I understand, they didn't approve of Adele, either."

"When Dottie starts bringing home her young men, they're going to give her just as much grief."

"I hear you were dating Warren Horncastle for a while. I couldn't believe my ears. He's a cad, a total jerk."

"And much more. A lapse in judgement on my part. I was duly warned, but didn't listen. Now I've learned my lesson."

"Have you ever been in love, Sydney?"

"No. I've lived a reclusive life. The only men I've been with – and there have been only two – were abusive."

"They didn't deserve you. Men should be showering you with gifts and flowers."

"That is not likely to happen in this lifetime."

"You are a beautiful, passionate, exciting woman. Any man with half a brain would fall in love with you and cherish you."

In the uncomfortable silence that followed, both of them lowered their eyes.

"I'll get you a refill." he nodded toward her empty glass.

"That brandy really hit the spot." she smiled weakly, handing him her glass.

He returned with her brandy. As he bent down, the front of his bathrobe fell open. She looked away. He fumbled with his sash to cover himself. His warm hand closed on her trembling fingers. She kept her eyes lowered. He knelt before her, wiping a tear from her eye with a fingertip. She attempted to speak, however, no words came out. He took both of her hands in his and pulled her to her feet.

"Do you know how beautiful you are?" he caressed her cheek.

She let out a moan as his lips sought hers, and his fingers struggled with her sash. He led her to the bedroom, darkened by the drawn blinds. He kissed her again and again. His fingers deftly explored her body. Not like Warren. He was nothing like Warren. With Jacob, there was tenderness. It was not about pursuing selfish desires or an obsessive admiration of his own technique, but a genuine need to please her. There was no hurry with him. He was willing to take his time for her. When both of them collapsed in exhaustion, he kissed her hair.

"Any regrets?"

"How can you ask me that?"

"I'm glad all your blind dates were duds. I want you all to myself."

"What about Mimi?"

"For all I know, she could be with someone else by now. This is the first time since Ella's death that I've felt this connection with a woman."

"Jacob, you and I are first cousins."

"I don't care."

"You know we can't let his happen again."

"I refuse to accept that there's anything wrong with what we've done."

"It was beautiful, and I'll always cherish it, but..."

The sound of the rain on the window pane was magnified in the silence. She shut her eyes and allowed the tranquility of the afternoon wash over her. In the security of his arms, she surrendered to an innocent slumber.

* * *

The young woman in the photograph smiled in innocence. Her finger traced the contours of her chin-length hair styled in a conservative bob befitting a woman in her profession. Her fluid brown eyes were kind. She admired her flawless ebony skin and white teeth. The bouquet of blood-red roses supplied by the photographer were almost a blemish on her immaculate nurse's uniform. She heard the bell announcing the arrival of a customer, followed by a strange falsetto.

"Excuse me. I'm looking for the latest album by that gorgeous dreamboat, Jack Chandler." Warren was leaning on one elbow on the counter, smirking.

"I'm afraid it's sold out, Miss." she smiled.

"Where've you been hiding since you came back from your little family reunion?"

"I haven't been hiding. It's just been very busy."

"I've got reservations at seven."

"Warren, I'm sorry I can't."

"This is your night off."

"I know, but I have a commitment."

"Cancel it."

"I can't."

"Who's the guy?"

"It's not a man."

"I had no idea you swung both ways."

"I'm meeting Dottie here after work to visit the cemetery and Ella's church."

"Why this keen interest in my late niece all of a sudden?"

"Tomorrow would have been her twenty-eighth birthday." she shot up a disapproving glance at him.

"I know when she was born: October the twenty-ninth, five days after my birthday. Don't look at me like that. Ella was a sweet kid. Nothing like my sister Frances, her mother. Ella was fine until she met up with that twit. He messed with her head. I'll bet he's the one who's been filling your head with talk about her. It must have been

263

pretty boring up in Toronto if you had to spend time with your cousin."

"Jacob's a kind, sensitive young man."

"Touchy about our family, are we?"

"People who live in glass houses shouldn't be throwing rocks."

"I'm impressed. You've come back a lot gutsier. Did you miss me?"

"There was a whirlwind of activity. I had no time to myself."

"Come on, admit it. You missed me. How much fun could it be to have people trying to marry you off to every half-wit and social reject?"

"I hope you enjoyed your birthday."

"Sorry I couldn't celebrate it with you. You know how it is: First, friends from work took me out. Then, the family wanted an intimate celebration. We'll have our own celebration, don't worry. Thanks for the present. I'll read it over Christmas. So, when are you two ladies going to be back?"

"I can't say. I've never been to a Pentecostal church before."

"Ella's foster parents taught her well. I just find it creepy that you're so interested in her."

"I feel she's a kindred spirit."

"You should focus your attention on the living. Like me."

"What's wrong with paying my respects?"

"Nothing. Go ahead. Take your time. No point in my waiting around. You don't look like you're up for an evening out, anyway. You've really let yourself go. Blotchy skin, dark circles under your eyes...You look like the crypt keeper."

"Thank you."

"I've noticed you're getting quite a gut. Too many matzah balls?"

"You sure know how to flatter a woman, Warren."

"Honestly, Stormy, you look like hell. I'd do something about it, if I were you. You're showing your age."

Her age. In fourteen days, she would be thirty-eight. What did she have to show for it? Nothing had changed. Nothing would

264

change. She would remain forever banished to the peripheral existence reserved for rejects and vagabonds.

Chapter 17/ The Parting

Sydney's hand rested lovingly on her father's shoulder as she stood behind him.

"Hi, sweetheart." he glanced up at her, his eyes overflowing with love.

"What are you reading, Dad?" she bent down to kiss his smoothly-shaven cheek.

"Bernard Malamud." he placed his gilded bookmark on the page he was reading and closed the thick hard-cover book to reveal its title, "I quite enjoy his short stories."

"Is it all right if I read it after you're done?"

"Of course." he stroked her cheek, "Sweetheart, are you feeling all right?"

"I'm just fine. Why wouldn't I be?" she sat on the Turkish carpet at his feet beside his wheelchair.

"You've lost the color on that beautiful face and the spark in those lovely eyes of yours. You haven't been able to keep anything down. I'm worried about you."

"It's probably just a virus I picked up in Toronto. Please don't worry about me, Dad."

"You ought to see the doctor about it, dear. I don't mean to nag, but we've been back from Toronto for quite a while, and your health has been getting worse, not better. This is too long to still be feeling the effects of a virus. I wish you'd make an appointment with Dr. Stein."

"It's nothing to worry about, Dad. I'm healthy as a horse." she kissed his cheek again and clutched his bony hand.

"You've been tiring easily and feeling light-headed, too."

"If it makes you happy, I'll call and make an appointment today."

"Sydney, dear, please leave the laundry and the morning dishes. Today's Alice's day to come in to clean."

"Dad, I'm here now. You should not have to pay a cleaning lady to do these things."

"Sydney, you are our daughter, not the hired help. We don't want you doing housework."

"I need to pull my own weight. I don't like to be a freeloader."

"Sweetheart..." he held her face in his hands, "You are our precious daughter. How can you call yourself a freeloader?"

"You drive a hard bargain." she kissed his hands, "I'll be off now, to run some errands. I'll take that bag of clothes to the Salvation Army."

"I'll get Ryan to drive you."

"I don't need a ride. It's only five blocks. The bag isn't that heavy."

"Honey, please. For me. Indulge me to pamper my daughter. I have a lot of years to make up for. I don't like to see you straining yourself."

"If it makes you feel better, I'll accept a ride. But you know you're spoiling me rotten."

"You deserve to be spoiled. It's long overdue."

"You know, I really could use the exercise." she put on her grey rabbit fur coat, "My coat's getting awfully tight."

"You need a new coat. You pick one out and charge it to our account."

"You've spent enough on me for my birthday. Besides, I can wear my wool coat with the big round buttons."

"That coat's not warm enough for Beavertown winters."

"I'll get myself a warm coat. Please put your wallet away."

"You drive a hard bargain yourself."

"Look who I take after."

"I'm sorry you didn't meet any nice men in Toronto, dear, but don't worry. There's someone out there for you."

"Your daughter's an old maid, Dad. You might as well face it."

"Back in my day, the fellows wouldn't have left you alone. Modern men have gotten too lazy. They want women to do all the pursuing, and then they settle for the first one that comes along. In the old days, we knew how to tell quality. Any man worth his salt would have done everything in his power to win your heart. You're a diamond among cheap glass. I knew your mother was a diamond the moment I laid eyes on her."

"I wish I could've lived back in those days when romance and chivalry were still in style. All men are spineless wimps these days, waiting around for vulgar women to lead them by their noses."

"Aunt Ethel didn't have much luck finding the type of young men she was hoping to."

"Maybe their age was the problem. Men my age are lost causes. I would've liked to meet older, distinguished gentlemen. They would've been kind and considerate."

"The next time we're in Toronto, she might be able to match you up with some. Warren has let you down, hasn't he, darling? I was afraid of this."

"Warren's not the one for me, Dad. I don't know who is, or if anyone is. Maybe I'm meant to be alone."

"Come here." he opened his arms to enclose her, "I love you so much, my Sydney."

"And I love you, Dad."

She gathered up the bag of clothing from the hall closet as he phoned Ryan.

"I'll be back soon, Dad."

"Good-bye, sweetheart."

Ryan, who had arrived promptly from his garage apartment across the courtyard, took the bag out to the car, and held the door open for Sydney.

"You don't have to wait for me, Ryan. I can walk back." she said as he pulled up beside the curb in front of the Thrift Shop.

"Your father wouldn't hear of it, Miss."

"We'll just have to humor him, then, I guess. Why don't you have a coffee and relax? I'll meet up with you at the deli in an hour, okay?"

"Yes, Miss. Thank you." he held the door open for her once again and retrieved the bag from the trunk, "I'll take it in."

"No, thank you, Ryan. You've done enough. Go get a coffee on me." she pressed a five dollar bill into his palm.

"Thank you, Miss." he held open the door of the shabby shop housed in a tired, dirty white clapboard building.

"Miss Goldstein." a plump woman with a grey bun emerged, "You've got more goodies for us. Your family's always so generous."

"I hope these will be useful." she handed her the bag.

The woman peeked in and moved the items around for a closer examination.

"These look hardly worn. You folks take good care of your things."

Sydney caught a glimpse of a tall, stately black woman along the back wall, thin and proudly upright in a drab olive sack dress ending abruptly at the knees, and a bulky brown cardigan. Her silver hair was pulled back into a severe bun at the nape of her neck. Aware of the woman's frequent glances at her coat, Sydney smiled at her. The woman looked away.

"Mrs. Carmichael," Sydney whispered to the clerk who was sifting through the bag, "Who's that woman?"

"That's Eunice Drummond." she replied knowingly, "She's always here."

"I've seen her at the Five and Ten and the Valor Meat Market before."

"Eunice is quite a fixture at I.O.D.E. rummage sales, as well. She can't even afford second-hand things, but she's too proud to accept charity."

"She's not wearing a coat."

"She doesn't have one, I suppose. Most likely, gave it to that useless daughter of hers."

"How did she end up this way?"

"Her late husband, Fred used to work for the railroad. Then, one day, he just dropped dead. Just fifty-three. Bad heart. Eunice went out to work cleaning houses, but her own ill health forced her to quit. Hypertension, diabetes, kidney troubles. Now, on her meagre pension, she takes care of her three grandchildren and her youngest daughter who's addicted to drugs. Eunice's church donates clothing and toys to needy families. She accepts things for her grandchildren, but she's too proud to accept anything for herself."

"Is her daughter getting help for her drug problem?"

"Shasta can't stick to any rehab program. She refuses to attend counselling sessions at Mental Health."

"Mrs. Carmichael, I think I'll buy a coat from you today."

"Miss Goldstein, I don't think she'll accept it."

"It's for me."

"Oh, I'm sorry."

"I think I see the one I want." she walked to the coat rack and pulled out a pebble-colored swing coat with a quilted lining, marked twelve dollars. She handed fifteen dollars to the confused clerk and tore off the price tag. Removing her own coat, she put on her new purchase. Eunice, by now, had slipped out to the street. Bidding Mrs. Carmichael a hasty good-bye, Sydney ran after Eunice breathlessly.

"Excuse me! Please wait up!"

"You talkin' to me? I don't want no charity." the woman protested without turning around.

"It's not charity."

"I ain't interested."

"Please listen to what I have to say."

"I don't take no charity from nobody."

"Eunice, I'm asking you to do me a favor. I've put on so much weight, I can't get into this coat anymore. It would look perfect on someone trim like you. I would feel so much better, knowing it was being worn by someone I know."

"You serious?" she eyed her suspiciously, her head cocked to one side.

"I'm dead serious."

"It looks brand new, like you just bought it."

"I bought it in September. I was thinner, then."

"You can lose the weight. I don't want no charity from no do-gooders who think they're better. No, honey, you keep it."

"I don't think I'm better than you. Not too long ago, I was exactly where you are."

"Sure, honey. You had to do without fancy dinners for a week or two."

"No. Until I located my family, I was on my own, barely making a living, for nineteen years. I lived over stores in tenement buildings. All my clothes came from thrift shops. Now that I've been blessed, I'd like to share with others."

"You serious?" Eunice squinted one eye.

"Dead serious."

"Sure is soft, ain't it?" she stroked the coat tentatively.

"It's warm."

"Is it real fur?"

"Rabbit." she held it up.

"It ain't big enough for Shasta to steal off me. Ain't no way her ass can get into it."

"Why don't you try it on?" she held it for her, "It's perfect for you."

"Sure is warm." Eunice put it on and smiled for the first time, releasing her frown lines to expose her smooth skin.

"Merry Christmas." Sydney blinked away tears.

"Same to you...Thank you." she looked at her incredulously.

"No. Thank you." she stood watching the perplexed woman cautiously making her way across the ice-encrusted sidewalk.

* * *

Brett stood behind the pillar, observing Sydney reaching for the edge of the piano for support as she sang "Someone To Watch Over Me". At the end of her set, Sydney bowed to her audience, shyly flashing her dimples, and disappeared behind the blue curtains. Taking an alternate route, Brett followed her to the corridor leading to the dressing room.

"Sweetheart, are you all right?"

"I'm fine, sweetie."

"You lost your balance there for a moment."

"Just a little light-headed, that's all."

"Have you eaten properly today?"

"I had a big, healthy supper. I'm sure it's just a virus."

"Honey, you haven't been yourself since you came back from Toronto. You've been looking peaked, and you get tired so easily now."

"I'm run down. I've missed my period, too."

"Sydney!"

"Must be early menopause."

"Most likely not. You might be anemic, or you might have a hormone imbalance. Honey, you have to see a doctor! I'll take you by the hand myself if you don't go before the end of the week!"

"Okay, I'll go. But I'm sure he'll just pat me on the head and send me home."

"How many periods have you missed?"

"I haven't had one since I came back. I missed October's, November's, and it looks like I might miss this month's, too, because I should already have started it by now."

"Honey, are you careful when you're with Warren?"

"Of course I am. Make that past tense. We haven't been getting on that well lately."

"You don't have morning sickness or anything?"

"Heavens, no! I eat like a horse. I do find I can't tolerate alcohol, so I only drink ginger ale. It's kind of nice being a tea-totaller."

"I noticed that. I thought you were either having a spiritual awakening or you were pregnant."

"Thank you for caring, honey." she kissed her cheek, "Ready to go home?"

Arms wound around one another, they locked up the room and slipped out the back door.

* * *

The man with the ruddy complexion and white hair was holding court at the corner table.

"My friends and I always managed to sneak into the girls' dorm at nights. What a wild time we had, back in those days!" he wiped soup from his chin with a paper napkin, his blue eyes gleaming with mischief.

The assortment of elderly and middle-aged men at his table laughed. All, except a younger man in a faded flannelette shirt. He peered at the others from behind thick glasses.

"Some of them actually have university degrees?" Dottie whispered to Sydney incredulously.

"Poverty doesn't discriminate, honey. It attacks people all across the board...All races, religions, socioeconomic backgrounds."

"That's scary. I mean, when you're a kid, they tell you: "Go to university. You'll get a good job. You'll never want for anything.".."

"Life's never that simple, Dottie. There are no guarantees."

"What causes intelligent, well-educated people to end up so destitute?"

"Sometimes, it's circumstances. The company they work for downsizes; they get laid off, find themselves too old or over-qualified for a new position. They're not trained to do anything else. Some get out of university full of hopes and dreams, but are too shy to make the contacts that are necessary to secure a position. Some have traumatic childhood experiences that incapacitate them as adults. Some lose jobs because of addictions. There are all sorts of reasons people end up in soup kitchens. I find the most sensitive, and the most human in our society always fare the worst."

"I agree with that."

"See that man at the men's table with curly hair and glasses, the one who seems distant and in his own world?"

"I saw him earlier."

"That's David. He has a Master's Degree in Math from McGill, and an I.Q. of 160."

"What happened to him?"

"He saw his father shoot and kill his mother when he was three. He was raised by his grandparents, who nurtured and supported him, and he did well academically. The effects of his early trauma didn't hit him full force until he was an adult and his wife left him for another man. He had a complete breakdown and lost everything."

"What did he ever do to deserve such a fate?"

"Most often, people who end up in the worst circumstances are the ones who deserve it the least. David's a gentle, sensitive soul."

"Minette says that, according to the Twelve Steps in A.A., there's a reason for everything, but I have a hard time believing that."

"So do I, Dottie."

"If there really is a Higher Power why does He allow stuff like this to happen? Why doesn't He intervene?"

"I wonder about that, too. I can't accept the pat answers provided by every major religion, even the Twelve Steps. Maybe that's why I can't commit to a belief system."

"I really want to believe, but all these doubts keep creeping up. I really admire Minette's unshakeable faith."

"My parents adhere to the Twelve Steps strictly. They have an inner glow, a serenity that mystifies me."

"I envy that. All my life, I've been searching for spiritual fulfillment. Peggy has it, too, with the Catholic Church. I just can't seem to find my way."

"It could be that, some of us need something more, something off the beaten track."

"We're just too weird for the general population to understand."

"We're not followers, Dottie. We're trailblazers."

"You always know how to cheer me up, Sydney."

"Thanks, honey."

"I guess I'll get back to work. Look at the cute baby over there! Why is the mom shaking like that?"

"She's an addict. Her baby was born with all sorts of problems. Her husband cannot hold down a job, either. He was brain-damaged following an industrial accident."

"That's so sad."

"The woman might refuse food, but if you coax her, she'll have a little soup. She's quite a pleasant sort. Her husband has a big appetite. Though we don't usually offer third helpings, we make an exception for him. He does little odd jobs, fixing things around here. He's a hard worker, honest, too. I hope he can get steady work as a carpenter. There's milk for the baby, and a sippy cup."

"I'll take care of them." she started toward the fridge.

"I'll go see how David's doing." Sydney wove her way between the tables.

"David?" she spoke softly.

He lifted pinpoint steel-blue eyes distorted behind thick lenses.

"Would you like more soup?"

"No, thank you."

"Would you like some doughnuts? They just brought in a fresh batch."

"No, thank you."

"Are you sure? You always like dessert with your soup."

"Well, maybe."

"I'll get you some. I think we've got your favorite: Venetian Crème. How many would you like?"

"Two, please."

"Coming right up."

When she returned, he lifted his eyes to her face.

"I don't want to be greedy."

"Greedy? David, you're never greedy. There's plenty more for the others."

"Thank you."

"Hey, David, she's trying to fatten you up!" the talkative man slapped his back.

The other men snickered.

"You're all coming for Christmas dinner, aren't you?" Sydney asked.

"Are you going to be working?" one of the men asked.

"I certainly am."

"Then, we'll be here."

"I'll be seeing you then. Take care."

"You, too, Miss." David waved awkwardly as she returned to the kitchen.

The lunch crowd was thinning. The emaciated young mother was attempting to keep down thin soup while her husband was polishing off his doughnuts. Their daughter sat eerily silent in the tattered high chair. Sydney blinked back tears as she carried dishes back to the kitchen. Brett burst in through the service entrance, weighed down by cardboard containers of varying sizes bearing the name of a nearby Italian restaurant.

"Hi, sweetheart!" she called cheerily as Sydney took the boxes from her and placed them on the counter.

"They're very generous." she remarked.

"There's lasagna and garlic bread, chicken and pasta. I can't wait to see the look on their faces tomorrow when we serve some of this."

"It looks like we're set for the rest of the week."

"Nice to see people in the Christmas spirit." Brett hung up her coat, rolled up her shirt sleeves and squirted dish soap from the yellow shapely plastic bottle behind the sink. Sydney returned to the dining hall to gather more dishes from the vacated tables. Harry, a middle-aged volunteer with salt and pepper hair collected the trash and tossed it into a green garbage bag. Sydney deposited the stained aquamarine melamine bowls and plates, plastic tumblers, and mismatched cutlery into the sudsy water.

"We can let the girls leave." Brett said, observing them arranging containers of lasagna in the freezer, "They've worked hard. You and I can finish the dishes."

Harry passed through the kitchen and went out to deposit the trash bag in the metal can in the back alley.

"Can youse ladies lock up today?" he said as he returned, "I promised my son I'd take him Christmas shopping."

"No problem, Harry. You go out and enjoy yourself." Brett said.

"Thanks. See youse later."

"Do you have enough volunteers to serve Christmas dinner, sweetheart?" Brett was scrubbing the dishes, "If you don't, I'll come in."

"We have plenty. There are seven of us."

"Should you be on your feet for that long?"

"It's all right. I won't exert myself too much."

"I should be here helping out."

"You've got a commitment to the boys, Maggie and Daisy. They need you more."

"Josh asked to join us, as well."

"That's terrific."

Dottie and Minette had returned from stocking the freezer.

"What can we do next?"

"You girls can leave now. Brett and I can finish up here."

"You sure?"

"Yes, honey. You two go out there and have fun. It's a beautiful day out."

"Thanks!" Dottie removed her blue gingham apron and hung it on the wall hook. She pulled the elastic bands out of her braids and shook her hair loose.

"Thank you!" Minette hugged Sydney and hung up her red and white polka dot apron next to Dottie's, "We've got some serious Christmas shopping to do!"

"Have fun."

Outside, Minette wound her striped scarf around her neck.

"I'm off early on Tuesday morning." she pulled on her white hand-knitted gloves, "For our yearly visit to Aunt Marie and Uncle Robert in Sudbury. It's a bit of a drag, but she's Dad's sister. I'll be glad to get back after babysitting my bratty cousins for two weeks. I can't wait till I turn eighteen! I'll finally be emancipated!"

"I'm going to miss you."

"Me, too."

"Do you want to go to my house for a while?"

"Sounds like fun."

"We can catch a ride to Beavertown Mall with someone later on. There's always somebody at my house going that way."

They ran diagonally across the intersection and through the back alleys of Queen Street, only stopping to catch their breath at the start of Waterloo Row. They walked at a relaxed pace until they reached the driveway of the mansion. The cracks and the soot stains on the white clapboard were glaring in the bright midday sun. Dottie skipped up the steps to the west wing, and opened the unlocked door.

* * *

"It was so nice to hear from Jacob." Dottie leaned against the support beam, "I haven't finished reading the books he sent me yet, because of Christmas exams. I hope he's not mad at me."

"There's no way he could be mad at you." Sydney stroked her cheek and returned to stocking the display unit.

"I don't know what this Mimi's like, but I wish he weren't rushing into marriage so soon."

"I think he wants to start a family. Mimi was a bit hesitant at first, but it looks like she's come around and warmed up to the idea of having children."

Hearing the jingle of the front door, both glanced up to see Warren.

"Somebody looks sharp." Dottie remarked, admiring his fur coat, "If you two are going to be smooching and stuff, I'm outta here!"

"See you later, Shortstuff." Warren responded distractedly.

"We'll talk later, Dottie." Sydney called out after her.

"How's the music business?" he glanced around him, feigning interest.

"How's the teaching business?"

"School's out for two glorious weeks. I'm celebrating tonight. Care to join me?"

"Why don't you ask one of your new lady friends?"

"You've got it all wrong, Stormy. What do you think it is that keeps me running back to you? I can have any woman I want; all I have to do is snap my fingers. Would I be hanging around here if you didn't mean something special to me?" he drew her close to kiss her.

"I'm working." she pulled away, "Besides, anybody could walk in the door."

"So, close up shop. Whoever shows up can come back later."

"I can't do that."

"This is your family's store. Your dad's not going to fire you."

"I'm expecting Greeney in a little while to go over some books together."

"Excuses, excuses. Are you nervous? We haven't been together for a long time. Are you worried about being out of practice? Don't worry: I'll refresh your memory." his hands crept up to her breasts and unbuttoned her top two blouse buttons.

"Warren, stop it."

He reached inside and unhooked her bra, caressed and squeezed her breasts.

"Please don't." she fumbled with her bra and her buttons frantically to regain her composure as his hands reached under her skirt.

"Don't worry. I'll go." he smirked, rubbing her inside her panties, "But I'll be back. Just a suggestion: If you want to entice customers by playing Christmas records, try traditional ones. Not Jack's pathetic attempt at a Christmas album."

"That's not a very nice way to speak about your nephew."

"Step, Stormy. Step nephew. Besides, I'm not a very nice person. Five o'clock sharp. Be ready."

She stood trembling as he swaggered out. The meat grinder in her stomach threatened to swallow her up and regurgitate her in bloody bits and pieces around the shop, her guts splattered on the soft green walls.

As Greeney stepped through the door, the sun rose once again.

"Hi, Sydney. Am I too early?" she removed her silver fox coat and placed it on a chair. Her Chanel # 5 wafted across the shop and Sydney inhaled deeply.

"Not at all. I'm glad you're early."

"Are you all right, honey? You look tired. Maybe you should close up when we're done, so you can go home and get some rest."

"No, I'm all right, really."

"I won't stay long, I promise."

"No, no. I enjoy your company."

"You're always so considerate."

"Is your son home for the holidays?"

"His plane arrives tonight. He's bringing his new girlfriend with him. I think he's quite serious about her."

Sydney felt an inexplicable pang, a wave of gloom washing over her.

"I hope you enjoy your time together. I'll make some tea." she slipped back to the tiny kitchenette.

"Sydney, don't go to so much bother, dear." Greeney called out to her.

"No bother. Tea is always nice." she called back, wiping her tears with a napkin.

"You've brightened up this place so much." Greeney spoke in a measured high volume, "I'm sure the increase in sales is due to your creativity."

"Thank you, but I'm sure I can't take credit for that."

"Nonsense. You're exactly what this place needed, to bring it from a forlorn, dusty, forgotten little shop to a bright, modern business. You've decorated it with lovely posters, arranged the displays in an eye-catching manner. You play a good mix of standards, pop, and disco to attract different demographics. You play jazz standards during the day when most customers are over thirty; then, you switch to disco late in the afternoon to cater to the young crowd. You intersperse pop with disco on the weekends. I follow your system when I'm on duty. Agnes likes to put up a fight about the pop and disco, but she's come around after seeing the increase in sales from young people. She's a die-hard classical music aficionado; it wasn't easy to bring her around to your method."

"You're very kind, Greeney. I wish I knew how to do the books better. I'm sorry you have to come over to help me."

"It's no trouble. We're a team. We help each other."

Sydney emerged from the back of the store with a tray and placed it on the counter. She poured shakily from the white porcelain teapot into two fine bone china cups with lilies of the valley. The delicate white flowers reminded her of Greeney. She wished Greeney would not have to leave once the books were done. There were no customers while they worked together. She watched Greeney put on her fur coat over her emerald green wool suit, and perch a circular hat atop her perfectly coiffed, face-framing blonde waves. She was the epitome of grace, class, and élan. She washed the cups and the spoons in the back of the store and placed them back in the cupboard. The sound of the bell alerted her to the arrival of a customer, and she returned to find Warren.

"Ready to go?"

"It's only four-thirty. You know I can't close until five."

"Didn't anybody ever teach you the fine art of keeping men interested? Who's been giving you lessons? A spinster with a moustache? The bearded lady at the carnival?"

"Warren, I'm not sure about tonight."

"What kind of a game are you playing with me?" he roared, "I'm getting sick and tired of it!"

"I'm not playing games." she folded her arms across her chest in an attempt to control her quivering.

"You jumped in the sack with me on our first date. You couldn't get enough. Now, you're blowing hot and cold. It's getting annoying. This is the seventies – not the forties. Cut out the virginal act."

"Warren, it's not an act."

"You broads are all alike. Always scheming and manipulating. When I first met you, I remember you were just a pauper. You couldn't do enough to please me. You were so grateful. Now that you've found respectability, you think you have the right to refuse. Ah, yes, the martyred princess finds her birthright. You're putting on airs now because you have the Goldstein name, but you'll never be anything but a pauper from Montreal to me."

"It's nice to know I am appreciated."

"If you think you can jerk me around like this, you'd better think again. You're not the one who calls the shots around here. You don't rebuff me. I decide when it's over."

"Warren..."

"You do as I tell you. Now, lock up. It's five to five."

She obeyed him.

"I've cancelled the reservations. We're going to have our own party right here."

"Here?"

"Isn't there a cot in the back room?"

"I can't...Not here..."

"Then, where, pray-tell do you suggest we go? Your place, with your parents in the next room? Get real."

"This doesn't feel right. It's all so...tawdry..."

"For Jesus' Sake, will you cut the bull! I've waited long enough!" he pulled her to himself.

"You're hurting me."

"You think that hurts? You're in for a shock. Try this on for size!" his hand landed across her left cheek. She covered her cheek with her right hand and recoiled in terror.

"What is it with you? You've gone frigid on me all of a sudden. Have you sworn to celibacy or something?"

"Warren, please, just go."

"Shut up, bitch! I told you before, you don't call the shots around here! Now, get in the back room!" he switched off the lights and locked the door.

Once in the storage room, he kissed her savagely.

"I know what you need, baby. I know why you've been acting like this. You think I've been neglecting you, don't you?" he unbuttoned her blouse and unfastened her bra.

His fingernails sank deeply into her skin, leaving red imprints on her breasts. He unzipped the back of her skirt. It swooshed against her pantyhose on its way down. He pulled her pantyhose and panties down to her ankles.

"Stop crying!" he commanded, unzipping his trousers, "You're getting on my nerves, you know that!" His open hand came down on her face again.

He was unable to enter her amidst her struggling.

"Stop fighting me, dammit! Your cunt's dry as an old nun's! Get up! Get up!" he pushed her off the cot, "On your knees!"

Sobbing uncontrollably, she was unable to take it into her mouth. Muttering obscenities under his breath, he forced her down on her abdomen.

"It's not worth doing if you don't do it rough!" he bit her buttocks before entering her anally.

She wept until he dismounted her, and attempted to straighten herself.

"I'm not through with you yet, bitch!" he pushed her back down.

He whipped off the belt from his trousers on the floor and turned to her, eyes blazing. It came down across her back, her buttocks and legs, as she howled in pain.

"Get on your back!" he ordered.

"No! Warren, no!"

Her strength was draining away from her; her consciousness was slipping. He lifted her off the floor and flung her across the room. She landed face down on the brown linoleum floor. She emerged from the darkness, overcome by the scent of her own blood. She fought to remain lucid, yet consciousness threatened to elude her once again. Water-stained acoustic ceiling tiles eyed her dispassionately. The pain was excruciating.

"Goddamn it! Why didn't you warn me about your period?"

"Warren..." she pleaded in a faint voice, "I need to go to the hospital."

"Jesus Christ!"

"Please...It's not a period. I'm having a miscarriage." her voice faded.

"Miscarriage! You fucking whore! How could you be so careless?"

"Please..." she was barely audible.

"This was all calculated, wasn't it? You were holding out for an engagement ring. You scheming little bitch!"

"Warren...I need help..." she called out in a whisper.

"You fucking whore! You got yourself pregnant, so you could trick me into marrying you!"

"That is not true."

"Go to hell!"

A demonic expression flashed across his face. The silence loomed, menacing and ice-cold. With his exit, the front door rattled. She struggled to raise herself up and crawled to the corner table for the black telephone.

* * *

"Good mornin', honey!" Marge glanced up from the dough she was mixing, "Why aren't you sleeping in?"

"I don't know, Marge." Dottie sat at the kitchen table, "I'm worried about Sydney. They won't tell me what's wrong, except that she's hemorrhaging. Marge, do you think there might be something really wrong with her? That robber must've worked her over pretty bad."

"She'll be all right, darlin'."

"Why would anybody want to rob Goldstein's? They don't have much cash in the till, and nothing valuable to steal. There's a jewellery store next door. Wouldn't it be more lucrative to rob them?"

"They're thugs. They rob whoever's the handiest target. They're looking for drug money."

"Drugs are ruining the world. No one's safe."

"She's going to be all right." Peggy, who had come in halfway through their conversation, patted her on the shoulder and sat beside her, "Is Minette at her aunt's place yet? Maybe you could call her."

"They're not there yet. They're driving, so they won't get there until Saturday."

"I have the day off. I can go with you to visit Sydney in the afternoon."

"Can you? Oh, Peg, that's wonderful! Afternoon visits are a lot better. It's not as busy."

"Her roommate's quite the social butterfly. There's no privacy for Sydney with all the people in the room."

"Sydney really likes the dusting powder you gave her. Lily Of The Valley is her favorite."

"Speaking of dusting powder..." Peggy reached across the table and dipped her index finger into the bowl of flour her mother had put aside, and playfully pressed her finger on Dottie's nose.

Dottie dipped her finger in the sugar bowl on the table, and returned the favor. The distinctive chime of the front doorbell cut short their chuckling.

"Must be a delivery at the wrong door." Marge, who had been cutting the cookie dough in festive shapes with metal cookie cutters in the outlines of Christmas trees, angels, stars, reindeer, and gingerbread people, wiped her hands with a green checkered dish cloth.

"Paul can get it." Peggy said.

"Miss Dottie, it's for you." Paul announced.

"Must be an admirer." Peggy winked.

Dottie followed Paul through the breezeway to the east wing, where her visitor sat on a slipper chair in the grand foyer, clad in her cherry red parka, a white scarf wound around her neck, and a white toque with a pompom perched on her blonde head.

"Clara?"

"Hi." she said wistfully, and stood to hand her the envelope in her white mittened hand.

Through the glass panel in the heavy door, Dottie could see a blue sedan idling in front of the house.

"Thank you."

"Merry Christmas."

"Merry Christmas."

"You've got flour on your nose."

"Oh." she wiped it with her hand, "I forgot. Want to come in?" she glanced at the envelope with her name scrawled in a childish handwriting, "Marge is baking her famous cookies."

"I can't. Mom's taking me to the mall. She's waiting in the car."

"Maybe another time."

"Yeah, another time. Bye."

"Thanks for the card. Bye."

Clara stepped down from the veranda and made her way to the blue sedan. She turned and waved. Dottie waved back and shut the door. She opened the unsealed envelope to find a card with a jolly Santa in front of a decorated tree. Inside, just the name Clara in irregularly shaped letters was at the bottom right corner. She returned to the kitchen, and placed it on the display shelf of the corner hutch.

"Who was it?" Peggy asked.

"Clara. She dropped off a card."

"Her mom must've made her do it." Peggy rolled her eyes.

"She did look sad. At least, she never told me she was embarrassed to be seen with me. Clara's never been a popular girl herself, so she doesn't do things just to be cruel."

"Them girls are in the past now, honey." Marge said, "You've got Minette now."

The doorbell sounded again. Soon, raised voices were heard.

"I'll go check what's going on." Dottie said.

"Honey, maybe you ought to let Paul handle it." Marge said.

"It's okay. We'll both go." Peggy offered.

"You be careful now. There could be trouble." Marge shook a dough-covered finger in their direction.

The girls ran through the breezeway, straining their ears to make out what was being said.

"Where's that slimeball, Warren Horncastle? I want to see him!"

"That's Brett Morrow." Dottie whispered.

"What's she doing here? Why is she upset with your uncle?"

"Madam, you can't barge in here like this."

"Where is he? Is he upstairs in his room? I'm going up there. I've got a bone to pick with him!"

"Madam, you can't go up there!...Madam...I'm afraid I'll have to call the authorities."

287

"You do that, and I'll tell them what he did! They'll haul his sorry carcass away in handcuffs and put his ass in jail!"

"Paul, leave her alone!" Dottie burst in through the connecting door, "I'm ashamed of you! This is Brett Morrow. You can't treat her like that."

"I'm sorry, Miss. I didn't realize."

"I'll take care of this."

"Yes, Miss." Paul nodded.

"Brett, what's wrong?" Dottie hugged her, "You want some water?"

"No, thank you, sweetheart. I have to talk to that uncle of yours. We've got some serious business to discuss."

"He's up in his room. Paul, could you please tell my uncle there's someone to see him?"

"Yes, Miss." he started up the majestic staircase.

"Let me take your coat, Brett."

"No, thanks, hon. I won't be here that long. I'll just say my piece and I'll be gone."

"Well, well, if it isn't the Wicked Witch of the West!" Warren was descending the stairs in a burgundy smoking jacket, "What an honor that you've decided to grace us with your presence!"

"What I have to say to you is not fit for the tender ears of your gracious niece. I'm coming up to your room."

"Why, Brett, I had no idea how badly you had the hots for me." he smirked, flashing perfect teeth.

"Quit clowning around, Casanova." she started up the stairs.

Paul was standing awkwardly behind Warren on the landing.

"Paul, it looks like Brett wants to have her way with me. You're excused."

The young man squeezed past Warren, pressing his back against the wall, and paused at the lower landing to allow Brett space.

"Would Madame like to come up to my boudoir, away from the prying eyes and ears of impressionable youth?" he winked, "It'll have to be a quickie, though. I have plans for later in the morning."

"Don't get any ideas." she followed him upstairs.

"Brett, Brett, you must try to curb your urges."

"You know precisely why I'm here."

"To ravage me."

"You wish."

Their voices became muffled and unintelligible to Dottie and Peggy, fading into a drone. The door to Warren's suite was slammed shut with a loud thud, rendering them inaudible. The girls returned to the kitchen.

"I'm going to see to it that you pay for what you did to her, you sleazy bastard!"

"Oh, really?" he leaned back on the brown leather recliner and crossed his legs, "And what, pray-tell is it that I'm supposed to have done?"

"What you did was vile and revolting! I'll see to it that she presses charges! They're going to lock you up, so you can't hurt any more women!"

"Just a little bit of fun. She's always liked it rough. I didn't know she was going to get wimpy on me." he leaned back further and repositioned the chair.

"You raped her!"

"Is that what she's saying now?"

"That is what you did!"

"Did she tell you what she did? She got herself pregnant, so she could trap me into marrying her!"

"She never wanted to marry you! The baby wasn't even yours!"

"She found some poor schnook to impregnate her; then, she tried to pass it off as mine."

"She never tried to pass it off as yours."

"The other guy must've seen through her, because he sure didn't stick around for very long, did he?"

"You're going down, you smug bastard! She's going to press charges!"

"Sydney's not going to do any such thing. Do you think she'd risk a rift between the Horncastles and the Goldsteins? Even Sydney's not that stupid."

"You make me sick!"

"The feeling's mutual."

"You're not going to get away with this, you know. The law's on her side."

"What do you think they're going to do to me?" he laughed, "My brothers are the finest lawyers in Beavertown."

"Don't forget Tony."

"You think he's going to betray his own family for a two-bit hussy like you? Think again, sister. Blood's thicker than water."

"You bastard! You evil bastard!"

"I'm very fond of you, too. Now, go away." he dismissed her with a wave of his hand, "You bore me."

"You haven't heard the last of me yet!"

"Yeah, yeah. I'm so scared." he laughed, "You're the one who'll be facing legal action if you don't stop harassing me and trespassing on my property."

"Justice will prevail in the end. One way or another. Karma will right the wrong."

"And Santa will come down the chimney. Now, go away. I don't have time for your childish games. Are you going to get on your broom and fly away, or do I have to have you removed bodily?"

"I'm leaving. But rest assured, somewhere down the road, you'll be paying in some way for the things you've done to Sydney."

"That sounds like a gypsy curse. Your hocus pocus doesn't work on enlightened people. Go peddle your trade among the ignorant and misguided masses."

"Some day, Warren Horncastle, some day!" she slammed the door behind her and ran down the stairs to find a perplexed Paul, "Don't bother, son. I can let myself out."

She stepped outside to be greeted by the kisses of virgin snowflakes.

*   *   *

Brett placed a warm mug of tea on the nightstand beside Sydney and sat on the edge of the bed.

"Brett, you don't have to wait on me like this."

"I enjoy it."

"You're spoiling me."

"You deserve to be spoiled." she pulled the duvet around Sydney, "Your immune system was suppressed because of what that animal did to you. You've got the worst case of pneumonia I've seen."

"I'm over the worst of it now."

"I'm sorry you didn't get to celebrate Hanukkah."

"I ruined it for my parents."

"Nonsense. Having you back is the best celebration they could ever ask for. Was Jacob in touch?"

"He called me at the hospital when Mom and Dad told him. He seems to be doing fine." she smiled, "He and Mimi have worked out their differences. They're going to be married next month."

"How do you feel about that, hon?"

"I'm happy for him."

"Are you sure you're okay?"

"I've found that life has a way of unfolding just as it pleases, despite all efforts on our part to intervene. I'm swearing off men, Brett. I'm a failure at relationships. Look at the mess I've made of things."

"No, sweetheart. It's not you that's a failure. It's the world. You're too perfect for this imperfect world."

Sydney marvelled at the fluidity of Brett's movements as she pulled down the blinds.

"Sweetheart, I'll get Keir to do Christmas dinner at the soup kitchen in your place. It'll be good for him. This is my first Christmas without Shayleigh. Sam's mother's dragging them off to a family dinner. But they're coming for New Year's. She and I always cooked Christmas dinner together. Shay never had a Christmas dinner with her parents because her mother hated to cook."

"She's very lucky to have you. So am I."

"I'm the one who's lucky. You'd better rest up now, so you can get your strength back." Brett stroked her cheek, "Good night, sweetheart."

"Good night, Brett."

* * *

Christmas music was playing on the ghetto blaster in the corner of the kitchen counter as Dottie and Peggy trimmed the squat artificial tree. It had been a tradition for as long as Dottie could remember, to decorate a small artificial tree two weeks following the trimming of the Douglas fir in the living room. For Marge, Peg, and the maids, who spend inordinate amounts of time in the kitchen, the holiday season was made more festive. This was the tree to showcase all handmade ornaments from Dottie and Peggy's childhood – even Tony and Jack's – all lovingly created in childlike wonder. The crudely colored cut-outs of bells, angels, and gingerbread men, Santas made out of bathroom tissue cardboards with cotton ball beards now matted, angels covered with tissue paper for gossamer wings and halos sprinkled with silver glitter that, each year, grew thinner as particles escaped to the floor, all found a home on this emaciated tree. Handmade cards with youthful drawings of family members carrying packages and snowy landscapes were placed on the lower branches with inscriptions in irregularly shaped letters: "To Mommy and Daddy"..."For the best mommy and daddy in the world"..."Mome and Dady"..."To the best parents ever". Their names were signed proudly underneath: "Tony", "Jack", "Dottie", and "Peggy". All traces of Garrett had been obliterated years ago. Candy canes, garlands, and icicles were added to complete the creation.

"Minette must be at her aunt's place by now." Peggy said, placing a threadbare pink angel on a lower branch.

"I'm going to call her tonight." Dottie hung a cardboard bell on her side of the tree.

"I wonder whose responsibility it's going to be to set up this tree when you and I leave the nest." Peggy mused, "I wonder if the future generations will throw away our masterpieces and replace them with their own."

"I hope they keep them in a box or something."

"Some of these are falling apart, Dottie. I don't imagine anyone would hang onto them once they get disgusting."

"I guess nothing in life is permanent."

"I wonder who the next generation's going to be...Tony and Jack don't seem ready to settle down to raise families...You and I may not stay at this house when we're older."

"I never want to leave this house, Peg. This is the only home I'll ever have. As long as I'm alive, our artwork will be on display. If I have kids, I'll make them promise not to throw these away."

"It would be nice if you raised your family here."

The Christmas music on the radio had stopped. The announcer began the news broadcast. The girls strung the multi-colored lights on the tree and plugged them in. They stood back to admire their handiwork.

"Perfect." Peggy said, "As always. We're the best."

"We make a good team."

"I like the new silver angel ornament you added this year."

"It's Ella's angel. It's there to guide her way and watch over her in heaven."

"Dottie, that's beautiful."

"...The names of the six fatalities in yesterday's two car crash on Route 314 in Ontario have been released by the R.C.M.P.: The occupants of the first car are: Myrtle Hansen, 55; Helen Graham, 26, both of Timmins, Ontario. The occupants of the second car are

Claude Couturier, 73; Etienne Couturier, 41; Anne Couturier, 39, and Minette Couturier, 17, all of Beavertown, New Brunswick..."

The Christmas lights innocently continued to flash hot pink, bachelor's button blue, emerald green and crimson in the still kitchen. The silver angel fell to the floor face down. The radio announcer began reading out hockey scores.

Continued in Book Two: **SANDCASTLES IN THE RAIN**

About The Author:

Summer Seline Coyle has a B.A. in Sociology and English Literature, and a Certificate in Counselling.

Her personal history of extreme abuse, neglect, and injustice is the driving force behind the empathy, tenderness, and passion in her portrayal of her diverse characters. Through her fiction, she hopes to raise public awareness, and be a healing voice for other survivors.

Also By Summer Seline Coyle:

Daisies From Ashes
Sandcastles In The Rain
Summer Is A Short Season
Sanctuary

Lightning Source UK Ltd.
Milton Keynes UK
UKHW010718040521
383104UK00005B/785